Renew by phone or online
0845 0020 777
www.bristol.gov.uk/libraries
Bristol Libraries

KT-221-009

PLEASE RETURN BOOK BY LAST DATE STAMPED

26 NOV

BRISTOL LIBRARIES
WITHDRAWN
SOLD AS SEEN

Bristol Libraries

1800488727

HOTBED

HOTBED

Bill James

KO HO	SW 4/11	RE 11/11	SO 6/12	BI 6/15
MA	b/13 HC	HO 12/13	WM	

CHIVERS

British Library Cataloguing in Publication Data available

This Large Print edition published by BBC Audiobooks Ltd, Bath, 2010.
Published by arrangement with Constable & Robinson Ltd.

U.K. Hardcover ISBN 978 1 408 49197 3
U.K. Softcover ISBN 978 1 408 49198 0

Copyright © Bill James 2009

The right of Bill James to be identified as the author of this work has
been asserted by him in accordance with the Copyright, Designs and
Patents Act 1988

All rights reserved.

Printed and bound in Great Britain by
CPI Antony Rowe, Chippenham and Eastbourne

My short story, 'Makeover' (*Ellery Queen Mystery Magazine*, March–April 2007), provides some material for this novel, in slightly different form.

CHAPTER ONE

About every six months the two firms ran a fine dinner for their staffs in a reasonable enough large room at the Agincourt Hotel. Ralph Ember loved this historical name, dating back to a famous British victory in the fifteenth century. He considered the reference gave extra class and a kind of solidity. Ralph really prized such qualities, not just at the Agincourt, but in life altogether.

Everyone connected with both businesses came. Usually, the atmosphere was good. Ralph or Mansel Shale presided in rotation. They invited their lawyers, accountants, PR consultants, street corner pushers and disco-rave dealers, personnel executives, couriers, debt netters, management advisers and chauffeur-bodyguards. Actually, Manse often drove the Jaguar personally these days after his man, Denzil Lake, got double head shot like that, possibly suicide, perhaps not. Nobody fretted wondering which. Tonight, though, Manse, as well as Ember and most of the others, came and went by taxi, because of the drinking. Also, it was unwise to fill the Agincourt car park with very recognizable vehicles. That could draw attention. Inevitably, the police knew of the regular dinners, but it would be stupid to get flagrant. People left at different times, so the late-night taxis did not swarm all at once, a bit of a sight and nuisancing the neighbourhood. Ralph hated discourtesy, except towards those who clearly deserved it.

As a general principle, he avoided any mixing of guns and social relations. He saw this as a supreme taste matter. Ralph thought of himself as a devotee of taste. Guns obviously brought threat, but also swank and swagger. Ralph hated brashness at least as much as discourtesy. Often they merged. For instance, he would regard it as deeply undecorous to go armed to weddings or funerals or christenings, unless he sensed a very plain prospect of outbursts of loathing and/or violence, as regularly happened at weddings, funerals and christenings, and at most formal family gatherings. And he did always take a pistol to the Agincourt meetings. He had a Beretta shoulder-holstered tonight.

Although the two companies—Ember's and Shale's—still worked peacefully alongside each other, Ralph often sensed that Manse craved monopoly, craved unshared commercial dominion, and might be ready soon to try destruction of Ralph: say, like tonight. The Agincourt's car park, where the taxi would put Ralph down and collect him, had poor lighting, perhaps a period touch, imitating night in public places six centuries ago, time of the battle. Ralph understood they used to burn rushes then as lamps, which couldn't have done much to illuminate places. Once in a while, Ralph himself thought with fondness about monopoly, too. And about Manse as a fucking obstruction. At the local university, Ember had begun a mature student degree course—suspended for now because of acute business demands—and learned in Economics lectures that capitalism always and automatically reached for monopoly, an aim recognized by many political philosophers, including Marx. Ride high, ride solo.

Ralph and Shale together had seen off a lot of new, small competitors in the powder and pill trade, including East European invaders, some touting girls as a supplement. Now, though, Mansel might be thinking large scale, might be thinking clean sweep, might be thinking autocracy: wipe out not just small fry, but Ralph Ember. There had been other, earlier occasions when Ralph felt on-off hints of this, but, lately, the impression grew constant and very strong. He'd come to believe he must act.

However, Ember favoured gentle, gradual moves, where practical. He believed in subtlety. As starters, Ralph decided he'd attempt to ease one of his people into Manse's core team to do some listening and reporting on Shale's intentions. Ember didn't imagine this would be difficult, because a sort of friendliness—or seeming friendliness—had

3

operated for years between the two workforces, reflecting the friendliness—or seeming friendliness—between their two chiefs, Manse and Ember. A happy and harmonious degree of overlap in trade activities inevitably developed. Ralph had heard of a top-flight London figure in the 1960s, Joey Pyle, who managed somehow to run with both the Krays and the Richardsons, though their gangs were forever at vicious war. That heartened Ralph, inspired him, as church people might derive inspiration from reading about the lives of saints. Pyle showed boundaries need not be absolute, and gave an ecumenical touch. Compared with what he had managed, Ralph considered it should be simple to place one of his lads close, or at least closer, to Manse Shale.

At this stage, the Beretta rated as nothing but defensive. After all, it had only ten rounds. Ralph would avoid daft haste and, to date, he drew back from the notion of destroying Manse before Manse could destroy him—a 'pre-emptive strike', so-called in nuclear strategy. Ralph wanted the pleasant, nicely civilized surface of his firm's arrangement with Mansel's preserved, if feasible. It might not mean much but it meant something, so far. OK, Ralph recognized so far was *only* so far, but so far was as far as matters had actually gone so far, and, so far, this should not be sneezed at. Maybe the concord would continue

4

to mean something. Maybe Ralph misread Manse's objective, perhaps maligned him on account of that university gab. Maybe the alliance would go on sweetly, chummily and rewardingly for ever. Ralph must not rush to destroy it through panic. In some ways, he retained a kind of liking for Manse, even respect, despite the trickery and complicated muckwormishness.

And Manse probably felt a liking and respect for Ralph. Shale intended to remarry soon—a piece called Naomi Something from who knew where?—and he'd asked Ralph to be best man. Clearly, this could be seen as an honour of sorts. Or, it might be just a lulling move, the fucking snake. Ralph longed to believe it really did signify, and that Manse had no scheme to eliminate him, best man or not. Ember would wear the full, tail-coat wedding gear, as tribute to the fine, lengthy commercial relationship between Manse and him. Ralph liked to be thought of as a conservator. He hoped others would see him as this: often he wrote constructive letters to the local press on environmental and heritage topics, signing them 'Ralph W. Ember'.

He and Shale paid turn-and-turn about for the Agincourt dinner. Although Manse might be an ungrammatical, totally crude jerk, he somehow knew wines, especially clarets, and only decent bottles, and a lot of them, appeared on the tables. Alan Clark, that MP who'd stuff almost anything female and its mother, said you couldn't get a tolerable bottle of claret for under £100, and this would be at least ten years ago and without hotel corkage. But Ralph never niggled over costs. Small-mindedness he despised. He prized the words 'bountiful' and 'unstinting' and would have had them on the back of his hands if he'd been into tattoos. He felt they caught his character. There were people at these functions whose devotion and bravery helped hold Ralph's firm together, and Shale's. They should not be insulted with cheapjack catering.

Whichever of them hosted and paid for the dinner made a speech at the liqueurs stage, summing up the previous six months' trade results and looking forward intelligently to the future. Obviously, the results quoted had been neatly edited by Ralph and Manse at a previous, one-to-one private meeting, and an agreed version prepared. Auditors they dispensed with. These results were not the exact results but the results Ralph and Manse thought tactful to disclose to such a crew.

Take the lawyers, including QCs. The firms unquestionably needed a team of these always ready in case the authorities tried to get awkward and harsh. There was a new Chief Constable who seemed strong and abnormally keen on lawfulness, so, obviously, he might have to be countered. Nobody—and definitely not Ralph—would dispute the usefulness of the on-call lawmen in these conditions. They had to be kept comfortable by him and Manse. But this could never mean giving them total disclosure of the firms' finances. They would up their already very distinguished fees if they discovered as fact the companies' true profitability. Probably they already guessed at the true profitability. This was not the same as being told, though, and *knowing*.

Or think of the debt collectors and enforcers—Arrears Reconciliation Legates, to use their proper professional title. Conscientiously they grievous bodily harmed, kidnapped, and all-round terrorized slow-pay and defaulting clients, urging them to cough immediately with gross interest. If these earnest helpmeets learned as fact—as precise *fact* —what Ralph and Manse individually took from the firms each year they might want improved percentages. They'd argue for the same sort of bonus rates copped by Goldman Sachs bankers. Again, the Arrears Reconciliation Legates—familiarly, shortened to ARLs on career path documents—yes, the ARLs might *suspect* Ralph's and Shale's income levels, but they lacked confirmation, and definitely wouldn't get it from a token presentation at this Agincourt beanfeast. A comprehensive run-down was unthinkably out of order and workaday for such a happy social evening. It would be poor form to burden the occasion with full, detailed accuracy. *Some*

7

detail—including, even, instances of *correct* detail—*some* detail could be offered, perhaps *should* be: those listening were not bumpkins and would be alert to concealment and/or deception. But too much authenticity might become tiresome.

Ralph already had in mind someone who could possibly handle well the task of subtly sounding out Mansel and getting the insights back fast to Ralph. Speed might be crucial. The 'pre' in 'pre-emptive strike' was clearly the guts of it. A *post*-emptive nuclear strike couldn't happen because there'd be nobody left to make it happen. Ember didn't know when Manse meant to move against him, or *if* he meant to. Ralph possessed only his belief that things could turn bad. Over the past few weeks, this idea had grown increasingly insistent. He'd been wary taking the few steps from the taxi across the Agincourt car park tonight to the hotel's rear entrances. Nothing occurred. He'd try to be just as alert when leaving, though—perhaps have his hand up to the holster. He mustn't let the booze turn him dozy. He could have called in a couple of bodyguards, but that would make him look nervous, feeble, dependent. Ralph Ember had an image to think of. He liked to be reckoned robust, dauntless. Consider also: wasn't some top Indian politician actually murdered by his/her bodyguards? In addition, to use minders would proclaim that Ember smelled a plot. Then, perhaps Manse would bring forward his plans, before Ralph had got himself up to readiness.

He spent half a morning not long ago computer searching character profiles of folk in his firm, seeking the most suitable to capture Manse's confidence and assess his attitude, expose his calculating dreams. Ralph didn't bring the personnel department in on this selection. He'd manage alone. Total confidentiality must be the aim. He feared leaks. Because he found it hard to forecast what qualities would be most appropriate, he worked from the negative side. That is, he rejected those who seemed dangerously wrong, and hoped this would leave him with a shortlist of one or two capable candidates. Ironically, the discards might have plentiful skills for the company's usual operations, but these skills would not necessarily do now, could even bring disaster.

Consequently, he dropped from his list anyone who sounded too head-on confrontational, in case s/he turned out blustering and blatant. He excluded those who normally dealt fast and direct with assignments, and who might be impatient: Ralph did want speed, but not careless or clumsy speed. Obviously, he passed over all with a habit or a history of a habit, or blood relatives with a habit; and/or with a current alcohol and/or mental problem; and everybody

9

who unconcealably—that was the vital word, 'unconcealably'—unconcealably loathed Manse for those know-all, boom-boom proclamations on wine, for the bragging, braying delight he took in his Pre-Raphaelite paintings, for the large, ex-rectory home, and for his parish-wide, hyperactive shagging, which might get to some staff's women for all they—the staff—knew.

Ultimately, Ralph had come up with one name, Joachim Bale Frederick Brown. He'd be here tonight at the Agincourt, and Ember could watch him—could see something beyond the dossier data and curt words of appraisal. His behaviour in company might be crucial. To carry the role Ralph wanted him for he would need to be, or seem to be, companionable, poised, relaxed, adaptable. The first name—Joachim—didn't worry Ralph too much. Perhaps one of his parents or both had a German connection. Never mind. Ralph detested quite a few forms of racism and backed apologies for slavery. Or Brown's mother and father might just have wanted to mark him out as unusual. The computer profile did not say much about his family, except that he had an actor brother who took big roles, including one in something called *The Duchess of Malfi*. Ralph hoped acting might be a family thing: whoever went into Manse's outfit would need to do some.

Although Ralph remembered running

across Joachim once or twice before tonight on company matters, those had been only casual, brief meetings. Ember would concentrate now and assess. Brown had a nickname—'Turret'—which Ralph took to mean not necessarily blast-off gun-mad, but all-round vigilant, the way someone in a turret should be.

Ralph ran this dinner, tonight. He thought it went well. The functions always took place on a Monday, when the 'banqueting hall' would normally have been closed after the weekend. The firms could hire it for exclusive use. Throughout the week the hotel put on 'medieval feasts' with syllabub and mead, wench-type waitresses décolletaging in a fruity way, and goose instead of swan, swans being protected birds these days. On the walls for atmosphere hung ancient armament and breastplates and helmets, mostly imitation and plastic, though some maybe actual metal. Many longbows featured, the weapon that won Agincourt. Although Ralph found this display dismally naff, he put up with it. The battle, Agincourt, *had* definitely taken place, and this hotel commemorated it as well as it could. The history was genuine even if the relic display wasn't, and this more or less satisfied Ralph. A minstrels' gallery for roundelays etcetera stayed unused this evening.

In his speech, Ralph spoke enthusiastically about the firms' health and prospects and referred warmly to the continuing, brilliant, assured cooperation between Mansel and himself. Massive applause followed Ralph's mention of Shale's engagement and approaching marriage to the woman Naomi, and he mentioned what a top-notch character Naomi was in the Bible: Ralph had been interested in religious education at school and recalled a fair whack of the teaching. Then everyone sang 'For He's a Jolly Good Fellow', with a real ringing shout on 'and so say all of us!' to suggest outright enthusiasm and genuineness. Ralph, standing at the head of the main table, led the chorus into two repeats, occasionally pointing heartily at Manse, seated a few places away, to indicate that, unarguably, *he*, Manse, was the jolly good fellow meant. Ralph saw Shale—egomaniac sod—give a couple of small nods as if he knew all this, but thought he'd better offer a bit of a thank-you to the fucking nobodies around him just the same.

The last two dinners at the Agincourt had turned raucous and unpleasant, with angry barracking from some guests. Back then, people feared that intruder firms from Eastern Europe and elsewhere might steal some of the trade, and there'd been a feeling that Ralph and Mansel underestimated this danger, and lacked a credible resistance policy. Some staff seemed convinced that the Agincourt occasions then amounted only to calculated distractions from the dark state of things. These worries no longer existed, though, as the menace had been removed. Tonight's dinner radiated harmony and peace and nobody heckled Ralph or did huge groan-yawns or put shots into the ceiling.

He liked to give a single, main theme to any speech he made—a substantial, inspiring theme. He thought of this theme as 'overarching'. Ralph scorned after-dinner performers who merely strung together a batch of anecdotes and coarse jokes. After the few sentences about trade topics, and the hearty congratulatory song to that cocky, ungrateful slob, Manse, Ralph went on to his central subject for this occasion, loyalty.

'I look around the handsome room here with its many reminders of another time and I ask myself what was it, in the end, that brought victory to King Henry V at Agincourt,' he said. 'Oh, I know, I know, some would answer, superior weaponry. And I certainly do not gainsay the British longbow's value. But the longbow alone could not have done it. No, it was the men led by Henry and firmly, gloriously, loyal to him who secured this triumph. Without their spirit and devotion not even the longbow could have won the day. And similar important, glorious loyalty I see present here tonight. Oh, yes. All right, I admit that, on the face of it, loyalty would appear a difficult commodity to create and keep, because there are two firms involved, not one. Outsiders considering our separate organizations might have expected any loyalties to be split, even—let us admit—to be at odds with one another. In fact, some would argue that destructive rivalry between the two firms was inevitable, part of their core nature, this governed by jungle law, which, as we all recognize, is no law at all, only a belief in unchallengeable, brutal power. But those of us actually concerned with the two companies *know* this to be deeply incorrect—know because we are part of a possibly unique bipartisan loyalty—know because we watch and experience it in daily operation—know that such shared, such double, such undivided loyalty, does magnificently exist—exists as magnificently as the loyalty of those Agincourt warriors, those "dear friends" in Shakespeare's words, who went "once more unto the breach" with Henry in 1415. I think of you as *my* "dear friends". Together we will triumph.' Ralph reckoned the applause that came now contained a fair bit of authenticity. Quite a few diners rose to give a standing ovation that went on a decent while: not Manse, of course.

Afterwards, at the bar, Shale said: 'I didn't know, Ralph.'

'What?'

'Naomi being in the Bible.'

'Book of Ruth. OT.'

'I've read some of Revelation about the end

14

of things. This is a bit of a frightener, but we mustn't shut our eyes to it. I like to be ready for any difficulties.'

'Oh, yes, Naomi suffers quite a packet but is then all right.' Ember could see Turret over Manse's shoulder. Brown seemed relaxed, though not pissed out of his mind and legless. He'd stay controlled, on top of a situation, affable yet discreet. As Ralph watched, Brown chatted with a group of Shale's people, then took a few paces and talked just as much at ease with half a dozen ARLs and couriers from both outfits. Ember observed confidence there, but no brassiness and no wish to dominate. He blended in. He talked occasionally. He listened non-stop. Ralph diagnosed flair, the kind that might not figure in dossier data. Ralph occasionally joked about his 'flair for spotting flair'.

'Naomi suffers?' Shale said.

'Several people around her, close to her, die. It's tough.'

'That right?'

'Oh, yes.' Turret obviously had acceptability, and therefore access. This was a terrific plus. Ember said: ' "Naomi" meant "pleasant", but she wanted to change her name to "Bitter" because of all her foul luck.'

'Die how?' Shale replied.

'But then her daughter-in-law, Ruth, has a baby and this gets Naomi OK again before the First Book of Samuel.'

'Die how? What do you mean, "close to her"?' Shale was short, square-built with a snub face. He looked powerful, but didn't sound like that for the moment. He'd fixed his animal eyes on Ralph, obviously keen for an answer. He seemed to sense some dire undertone in what Ralph told him.

'Yes, really close,' Ember said.

'I think she's all right now—*this* Naomi, I mean. Mine.'

'I'm sure, Manse.'

'She've got me to look after her.'

'Certainly. But you think there's going to be trouble, Manse? What sort?'

'Women *can* turn bitter, though,' Shale replied.

'It's sad.'

'Well, you most probably know that for yourself, Ralph.'

'Mood swings.'

'They got their own way of looking at life, most of them. They're entitled. Usually it's shit,' Shale said.

'We should always be ready for their carry-on, Manse, often in a sympathetic fashion. I see that as a male duty.'

'I don't say they ought to be the same all the time. They got their rights, in a way. You'll never hear me argue different. Women are human beings as much as we are, no question, absolutely no question, Ralph. Their knees developed like ours so they walk upright. They

16

got a quite worthwhile role. They can have passports, and drive cars, and be judges. Things have come on a lot since they was all just squaw types. But often they're a real unholy pain.'

'We have to try to—'

'I don't mean by accident—like being a pain without knowing it. Some of them fucking *mean* it, Ralph. These say to theirselves, "How can I deliver this bastard agony plus agony?" And they're great at giving theirselves an answer. Remember in arithmetic lessons where they taught us to put an asterisk on a figure that can't be got rid of in a division sum, it just goes on for ever? That's what *they* do with agony for us. They put an asterisk against it. Oh, yes, they're *so* smart at thinking up wounds for men. No poncy longbow would knock them back when they're like that. No poncy armour would keep out the poison.'

As far as Ralph could see, J.B.F. Brown wasn't carrying a pistol under his jacket tonight, despite the Turret name. Either that or his suit was brilliantly cut to conceal any gun lump. Ralph didn't really mind which. Both showed grand tact. He said: 'On the other hand, Manse, women do have their more helpful side. I'm sure Naomi will be a real asset to you and the—'

'Look, Ralph, I was afraid you might of heard them bad rumours. You probably hear a lot of rumours at the Monty.'

17

Yes, Ralph did hear a lot of rumours at the club he owned in Shield Terrace, the Monty: grubby, low-life rumours. It was that kind of place—for now. He longed to smarten it, respectabilize it. 'Rumours? Bad rumours?' God, had Shale picked up that Ralph expected a kill move from him? Manse might sound thick, but he could read a scene all right and plumb a situation. He wouldn't have been at the top of his firm otherwise all these years. He was never going to win that prize for oratory at Oxford University, but he saw things.

'Bad,' Shale said.

'Rumours about what?'

'Take this discussion we been having re women, Ralph.'

'Bad rumours about women? But which? Not bad rumours about Naomi? I can assure you, Manse, nothing of that sort has come to—'

'No, no, Naomi's different. Remember my first wife, Ralph?'

'Sybil? Yes, of course.'

'I don't know what that name means, but it didn't ought to be "pleasant", I can tell you. *She* could get bitter.'

'A trying time. We all—'

'*Very* bitter.'

'I'm sorry.'

'She went off with some optician or roofer—living in North Wales. Ivor. Or maybe

18

a vet.'

'Best put all that behind you now you have Naomi as a fixture, a lovely fixture, Manse, and a new mother for Matilda and Laurent.'

'Put it behind me?' This was almost a shout, a tormented shout. A few people looked across at Shale, Brown one of them. '*I* can put it behind me,' Manse said. 'That's all I'd like to do—put it be-fucking-hind me. But Syb? She's heard I'm getting remarried and, suddenly, she starts wondering if she done right, flitting like that. Why I referred to it—the way they change. They goes one way and then another. No explaining it. She came back for a while, you know. This wasn't just flitting, but *re*flitting.'

'Well, yes, I heard that.'

'She got fed up over there in Wales. It's to be expected, in a place like Wales. But then, after a while, she's off again, back to him. That don't mean she's decided she's happiest with him. It means she just felt like another move. Then she demanded the divorce. That's her, not me, Ralph. I didn't want it—the final wrap-up. But she kept on, and it had to happen. And now? It's like this, Ralph: jealousy was always big with Syb. Miserable jealousy. So, now she gets to know about the wedding and this really franticizes her. She hates it. Most likely she's thinking about the money. Well, of course she is. Don't tell me opticians make *real* funds. Or roofers, or even

19

vets. It's all taxed, Wales or not. She *says* she can't stand the notion of a strange mother for *her* children. So fucking caring! And late. She didn't worry about the children or me when she walked out, and walked out again, and then wouldn't let up until divorce. What bothers her now? It's the money.'

'But she chose to leave, Manse. The money didn't seem to matter.'

'It didn't matter *then*. She had a taste for someone else and went to him. Twice. How they are, Ralph. They got undoubted impulses. Famous for it. Just watch for a thin line of sweat on their top lip. You ever noticed that on *your* wife's top lip? That means impulse. Or perhaps the signs are different with your wife. Maybe she turns nervy and twitchy, can't sit still, shuffling her feet all the time, and not listening properly to what you're talking about. That's impulse.'

'No, I haven't noticed anything like that with Margaret.'

'Syb could be lovely to me and really special in the womanly sense, such as passion and sweetness. Of course she could or would I ever of married her? Then, though, all that gets a bit shaky. Time's a sod. You probably know what I mean, with *your* wife, Ralph. So, impulse sends Syb off to Wales, brings her back and then sends her there once more. But now? A new situation, yes? Yes. It's a wedding. This word really gets to them—"wedding", or, even worse, "marriage". Wedding is just a day, but marriage is for keeps in quite a number of cases. Yes, she collected a nice heap through the divorce, but suddenly she sees some other woman will get her mitts on everything left here, and legally get her mitts on it, being a totally documented wife—on the business, the art, seven-bed home with Edwardian-style octagonal conservatory, cars, built-in wardrobes, hardwood strip floors, wine cellar—*everything*. That's why I say "a new situation". That's why I say "bitter" and "jealous". You sure you haven't picked up no rumours?'

'What rumours?'

'These rumours are definitely around, Ralph.'

'Unpleasant rumours?'

'That she'll come back and vandalize the wedding.'

'Sybil? But how, Manse?'

'She'll work out how. She's bitter but she's also brazen. Such as carrying on—screaming and shouting in the aisle and that, while the service is actually going its holy way, the vicar in full togs. Abuse at full screech. Flinging language. The fuck word. The cunt word. Tearing at posies. Disregarding in toto the holy setting. Most probably roaring to the congregation how I bought Naomi's rings—engagement *and* wedding—with charlie profits. She've got the strength and the

21

bitterness. This is a big woman, Ralph. Plenty of lung. You can't put bouncers on the doors of a church. Don't the Bible say, "compel them to come in", not "compel Syb to stay fucking *out*"?'

'Oh, Manse, I wouldn't really think she—'

'Them rings was paid for with clean cash, I swear, Ralph—from a Premium Bonds win, which are proper, straight, government things, right? Oh, some might say, but which money did I use to buy the bond what won? Was *that* from, say, cocaine deals? But can I remember when them deals was years ago, and the money just piled up with other money, not money kept special for rings, but left in the bank for whatever kind of requirement arrived, such as school fees, or holidays or anything else, and an engagement and wedding would come in the anything else brackets, not at all expected at the time?'

'You could hardly be asked to keep labels on very various moneys, Mansel, showing their origin.'

'Labels—exactly, Ralph. Crazy. You're quick. You get the point fast. Always did.'

'Moneys flow in as a tributary might into a major river, and it would be absurd to try to distinguish one bit of water from the rest once this has occurred.'

'My feeling, too, Ralph.'

'It would be the view of anyone reasonable who examined this situation fairly, Mansel.'

'One of the ARLs knew I was getting engaged and he come up with a nice ring, genuine stones. A *very* nice ring, and deeply, all-round genuine. He'd took it from someone after negotiations to cover half a debt. I'm not saying he ripped it off her finger, the fucking debt-dodger, but he claimed it, as correctly per the tradition and entirely no blood or flesh entailed in this recovery, he swore. Possibly he even gave a receipt. He said it would do me just right. He was trying to be helpful, Ralph, but I had to tell him I couldn't do that—not use a ring coming from that sort of quarter on Naomi. It would be unkempt. I told him to raise cash on it and make sure this cash went into the firm's account.'

'You were always a one for protocol and the ordinary, fundamental, decencies, Manse.'

'Someone got to be or where are we, Ralph? There's proper behaviour and there's behaviour.'

'True.'

'I know the one I'd pick.'

'And most people would guess which you'd pick, Manse.'

'I go for a big single diamond.'

'That chimes with your personality, Mansel—unfussy, obvious, genuine worth.'

'Well, I hope so. But, look, Ralph, don't let tales like that about Syb put you off.'

'Off what?'

'Off the best man job. Please.'

'Put me off? As you say, these are tales, *only* tales. Speculation. Besides, nothing would prevent me from—'

'I know—we all know—I know how you detests vulgarity and rough behaviour, especially in a church among vestments and effigies. If you hear this gossip, you might pull out, dreading a scene. But we need you there, Ralph, me *and* Naomi. Yes, *need* you. Like the ceremony wouldn't be complete without you. We're lucky to get a church that will take a couple of divorceds, but this luck is not worth a fart if you was to quit in disgust at what Syb might do and not wanting to be involved, which I'd recognize was within your rights.'

'Nothing will stop me, Manse,' Ember replied. 'Nothing. I've heard no stories, and even if I had I wouldn't care. This is a rare—a unique—privilege.'

Ember had one hand on the bar, about to pick up his drink. Shale put *his* hand over Ralph's and pressed down for a moment. 'Thank you, thank you, Ralph. I know for definite Naomi will be *so* content now, content and proud. This is like that event in the Bible making a fine future, what you mentioned just now.'

'Ruth's baby?'

'True.'

God, Ember did need some rapid clarity on what schemes Manse had under way. Did this creepy hand contact really mean something, a wholesome, eternal bond, after all, an authentic thank-you, a bracing pledge, nearly at the blood-brother level? It was Ralph's shooting hand, immobilized for nearly a minute. When it happened, Ralph thought of that *Godfather* scene where Luca Brasi puts *his* hand on a bar and Sollozzo, the Turk, drives a knife through it, pinning Luca there while he's garrotted. Were those earnest pleas about the best man role real, or tricks, or traps? He must try to line up something with Brown and make the first approach now.

CHAPTER TWO

Alone in an old, unmarked police pool Ford, Harpur saw Ralph Ember take two or three steps from a rear door of the Agincourt Hotel into the car park, and then stop. They were graceful steps—what one would expect from Ralph. He believed he had style. Ralph probably thought he had more of it than others might, but, just the same, Ralph felt a responsibility to move elegantly and offer his profile at favourable angles. He seemed to be waiting for somebody. Although most of the car park was dark, a single security lamp near the door made him identifiable, but his profile couldn't at all come over in full glory through the dimness.

Naturally, Harpur wondered whether Ember had managed to get something going with a girl dinner guest or a waitress, and expected her to follow him out now, possibly for something quick and doggie, or, more likely, to fix an arrangement for a better time. Ralph could undoubtedly pull. He looked quite a bit like the young Charlton Heston in, say, *Ben Hur* or *El Cid*—the same fine boniness of face and tall, wide-shouldered body. A long scar along one side of his jaw intrigued some women and gave a pretext for fluttering their investigative fingers on him, stroking that slightly raised line of shiny pink skin until other shiny pink skin reached the agenda, while clucking with sympathy and big, admiring curiosity. They thought the mark must hint at a story, and a story with Ralph as magnificent, though damaged, hero. The damage rated for them as highly as the magnificence because it ignited their caring side. Harpur had seen women react like this to Ember several times and occasionally wished for a face scar himself. About Harpur, though, people said he resembled a fair-haired Rocky Marciano, not a film star: undefeated and unscarred world heavyweight boxing champion just after the war.

But it wasn't a woman who joined Ember after a few minutes in the small patch of light. Instead, someone Harpur recognized as a commonplace courier member of Ralph's firm,

Joachim Bale Frederick Brown, came and stood with him. It looked planned. As Harpur remembered him, Brown had a flimsy moustache and small beard, just about discernible, despite the shadows. Although he owned three first names, most people called him Turret, probably following a gang spat somewhere—not on this ground or Harpur would have recalled it. Brown must have done well in the fight. 'Turret' suggested a blast-away all-rounder.

Ember and Brown talked briefly, earnestly. From where he sat, Harpur could hear nothing of what they said, but it definitely seemed more than chit-chat. The meeting had purpose, and, most likely, a secret purpose. Why come out into this murky yard otherwise? So, what kind of secret would a chieftain like Ralph share with this fetch-and-carry lad, Brown?

Harpur had no answer to that one—nor to a few others. For instance, he didn't altogether understand why he decided to come here tonight. These company dinners happened regularly and wouldn't normally interest him. They were for show only—no disclosures. Any information presented there had been sieved and pasteurized by Ralph and Shale. Occasionally, it was true, Harpur's boss, Assistant Chief Constable Desmond Iles, might suggest a joint stroll into the banqueting hall at about the oatcakes and various cheeses

27

stage to queer the do and cause disruption.
Iles loved—lived—to cause disruption. But he
hadn't suggested a visit tonight. Once, when
they'd invaded a dinner, Iles compelled silence
and recited what was apparently a send-up of
some famous poem:

'Stilton! thou shouldst be living at this
hour:
England hath need of thee . . .'

Iles had a lot of knowledge, some of it not
much use, but plenty of it terrific.

Did Harpur's trip here now amount to more
than an on-spec lurk? He lacked a precise
motive for the stint, just sensed that somebody
ought to take a peep. And he felt unable to
send anyone from his department to watch,
because he couldn't brief him/her on what to
watch *for*. Why target a dinner? Harpur simply
had what he described to himself as 'a vague
prompting', and he'd respond in person. This
basic surveillance wasn't the kind of duty
a Detective Chief Superintendent usually
handled. But now and then he would feel
forced to take on a private session of low-level,
street-level, car-park-level policing, especially
if such a session seemed perverse and non-
delegatable.

'A vague prompting'? Oh, hell! Some bright,
fucking folderol wordage. Where did it start
then? He thought he could spot the moment.

His daughters, just back from school the other day, were discussing in that loud, Now-hear-this, know-all yap of theirs what one of them had read or heard—maybe in the classroom, maybe elsewhere—about a famous book by Karl Marx attacking capitalism. Apparently the argument there was that capitalists try to eliminate one another's businesses so that a smaller and smaller number of them can dominate. All capitalists have this deep, inborn, compulsive need to destroy rivals. The few surviving firms—or even single survivor—have the power then to fix prices as they like and milk the customers. Harpur's elder daughter, Hazel, had seemed to agree with this analysis. She said, 'A bit like our well-known Ralph Ember and Mansel Shale, the drugs biggies here. They've seen off rivals and one day each might try to see off the other, so as to win total control of the market.'

This snippet of economic wisdom had got to Harpur, and especially Hazel's mention of Ember and Shale as examples. Harpur often thought of Ralph and Manse, of course he did. Any detective would. The discussion by Harpur's daughters had put some focus on his thoughts. Between them Ember and Shale had destroyed several small-time opponents, some foreign, and now dominated the trade without rivals. So far they didn't challenge each other, because they had a kind of pact—a practical, long-lasting, profitable, gentlemanly, cartel pact. But *how* long-lasting? Could each of them tolerate the other for ever—for ever meaning until death, or born-again conversion and a purified life, or retirement on amassed proceeds to France or Cyprus or the new Bulgaria? Were Ralph and Manse doomed by Fate, natural, commercial greed and survival instincts, to do final battle? Perhaps trade had slipped during the invasions by those small firms, and never properly recovered. This could make Manse and Ralph anxious—and extreme.

Ember and Brown seemed to have finished their short talk. Ralph obviously did not want to hang about there and began to move back towards the hotel door. Perhaps they'd made some sort of arrangement to rendezvous at another time in easier conditions. Had this been a talk about talks—future talks? Brown stayed put for the moment, probably under orders. They'd avoid re-entering the banqueting hall together, a give-away: yes, the meeting was confidential. Harpur had been lucky.

But, then, just before Ember disappeared, Harpur saw the outline in the blackness of another man over at the left corner of the building, apparently about to cross the car park towards the gates, perhaps to wait for a taxi. He might have come out from the Agincourt's front entrance and walked around the side of the hotel. When he'd taken a couple of steps into the car park he seemed suddenly to see Ember and Brown. Darkness and distance made any try at recognition impossible.

After about three minutes Brown followed Ember into the hotel. A little later, the other man came out from where he must have been waiting and watching at the edge of the Agincourt, and this time did walk across the car park to the gates and stood there, gazing left up the road. Harpur could get a better look now, and had an idea he was someone fairly significant in Mansel Shale's outfit. Harpur's mind failed to come up with a name, but he'd keep the description in his head and check with the Drugs Squad and/or some dossier pictures: about five foot ten, wiry dark hair, round-faced, say thirty-two to thirty-six. Did it matter? Had Harpur learned much? Perhaps, yes, he'd been lucky to witness these Agincourt happenings, but what did they amount to? He'd discovered Ember wanted a quiet chat with Brown. The two were noticed by No-name, who made sure they didn't know they had been spotted. So? Was this a good night's work? Had he been fortunate to overhear that bit of conversation between his daughters, and smart to come here as a result on arm's length reconnaissance? A Saab—maybe a taxi, maybe not—arrived at the gates and picked up the waiting man. It drove off.

In fact, though, it wasn't Hazel and Jill's

words alone that brought Harpur to the Agincourt tonight. He'd been influenced by another conversation, maybe less woolly, more concrete and workaday. Harpur knew an art dealer, Jack Lamb. Occasionally, Jack spoke a useful word to Harpur. In fact, he reckoned Lamb the greatest informant known to any detective anywhere at any time. And he breathed his hints and more than hints exclusively to Harpur. However, Jack had his rules and conditions. He was selective about what he passed on. He could not be regarded as a mere grass—at least, not regarded by Jack, himself, as a mere grass. He took no money, but he did like to keep his business unharassed by very valid police nosiness. Harpur could help with that up to a point. Jack offered his whispers when he considered a crime or planned crime to be especially vile, cruel, sickening. Or when he feared some behaviour threatened the general peace, balance and overall worthwhile orderliness of things. Jack wanted a decent, serene scene where people had time to focus on their special interests, such as picture collecting, and had adequate disposable income to buy from him.

'Manse Shale, Col,' Lamb had said.

'What?'

'Suddenly, he wants to buy big.'

'Art?'

'Pre-Raphaelites.'

32

'Well, he's always been into those,' Harpur said.

'This is major.'

'He likes colour, shimmering frocks and auburn tresses. He's sold on tresses. Manse has all kinds of unexpected tastes. And he heard the Pre-Raphaelites formed a Brotherhood. He envies this. Manse yearns to belong to something intensely worthwhile, even noble. His firm doesn't fit that bill.'

'He has an Arthur Hughes and a couple by Prentis. They came from me, and I'd give decent odds at least two are genuine. At least. But he's going up a level. He wants a search for anything by Burne-Jones or Rossetti or Hunt. These are much desired. These are rare on the market. We're talking heavy prices, we're talking lavishness here, Colin.'

They were talking heavy prices and lavishness in a small launderette they sometimes used for their conferences, on a drab street in a run-down neighbourhood. Each brought a bag of washing and they sat and watched through the glass front panels as the clothes and bedding did their slow antics among the suds. Harpur thought they could be regarded as a miniature but strong Brotherhood themselves—the detective and his informant. The washing, rather than art, gave them their link now. Harpur considered it reasonably secure here, though they didn't use any of their rendezvous spots too often.

'He's getting remarried, Col.'

'Well, yes, I'd heard.'

'A woman called Naomi Gage. They met via art.'

'Nice,' Harpur said.

'In some London gallery.'

'Is she a tresses person? Great to have a common interest, the same enthusiasms.'

'Manse wants to impress her. So, Burne-Jones or Rossetti or Holman Hunt, to hang in the rectory. It's the sort of thing he'd do, isn't it? The massive Manse-type gesture. A need to show he really rates, and compensate for what he looks and sounds like. That's a fair whack of compensation, Col.'

'I've heard of one of those,' Harpur replied.

'One of those what?'

'Artists.'

'Good.'

'Hunt. Religious? Lantern slides at Sunday school.'

'*The Light of the World*,' Lamb said.

'"Behold, I stand at the door and knock." My Sunday school was fundamentalist and generally didn't approve of religious art and images—too churchy and idolatrous. But Hunt was OK.'

'He helped start the Brotherhood.'

'Grand.'

'I've got some inquiries out for work by any of the three,' Lamb said.

'Manse will be grateful.'

34

'But where's the money to come from, Col?'

'He does all right.'

'He does all right. This has to be more than all right, though, a lot more. They say he draws £600K a year from the firm.'

'Yes, I have it at about that,' Harpur said.

'Fine, but finite.'

'Maybe his fiancée's loaded.'

'I haven't heard this.'

'Would you?'

'I would if she's seriously into art, not just a show-hopper.'

'We ought to get some research going and see if she—'

'Besides, Manse wouldn't touch her money, if there is any. You know what he's like.'

'What?'

'He's Manse.'

'And?'

'He's proud-stroke-vainglorious-stroke-fragile-stroke-absurd. He has to prove his grandeur. He pays.'

'He does have a sort of crooked grandeur,' Harpur replied. 'Sometimes he rides a 1930s-type heavy Humber bike, with chain guard to keep the oil off his trousers.'

'I wonder if he's got something in mind, Col. Something fund-producing. Something *extra*-fund-producing.'

'What kind of thing?'

'A new situation.'

'Which? A new *business* situation?'

'Only Manse.'

'Only? Only in what sense?'

'Manse and his firm alone. And so the money booms—doubles and more.'

'Monopoly?'

'Monopoly. Twice as much business, plus push up the prices to whatever he fancies because there's no other supply.'

'My daughters mentioned this.'

Lamb twitched. He stood six feet five inches, not at all how most people thought of an informant. They'd expect someone small, furtive and slight, say Toothpick Charlie in *Some Like It Hot.* A Lamb twitch needed space. 'What? Your daughters?' he asked. 'You mean two kids spoke about Manse possibly seeing off Ralph—possibly *killing* Ralph?'

'The theory. The built-in, unstoppable, free-enterprise drive. Firms may thrive alongside one another in the hotbed conditions of retail, but all those firms have chiefs who wonder whether one firm—theirs—wouldn't thrive even better if it didn't have to waste energy fighting competition. No, no, they don't wonder, they *know* one firm—theirs—would thrive better. Of course it would. They *wonder* about ways to achieve that excellent state. How do you rid yourself of the others? My daughters get all this from school or it's something they've read.'

'My God—their school teaches how drugs firms' chiefs slaughter each other? But I suppose it's a state comprehensive.'

'Mainly, the children talked ideas. Hazel needed examples, that's all.'

'*Is* he going to wipe out Ralphy, Col,' Lamb said, 'in the cause of art and his new woman? Try to? Have you got other pointers—I mean, besides your daughters? I don't like the idea of Ember dead. Why I'm talking to you. Equilibrium would be smashed. Equilibrium's a very dodgy item. Disturb it and you're into chaos. Carnage. No good to anyone. These two are pillars, Colin.'

'Pillars of what?'

'The imperfect, priceless civic structure.'

'I heard Ember's to be his best man.'

'I heard that, too. Clever?'

'To tranquillize Ralph and the rest of us, you think, Jack?'

'Manse could not *not* ask him or Ralph would know something rough was coming his way soon.' The wash programme finished and Harpur and Lamb collected their laundry. 'I'll think about it,' Harpur said as they left.

And he'd thought about it and decided on the basis of Lamb, Hazel and Jill to come to the Agincourt tonight. Or to the Agincourt car park. This couldn't be termed high-tech bugging, but perhaps it had produced something. Taxis began to arrive now and the diners dispersed. He waited until both Shale and Ember had emerged at different times into the bit of light and departed safely and separately. Then at just before 2.30 a.m. he drove home.

Luckily, Denise was staying over tonight— luckily in the happy sense that she'd be in bed when he got there, and in the sense that she'd be with them for breakfast. His daughters liked this. It felt like family. They missed their mother, dead a long time ago now. Denise had a room in student accommodation at the local university, but she'd often sleep at Harpur's house, in Harpur's bed, at 126 Arthur Street. Harpur knew she didn't like the substitute-mother role. The idea scared her, maybe seemed to snare her. After all, she was only nineteen, less than five years older than Hazel. Denise tried to treat them as pals. The girls got the hint and reacted right, but they still took obvious comfort and satisfaction from having her at home with them. So did Harpur.

Although he tried to be silent entering the house now, Jill, his younger daughter, must have heard something and came downstairs in her dressing gown. Possibly, she hadn't slept but waited for him to return. She often did some monitoring of Harpur's hours away from the house.

'We said surveillance,' she told him. They were in the big sitting room, but not sitting.

'That's right, surveillance.'

'When Denise arrived we thought we'd better explain it by saying surveillance.'

'Explain what?'

'Why you weren't here.'

'Thanks, but I'd already told her I'd be late. She mobiled me to say she was coming over. I mentioned I'd have to be out a while. Tuesday mornings she has no classes. We can sleep on.'

'Yes, she said you'd mentioned you might be late, but we thought we'd better explain it was surveillance. Just to be sure.'

'OK.'

'Was it?'

'What?'

'Surveillance.'

'Of course.'

'Dad, do Detective Chief Superintendents have to go on surveillance in the middle of the night?'

'Not "have to". This was special.'

'Why?'

His daughters worried about Harpur's morals and feared his occasional unexplained absences might offend Denise and make her finish things with him, and them. They'd had a loss and didn't want another. 'It was something you and Hazel said,' he replied.

'Something Hazel and I said kept you out on surveillance until two thirty in the morning? What?'

'About competition and monopoly.'

'So, where did you have to do this surveillance about competition and monopoly because Hazel mentioned Karl Marx?'

'That was how it began.'

'Where?'

'This was a matter of watching how certain people behaved.'

'How certain people behaved?'

'Exactly.'

'Which people?'

'Certain people who interest us.'

'Yes, if you stay out in the middle of the night to do surveillance on them they must be people who interest you. I suppose surveillance is always about watching how certain people behave, isn't it, dad? It's what surveillance is. But which people? Where?'

'You had it absolutely correct when you spoke to Denise,' Harpur replied. 'Surveillance.'

'You're brickwalling, are you? Why?'

'You should get back to bed now we've settled everything.'

'*Have* we settled everything?'

'I think so.'

'Yes, *you* would. You think something's settled if you can keep talking without saying anything at all.'

'We've been all around the subject.'

'Around, around, around, without really getting anywhere.'

'I think you should get to bed,' Harpur said. 'That's where to get now.'

'Well, say "Surveillance, as a matter of fact, Denise," if she wakes up and asks where you've been so late.'

40

'She won't wake up.'

'Or in the morning.'

'It *was* surveillance.'

'But say it, so it's the same as what we told her, and then it will sound true, totally true, because three people said it.'

'It *is* true.'

'But best say it—"Surveillance." Then she'll reply, "Hazel and Jill told me that. Surveillance." But what if Denise asks, "Surveillance where?" You could cook up some answer for her, couldn't you? You won't cook one up for me, but you could cook one up for her, couldn't you? This might be important. We don't want her wondering where you've *really* been. Perhaps she'd get upset.'

'I don't have to cook up some answer. I went there.'

'Where?'

'Get your sleep now,' he said.

When he climbed into bed with Denise she grunted and muttered 'Col,' as if to prove she definitely knew who was sleeping with her tonight and didn't object. To welcome him, she gave a feeble half wave of her right hand, but without raising her head.

'Surveillance,' he said.

'Ugh?'

'Surveillance.'

She grunted again and then went silent. He put an arm around her and they slept spoons.

Denise liked morning lovemaking and then a cigarette or two to begin the day right. Harpur didn't smoke but thought the rest of it would be fine. They'd get up to have breakfast with the children before they went to school, then go back to bed for a while, their lips tasting of black pudding at first.

*   *   *

Iles said: 'Something's around, Col.'

'Around?' This was a Jill word, wasn't it?

'No question, around.'

'In what respect, sir?' Harpur said.

'I get that feeling.'

'Which?'

'Perhaps you do yourself.'

'Which feeling?' Harpur said. Iles could intuit. Iles had unstrangulated genius somewhere within and always liable to break out full of puff and brilliance and concealment. Iles heard things, but also sensed things, foresaw things, stored things. Harpur tried not to tell the Assistant Chief too much, hoping to balance up and give himself a chance. Harpur, of course, realized that one of the things the ACC in his magical fashion most probably sensed was that he (Harpur) held back from telling him (Iles) everything he (Harpur) knew. This meant each of them suspected the other of using the spoken word to cloud and even obstruct understanding

42

rather than assist it. They conscientiously and skilfully struggled to avoid all-out disclosure. Harpur thought that anyone listening to them talk would feel each took his own dedicated route, and that these routes only rarely and briefly criss-crossed.

'They had one of their Agincourt hooleys last Monday,' Iles said.

'Is that right? I don't diary them any longer.'

'Why not?'

'Absolutely routine.'

'In what respect, Col?'

'We know who'll be there. And we know the sort of trimmed stuff they'll be told. But, yes, they do come around. Is that what you meant—"around"?'

'Its flavour—I didn't like its flavour.'

'You *know* its flavour, sir.'

'Something's around, Col. Something basic, considerable and perilous.'

'We'll have to deal with it.'

' "Deal with it"! So confident! So matter-of-fact! I love your primitive optimism, Col.'

'Thank you, sir.'

'At my rank, Harpur, one looks for factors beyond the actual matter-of-fact facts. Yes, factors beyond the matter-of-fact facts. The matter-of-fact fact in this case is the Agincourt dinner—a matter-of-fact fact in the sense that it happened.'

'Yes, as a matter of fact, it's a fact it would probably be about time for it to, as you say, sir—come around, as a fact.'

'I agree, we don't take much notice of it any longer—as a fact, that is,' the ACC said.

'We can't learn much from it.'

'Behind this fact—the dinner and festivities—is a bigger element, though—what I've termed for you—so the idea is not beyond you . . . what I've termed for you, a factor.'

'Is that right, sir?'

'This dinner has a context both ahead and back.'

'Ah.'

'Oh, yes, a factor, a context, Col. Dimensions. Width. That's what I'm getting at when I say something's around.'

'A factor? A context?'

'I have a contact in these dinners,' Iles said. 'I get special whispers. *You* might have given up entirely on the occasions. Not I, not entirely. Abandonment of a project is not my style.'

'Oh. Are you close to one of the waitresses, sir, close in your style of being close—which might bring special whispers?'

'I'm given excellent feedback.'

'Nice.'

'By means of this contact I have an overview.'

'I believe some of them are very OK.'

'Who?'

'The waitresses. OK in the way you like.'

'And which way is that, Harpur?'

'Chirpy. Forthcoming. Game for merry-making etcetera. They wear greenish Nell Gwyn costumes at the medieval banquets, don't they?'

'Nell Gwyn wasn't medieval, you dull sod.'

'Her name has come down through the centuries.'

'My source reports an exceptionally happy and convivial Agincourt dinner.'

'Ah.'

'That's sinister. I'm uneasy, Col.'

'Ralph and Manse have seen off a lot of competition, mostly East European. Possibly they had rowdiness from their back benchers at previous meetings, including racism, which Ember is quite a bit against and believes should be applied only very selectively. This time, things would all have been serene and pleasant.'

'Well, of course, you'd have a dull, limited, unimaginative formula explanation for their apparent contentment and good spirits. I have to see beyond that. I want you to think of me as like those youthful locals in South Sea tourist resorts who will dive into the sea and bring up from its considerable depths coins that have been flung in by spectating visitors.'

'Exactly as I always *do* think of you, sir.'

'The surface is an invitation to me. I am not content with it, as its self—mere surface. An invitation to look beneath. I need to see what is hidden.'

'What *is*?'

'As ever, there's a surface amity between Ralph and Manse Shale. What does it conceal, Col?'

'You'll have an answer to that.'

'I do believe in the standard routines of basic detective work—the kind of thing you so thoroughly, even commendably, represent, Col, in your tidy fashion, but . . . sources, Col.'

'True.'

'We are nothing, nowhere, without a source.'

'*Are* you satisfying one of the waitresses, sir? And she's grateful—as she damn well should be—and gives you tip-offs in return? You're not one to mind being mentioned in the Agincourt kitchens as a lover boy with special requirements. People are very understanding these days about kinks.'

'What do I mean by "factors", Col? By "context, as applied to the Shale–Ember cartel"?'

'Some people, when they talk to me about you, say, "Mr Iles is one for factors, not mere facts. And context. Hence gold leaf on his cap."'

'Which people?'

'It would add up to more than quite a few, in my opinion.'

'How many more?'

'"In depth". This is another term they'll use when talking of your approach. Perhaps they've spotted your resemblance to the South Seas boy divers. They'll refer to your "in depth" methods and outlook. I think they mean it well, on the whole. "In depth" links up with "factors" and "context". The same ballpark.'

'You discuss me, do you, Harpur?'

'Many regard you as a considerable topic, sir. They're used to ordinary folk such as their spouses or newsagents or chartered surveyors and then you come along, and very few would say *you're* ordinary in the least. Probably.'

'Which very fucking few?'

'Statistically almost negligible.'

'Do you note the names?'

'People say things for effect. They hear someone spoken of reverentially and feel driven in a destructive way to counter this. It's mere mischief.'

'Reverence I don't seek, Col.'

'Although you don't seek it, it comes, sir.'

Iles nodded, but a fairly minor nod. 'Ralph led a kind of gush testimonial to Shale. This is sickening, worrying, Col.'

'Manse is getting remarried.'

'Yes. Dangerous. Someone he met through art.'

'Is that right, sir? Manse does a lot of appreciation. Apparently, it's a tonic to see him gaze at canvases. Empathy's his chief relaxation. He's very keen on one sort of stuff—auburn hair and long purple dresses.

47

It's his other side from the trade. He wants to be thought of as an all-rounder. Some pictures in his collection at the old rectory are quite possibly not forged, I'm told.'

'Who told you?' Iles was in one of his double-breasted navy blazers that enveloped him like a tribute.

'You know, sir, I *like* to think of Manse Shale as an art fan,' Harpur replied. 'It proves he still has bits of uncorrupted soul.'

'Well, we all possess some of *them*, Col.'

'Is that right?'

'On the whole, police should have more bits of uncorrupted soul than villains. It's tidier that way. It's expected. And it helps mark a difference. This is a difference one favours.'

'I can see the point.'

'Oh, yes, bits of uncorrupted soul are universal, or we're into heresy. It would mean God made evil. At the Agincourt, Ralph led a rendering of "For He's a Jolly Good Fellow".'

'About God?'

'With resounding, mawkish repetitions of the chorus, and pointing at Manse in case of doubt. *For he's a jolly good fellow.*' Iles could do quiet irony, but this was more like out-and-out baying. 'What's behind something as disgusting as that?'

'In which respect, sir?'

'That evidence of grand heartiness between Ralph and Manse and magnificently authentic respect—even affection. What are they

48

disguising? What are they compensating for? Shit will fly.'

'Was this at the liqueurs stage?'

'Why?'

'Well, they kick the waitresses out just before that, for confidentiality. If one of those is your source I'm wondering how she'd know so much. *Do* your whispers come from a waitress you're giving it to, sir?' Or did they come from someone who spotted Ralph and Brown in the hotel car park and hid and watched? Harpur could not ask that, though, as Harpur was not officially there.

'In the past we've invited ourselves impromptu to their Agincourt dinners now and then near the cheese or liqueurs juncture, haven't we, Col?'

'To show interest. In your friendly, positive way, sir, you thought Ralphy and Mansc deserved that.'

'Now, neither of us bothers. Why is this?'

'No, neither of us. Nothing much ever came from our visits.'

'And you'd rather be at home, sporting with the lovely undergrad.'

'I might drift down and have a look at the Agincourt from a distance at the next one.'

They talked now in Harpur's room. Harpur had an armchair. Iles paced. He liked pacing, cultivated inborn pacing skills. He was nimble, slight, less than six feet tall, his grey hair back to normal length after a period when he went close-cropped after seeing an old Jean Gabin film. Iles looked the sort sure to hate the singing of 'For He's a Jolly Good Fellow', no matter who led it, or who was the supposed jolly good fellow. Iles wouldn't really believe there could actually be such a thing as a jolly good fellow, only a song about a jolly good fellow. And this had to get those singing it to bellow and rebellow 'so say all of us', because in fact most considered the jolly good fellow a turd.

Iles said: 'Of course, my source thought it all very lovely, the choral aspect and general harmony of the evening. One *listens* to a source. One doesn't always accept altogether what's said. A source feeds material in. It is I who must decide its worth.'

'Like Tony Blair used to say. Your source can't be a waitress if he/she was present for the singing and the formal speech. Have you got someone grassing to you from Ralph's lot, sir? Or Shale's?'

'And then I gather Ralph's to be Mansel's best man.'

'Ember will look great in the full ceremonial clobber, his jaw scar vivid above a very white shirt.'

'What kind of a ploy is that, Col—Ralphy best-manning?'

'They're long-time mates.'

'I won't have gunfire in a fucking church, Harpur. This is going to be a proper C of E place, I'm told.'

'Who by, sir?'

'Not some non-Con shack.'

'St James's.'

'I'd hate it if such a congregation had to scurry.'

'In what respect, sir?'

'Away from bullets. Manse's people will know *exactly* where Ralph is going to be, all morning-suited and smiley. This might be rapid fire, spray weaponry. There are fine stained glass windows at St James's and fonts and screens. Terrible to hear of a font chipped by gunfire. Think, Col: it would be very poor form to wear a flak jacket over wedding duds, plus buttonhole carnation, and in such a joyous, kosher—as it were—setting.'

'You think Manse is going to—?'

'I wouldn't mind if we could guarantee they'd blast each other, preferably a double death, of course, but mutual serious disabling OK. We'd have a *tabula rasa*. If there's one thing right up my street it's a *tabula rasa,* Col.'

'I've definitely heard somewhere of one of those. Or maybe more.'

'*Tabulae rasae.* A clean sheet, or sheets,' Iles said.

Harpur wished he hadn't pushed Iles into that explanation. The words 'sheet', 'sheets' and/or 'bed' and/or 'back seat driver' could activate him. The ACC said: 'Of course, you wouldn't know *tabulae rasae*, but perhaps you

51

know the meaning of clean sheets. However, and *very* damn however, I wonder if the sheets stayed immaculate when you were exploring my wife in your comradely, heated, sneaky way, Harpur.' Iles began to scream, always a very recognizable, Iles-type, agonized scream, regardless of the particular words it carried at different times. Some spittle fell on to the right lapel of the blazer and lay there glistening, set off by the splendid, dark blue material, like dew on lavender. But Harpur knew that blazers were not special to the ACC's jealousy squalls. In the past, Harpur had seen spit cascade on to both a grey and a navy suit when Iles grew reminiscent in this painful way. Harpur stood and moved across the room, as was standard for him during an Iles spasm. He made sure the door had been properly closed. People at headquarters hung about in the corridor hoping to eavesdrop if they knew the ACC was spending some time privately with Harpur and might go into a hate fit.

There had been a time when Harpur tried to work out the state of the ACC's mind from the clothes he picked for the day. All the civilian garments Iles put on were high grade, custom-made and costly, but Harpur had attempted to tie each outfit to a mood, and so forecast a brilliant and/or amiable or deranged or even neutral spell from the Assistant Chief. Harpur devised a multi-coloured wall-chart in his room to display the relationship of outfits to behaviour, suppose one existed. He had disguised the chart as a breaking-and-entering graphic, and he coded as major warehouse robberies occasions when Iles actually had notable froth on his lips in an outburst—something more than a couple of droplets. Harpur kept the chart going for three months and at the end had to accept that Iles's brain and temper operated without regard to particular gear. (Obviously, Harpur excluded Iles's uniform from the survey because he wore this only when due at ceremonies and functions, and it was not a matter of choice.) The chart showed that Iles could be benign and/or constructive in a blazer and malignant and/or doolally in a blazer. It was wrong—unjust and naive—to suppose that when getting dressed for work he'd look at his wardrobe and deliberately choose something to flag up and increase, say, his viciousness and frenzy for the next eight hours or so.

'What reaction by Manse, sir?' Harpur said.

'To what?'

'To the "For He's a Jolly Good Fellow".'

'What do her parents think of it?' Iles replied.

'Whose?'

'The undergraduate's. For instance, you're about twice her age, aren't you, quite apart from no-nos such as your clothes and back-street barbering?'

'You see the likelihood of an attack by

53

Manse on Ralph, do you, sir, not the other way about?'

'People marrying above themselves get strange compulsions, Col. They try to up their personal status.'

'*Is* he marrying above himself?'

'It's a fair bet, isn't it, given who Manse is?'

'Who?'

'Manse.'

'I sometimes think he has a kind of dignity, a kind of crooked dignity.'

'What *you* think of as dignity, Harpur, most call moral decomposition. He'd need exceptionally good, accurate people.'

'Who would?'

'Manse. The best man stands very close. Shale won't want to get hit by friendly fire at his wedding. Or the bride. Yes, he'd probably worry about her, too. Manse in the Marriages and Deaths columns of the same *Times* issue —he'd loathe the idea of that.'

'It might turn out to be a really fine occasion.'

'Might it? In any case, that doesn't guarantee anything afterwards. Consider the younger Royals. Or, for instance, my wife and myself. This was a considerable occasion, her father something more or less worthwhile in Town Planning, and stretch limos for guests before stretch limos were everywhere.'

'I for one would have bet on it.'

'But what happens after a few years?' Iles's

voice began to rise once more. 'You'll see what I'm getting at, won't you, Harpur? Won't you, Harpur? She and someone I thought of as a dear, admittedly loutish, but unswerving colleague decided they would—'

'If only one of them were killed in a gang battle—Ralph or Manse—which would you prefer it to be, sir?' Harpur replied.

'Of course, Sarah can't understand now how or why she ever took up with someone of your make, Col. We often have a chuckle together at the preposterousness of it when looked back on.'

'I believe one sign of a good marriage is husband and wife can chuckle together. That kind of joint chuckling is a true bond.'

'Ralphy will dither, naturally,' Iles said. 'He'll have spotted that Manse most likely wants to see him off. But, because Ralph is Ralph, he'll hesitate for as long as he can. He'll try to prove to himself that his dreads and suspicions are unwarranted. That will be *so* Ralphy. Part fear, part decency. In his generous, nervy style, he craves to think Manse really is a jolly good fellow despite the ferret features and art collection. Do you know what I'd guess, Col?'

Iles's guesses often amounted to clairvoyance. 'I wonder, sir,' Harpur said.

'Yes, I suppose you would.'

'Many admire your guess facility.'

'I'd say Ralph will try to put someone into

55

Manse's firm to take some soundings, get at his intentions.'

'A spy?'

'But for the best of reasons—Ralphy-type, should-I? must-I? shall-I? reasons.'

'Plant an observer? Your contact told you this, has some evidence of this?'

'Of course fucking not, Harpur. My contact describes what is there to be seen and heard at the Agincourt. Nothing else. The factualness of the facts. This is as much as you can expect from a source. It's *my* function to see past these, Col—to envisage, to posit, to anticipate. This is the factor realm.'

Yes, the thing was, when Iles did some of his positing and all the rest of it he generally posited spot on. Harpur had seen this happen so regularly. And perhaps he'd seen it happening at the back of the Agincourt the other night—that secret, secretive, exchange between Ralph and Turret Brown. Iles might be right about Ember's methods. He would favour slow, stage-by-stage tactics—hesitant, cagey tactics. Hardly tactics at all. Ralph *could* take action, but he didn't like it much. Was he lining up someone to do a bit of a crafty drift into Mansel's grace and favour? Joachim would be a fair bet. His work as a courier brought a lot of intermingling. There'd be some half-open doors for him to try to edge through. Iles might have spotted the meaning of that meeting if his car-park source told him

56

of it, or if he'd seen it himself. Perhaps Iles deserved the gold across his cap for gifted inklings, even if his outfits did get saliva'd sometimes.

'Do you think he knows someone who could infiltrate like that and stay safe and effective, sir?'

'Don't be smartarse, Harpur.'

'In which respect, sir?'

' "In which respect" what?'

' "Smartarse" in which respect?'

'Because it sickens me when you ask a straight question,' Iles said.

'In which respect, sir?'

'I know it means you already have the answer, or half the answer. You wouldn't humble your paltry little self more by showing ignorance. You've found out who's going in for him, have you?'

'This would need to be someone who can hear the unspoken, read the unexpressed. Nobody's going to say outright to him, "We're planning to do Ralph." Or not at first, anyway.'

'You've found out who's going in for him, have you, Harpur?'

'I'll do a data sift, and see if I can sort out some likelies.'

'You've done one, have you? Or you've got some other indicators. So, who?'

Harpur said: 'On the other hand, sir, I don't mind at all when *you* ask *me* a straight question.'

'That means zilch. You never reply, anyway. You've seen something, have you?'

'In which respect, sir?'

'Something that says who Ralphy's spy will be. A meeting somewhere? That kind of thing?'

And maybe Iles also knew about a meeting somewhere, such as the Agincourt car park. Often the weaponry in these set-tos with Iles was a show of ignorance.

'Patience is another vital quality for that kind of infiltrator,' Harpur replied, 'plus the ability to see behind bullshit big talk and spot whether a real Kill Ember mission is on.'

'I'm fond of Ralphy, Col. His delusions are worthwhile delusions, not like my own.'

'I wouldn't say he holds you in total contempt, sir.'

'And then, Mansel,' Iles said. 'So winningly in touch with culture.'

'I've never heard him speak badly of you, sir. But, then, he's a wily sod.'

'Equipoise—that's what we've achieved, Col—equi meaning settled, poise meaning the state of things. A settled state of things. Yes, we've achieved that, Harpur. I include you in this, Col, despite your ungovernable, traitorous dick. If someone were to ask me to say in one word what is the basic nature of our operations here I would instantly reply, "Equipoise." We've had peace on the streets from that equipoise between Ralph and

58

Manse.'

'And from your treatment of them, sir. The brilliant blind-eyeing, as long as they disallowed violence.'

'And now, is what we've accomplished all at risk?' Iles replied. 'Am I supposed tamely to let this happen? Does an architect stand by and watch his most prized building burn down? Did anyone else see it?'

'What?'

'This meeting.'

'Which?'

'Ralphy and his chosen one,' Iles said.

'Did your Agincourt source say there'd been a meeting?'

'It was at the Agincourt, was it? Some quiet area? Outside? The car park's dark there, isn't it?'

'Is that what your source said?'

'What?'

'Outside at the Agincourt.'

'You were down there, were you, Harpur? You saw them? This was one of your damned independent saunters.'

'I know Ralph likes the period flavour of the Agincourt name but thinks the phoney armour vulgar,' Harpur answered. 'Yet he puts up with it, no tantrums. I think he has in mind that equipoise you mentioned. The responsibility is weighty, but he will not shirk it.'

'Identification?'

'Of?'

'Jerk—the one with Ember at the meeting.'

'That would be important—if there *were* a meeting.'

'Could you make him out?' Iles said.

'Anyone down there would have trouble getting a proper view. As you mentioned, sir, the car park used to be very dark—possibly still is. You weren't present watching in a personal capacity, were you? I doubt that. A loiter of this kind—hardly a role for an Assistant Chief.'

Yes, Harpur realized he should consider whether Iles hadn't simply guessed in his inspired, magical way about the meeting, but *knew* of it from his 'source', or even because he, Iles, himself, had been at the Agincourt that night—'around' the Agincourt that night—and had spotted not just Ralph and Turret, but Harpur in the old pool car. It was the kind of knowledge Iles in his hoarding style would possibly choose to keep buttoned up for the present, in case he could use it later to injure/humiliate/ demoralize/bewilder Harpur as part of some scheme. Iles loved schemes, especially when they injured/humiliated/ demoralized/bewildered anyone he had a grievance against: a lot. That was part of the rank. If the ACC's information came from someone at the dinner, not from his own observations, this source might well turn out to be the lad Harpur had seen emerge at the side of the Agincourt. He quickly retreated into cover, then reappeared, obviously having watched Ralph and Turret until they withdrew back into the hotel, leaving the car park apparently clear. Harpur had asked the computer to tell him about someone with the characteristics he'd noted at the Agincourt and a search came up with Samuel Quint Aubrey Evox, one of Mansel's Health Pensions and Security (HPS) staff, very clued up and vastly roughhouse. Could Iles really have got something going with Evox? Iles was at least as clued up and roughhouse, so perhaps they drew together naturally. As Iles had said, he recognized the value of sources, and knew where to find them. He didn't stay at his desk. This might mean the ACC realized the back door meeting had been between Ralph and Joachim Brown. Iles could get hold of facts, as well as factors and contexts.

CHAPTER THREE

No shilly-shallying, Ralph took Joachim Brown into the drawing room at Low Pastures, the drawing room itself. Ember thought this would be a soul-refreshing education for Brown. The big windows looked out over paddocks and fields to the sea. Brown was bound to feel the sheer, damn . . . well . . . the sheer, damn established *grandeur* of it all. Ralph did not consider himself, personally, as being central to this grandeur, not its, as it were, essence. That would have been preposterous vanity, and Ralph loathed any kind of pompousness. When he referred to grandeur, he meant the vista, the serenity and sweep of Low Pastures. Of course, Ember realized that by owning the vista, serenity and sweep of the place, he was bound to acquire some of the grandeur himself. He always tried not to make too much of this, though.

He opened a bottle of Sauvignon and poured out a glass each. Lately, he'd come to think of Chardonnay as too 'populist'. They sat in armchairs facing each other. Ralph knew he must achieve a working balance of apparently opposed effects. Brown would be to some degree overwhelmed by Low Pastures, and Ember, in fact, wanted that, worked for it. But he'd also like Turret reasonably at ease, not made wholly speechless and/or gibbering by the timeless, prestige spread, and the inevitable status of its present freeholder.

Near the end of the after-dinner partying at the Agincourt, Ember had found a moment to talk to Brown, who could still be mistaken for cold sober. 'Come out to the rear door for a second, would you, Joachim,' he'd said. Ember spoke the name with no hint of retch or giggle. The shadowiness might be favourable now. Ralph went first. Soon, Brown joined him. He had a long but lively face, slightly arched nose, clear blue eyes, a small pale moustache and chin-tip beard. He wore a dark, three-piece suit, almost certainly made for him, and more or less adequately made. It would be unjust to blame someone like Brown for not knowing the difference between a reasonable tailor and a major one yet. 'I've been glancing through the records of various people, with a certain prime project in mind,' Ralph said. 'Your CV interested me. One or two things I'd like to discuss with you. Look in at Low Pastures, on Friday at two thirty in the afternoon, will you?'

'Low Pastures?' Brown had seemed surprised, even thrilled. Ember understood this, actually expected it. On moral hygiene grounds, he hardly ever asked people from the firm to his home. Ralph's wife and daughters might be there. They had to be kept clear of the trade. Usually, he wanted the property itself kept clear of the trade. Ralph saw himself as guardian of Low Pasture's dignity and wholesomeness: a vast responsibility. But he thought it could be useful to allow Turret entrance, and he picked a time when the girls would be at school and Margaret weekend shopping. Admittedly, he had once let Mansel Shale into Low Pastures for dinner, though Ralph would never regard this as a precedent.

On the edge of the Agincourt car park, Ember had said: 'Confidentiality's important. We won't hang about now. People are beginning to leave and some will come out

63

here or around the side of the building from the front. Let's talk in comfort on Friday. We won't return to the banqueting room together. Wait a little while.' Ralph went back. Brown followed, but not at once. They didn't speak again at the hotel.

So, yes, Ralph had realized Brown would be impressed, awed, by the invitation. But if you were going to ask someone to take on a damned hazardous job for you, special preparatory kindnesses might be wise. Brown must know from talk within the company what a rarity this was, an accolade. And then, Ralph guessed that sight of the manor house and grounds on Friday afternoon would have its effects. If Brown didn't already realize Ralph's social and business standing he'd definitely sense it as he drove up the wide, curving Low Pastures drive, at first tarmac, then large-stone, golden gravel, between an avenue of larch, conifers and beech. The Spanish consul had lived here more than two hundred years ago, and, later, a lord lieutenant of the county. Ralph did not believe in mentioning such former residents too frequently, and did not need to, because most locals knew the history. The house was shown on old Ordnance Survey maps, and under its current name.

Secrecy of the meeting could be better preserved at Low Pastures, as long as Brown kept quiet. In the drawing room, Ralph said: 'Joachim, I'm looking for an assessment—an

64

opinion—a survey—yes, an assessment, opinion, survey of the firms as of now from someone younger, and from someone who in the ordinary course of business has regular contact with our own people and Manse's. You, as a courier—and, at what are you now, twenty-seven?—you seem to suit. A fresh pair of eyes. I value that kind of scrutiny. Of course, I carry out such rigorous examinations myself continually, but comments from someone else, and from a different, perhaps sceptical, generation, can bring a new perspective. I thought that, out here at my home, we might be able to examine matters with a little more detachment. I look at the way things run and, of course, I'm used to them running like that, so I might subconsciously feel this must be the right way—the only way—for them to run. You're not pre-conditioned in this fashion.'

Ralph thought he could shape the talk so Brown would see improved wages plus a hint of possible advance in the firm to departmental head, even eventual leadership succession, or at least deputyship. And this might not be altogether false. No, certainly not altogether. Ember's wife, Margaret, would love him to get clear of the detailed running of the business—not the Monty, perhaps, but the rest. She'd left him for a while recently because he refused to change, taking the children with her, though she came back fairly soon.

Brown said: 'You want a verdict on the firms? Well, they go along all right, as far as I can see, Ralph.'

'They do, they do. But, then, the future. How does that shape up in your opinion?'

'I don't see any difficulties. I'm way down the ladder, though, so possibly I wouldn't. I don't know enough, maybe.'

'Are you satisfied as a courier?'

'I'm learning the business.'

Ralph enjoyed this. Brown was terse, perhaps through nerves at this stage, but cogent. 'A good answer,' Ember said. 'A great answer—one I might have given myself, back in the early days of the business.'

'It's true.'

Ember said: 'The business, as you call it, is complex, Joachim.'

'Well, yes. But I expect every company above a certain size is going to have its intricacies and—'

'Because, of course, it is *two* businesses, though two businesses acting as if one. At present.'

'At present?'

'At present. That's why I asked how you saw the future,' Ralph said.

'You think there *are* difficulties?'

'I think there might be changes, developments.'

'But I'd say again, this must be true of most

businesses. They have to push forward or get left behind.'

So, he could opine and quack, given careful, encouraging treatment, and a little time. Ralph didn't mind the niggly argumentativeness too much, as long as he curbed it when necessary—and 'when necessary' would be when he went into Manse's operation. He'd be there to listen and watch, not fucking well quibble over every damn thing said to him, like a *Newsnight* interviewer.

However, some independence and belligerence in Brown might be pluses. These could be seen as leadership qualities. Ralph would admit that, occasionally, he did feel he needed a lieutenant, and a lieutenant who could one day take over the grind of day-to-day control, with Ralph a figurehead, although, of course, still powerful, still in final charge. Perhaps the invitation to Low Pastures carried all these hints, anyway. It suggested Ralph already esteemed Brown, had selected him from many and considered that this superb venue was spot on, to match his rare abilities. Compare the Prime Ministerial country house, Chequers. Only visitors of stature reccived a welcome there, not dogsbodies. Thcy must shape up and fit in. It was true that just before Ralph, a fairly considerable local villain, Caring Oliver Leach, had Low Pastures. This unseemly recent period could never cancel all the property's previous distinction, though.

No, arranging an encounter with Brown at Low Pastures gave their talk undoubted calibre. Discussions which might lead ultimately to the slaughter of Manse Shale needed a prestige setting, surely. The main gates bore a Latin inscription on a plaque, *Mens cuiusque is est quisque*, meaning 'A man's mind is what he is.' This plaque had come to Ralph with the estate. There was another at a second, minor pair of gates, to the rear of Low Pastures, leading to what used to be the home farm. Maybe they had been put there by the Spanish consul. Definitely not by Caring Oliver! Ralph agreed with the message on the principal gates, which he'd had translated for him by a lecturer at the university. Minds certainly counted in life. But, clearly, minds could not add up to the *whole* of life. If Manse had to be wiped out, this would inevitably be a very physical, not intellectual, matter, as far as the actual killing went, though there would be considerable thinking behind it, and a mind— Ralph's. Today's chat, for instance, derived very much from Ralph's mind, and might turn out to be preparation for that extermination of Manse. He thought of asking Brown what he made of the main gate inscription—did he see minds as important? But then Ralph decided it might be cruel to expose Turret's ignorance of what the words meant.

Ralph knew that many great thoughts came down to us through the classical tongues. Although he had never learned Latin himself, he greatly supported it. He wanted his daughters taught the language, plus, possibly, Greek later. For fuck's sake, if you sent your children to a fee-paying school this was what you looked for on the timetable. But the head teacher wouldn't give way and Venetia and Fay learned classical tales, and so on, in English—what Ralph called 'soundbite Aeschylus'. He considered that story about Atalanta and the golden apples stupid when you read it in English, as he had from one of the children's books. Atalanta said she would only marry a man if he could beat her in a running race. Nobody could until a lad came along and put golden apples on the track. Atalanta went to get them, which obviously slowed her down, and she lost the race and had to marry Hippomenes. This dopey stuff needed to be in ancient Greek, so it didn't come over straight at you—you'd be too tied up translating it to think how daft it was.

Ralph, personally, cleaned the main gates plaque every few weeks and made certain the screws holding it did not corrode and become insecure. He would have seen such deterioration as symbolic, hinting at the decline of so much that had been traditional and worthwhile in Britain. This plaque helped give Low Pastures its unique status. Turret was sure to see it and wonder as he turned into the grounds. For Brown to discover that someone of Ralph's blatant worth wanted him to take on a special commission would inevitably bring excitement: make Joachim ready to accept, eager to accept, regardless of the hellish peril. *Joachim*, for God's sake! His parents must really be something, or barmy. Ember had the idea they'd be the sort who'd take holidays in the Black Forest, camping by a brook and drinking the water regardless.

Ralph liked to apply psychology when selecting someone for a task. As he understood it, this lad, Brown, had a brother who played major roles in West End theatres and at Stratford. Perhaps, then, Joachim felt left behind—a failure. He might be desperate to excel in a career, and impress those fruity parents: *Mother, father, your Joachim has broken through via a dear friend and colleague, Mr R. Ember!* Ralph didn't mind helping someone to that sort of little triumph. By sending Brown to spy on Manse and his crew, Ralph would surely be opening up new and glittering career prospects for him, as long as he survived.

In fact, Ralph felt a duty to let some of his own strength and success seep down to any promising apprentice. It was how humankind progressed. Margaret Thatcher had surely been right on this: if you made it easy for the rich to get richer some of the wealth would

70

reach the less rich, through more gardening jobs in the big houses and deckhands for private yachts. But Brown would understand that for any leg-up to come Ralph must certainly be preserved in place, so as to retain the power to lift him. Clearly, this meant there should be no destruction of Ember by Manse, or Brown was scuppered himself. It would be another reason for Turret to jump at the reconnaissance assignment inside Shale's outfit and bring Ember reports and possible forebodings. Destruction *of*, not *by*, Manse might then be a solution, a regrettable, forced solution, but one which Brown would undoubtedly be proud to have helped initiate.

'You have a brother who's an actor, I understand,' Ember remarked. 'A star, I gather. In that famous play, *The Duchess of Malfi*.' Best rub it in a bit.

'We don't keep contact.'

'Oh.'

'Probably my fault. I drifted away.'

'You haven't seen him—seen him perform? That's surprising.'

'I did go to the Almeida when they had a few weeks there.'

'Good? Were you able to get backstage and congratulate him?'

'I just drifted away.'

'Brother v brother rivalry? A sibling's success intolerable to you? Very common, very understandable.'

'We're different.'

'I find that strange.'

'What?'

'You to be out there in the body of the theatre watching your brother, and he never aware of it. But perhaps he *was* aware of it. They can peep at the audience unobserved sometimes, can't they? He might have seen you there. Perhaps he expected you to go and call on him afterwards.'

'No, he wouldn't expect that or wish it.'

It was flat, it was definite. He'd say what he wanted to say, just that, this one. Did he sound wounded, undervalued? Ralph could help, longed to help, if this could be made mutual. 'Acting has its rewards, I'm sure, financial and otherwise,' Ralph remarked. 'But running a company can have good rewards, too.'

'Absolutely.'

'These rewards have to be guarded.'

'How?'

'What I want is a colleague, younger but very much on the up, who can get used to the way things are done, especially get used to the special circumstances of two separate yet combined firms. I need to feel there's somebody else besides myself who knows the details, could handle them alone, if necessary.'

'Details?'

'What you'd call "the intricacies". The fine points and the possible dangers in this kind of alliance.'

'Dangers?'

Oh, fuck off. Did mummy buy him a big box of question marks for Christmas? 'Somebody who has familiarized himself with the way our company operates—that "learning" you referred to,' Ralph said, 'but who also knows his way around Mansel's firm.'

Brown went silent, as if registering what Ralph had said, picking at it for undertones, searching for the unspoken. There were plenty of these. Let him find them himself. He probably would. Ralph decided he'd chosen a shrewd lad. That could be good or not. He might be *too* shrewd. He'd see the risks in sniffing around the Shale camp and turn Ralph down. 'Ah, I see now, you're scared of him, are you?' Brown said. He stared at Ember and nodded his head slowly three times, maybe to signal that he did not need an answer, because he knew he had it right.

Ralph loved truth, but, obviously, truth demanded sane and delicate handling. 'Scared?' he said. 'Of Manse Shale!'

'I noticed it.'

'Noticed what, where?'

'Fright. At the Agincourt,' Brown said.

'At the Agincourt?' Ember said. 'When exactly at the Agincourt?' Hell, he'd gone into questions mode himself now.

'I thought there were moments of hidden panic, Ralph. But not very *well* hidden.'

Yes, although Ember admired plain

speaking and honesty above all else, sometimes they should be bludgeoned, dungeoned. Like fucking now. This curly-headed creep infuriated him. He'd generously brought Brown out to a brilliant property as sign of possible admiration, but, suddenly, the sod acted breezy and became all incisive and eyeballing instead. For God's sake, this house had a consul and a lord lieutenant in its pedigree. Have a gander at that Latin plaque, will you? Seeing his self-assurance, you'd swear this damn nonentity, Brown, was used to such manorial elegance, and to this kind of drawing room, with its Wellington cabinet, rosewood table and long, Regency sideboard, the cheeky clown. But maybe a couple who'd call a baby Joachim *did* have a considerable property with land. Perhaps Brown wouldn't feel as impressed as he damn well should in Low Pastures.

Just the same, people never, *never*, used the word 'panic' about Ralph when in his presence, and especially not people who worked for him. This, above all, was an image matter. He knew that some, behind his back, called him Panicking Ralph, or even Panicking Ralphy, on account of episodes in the past they did not understand properly. They saw ordinary carefulness and wisdom as cowardice. Foul slanders went the rounds. He could not stop this. But they were now in the fine drawing room of his own fine home and to have this prick actually accuse him *here* of panic dazed Ralph for a few seconds. It nearly brought on . . . nearly brought on a massive Ember-type panic. But he said pleasantly: 'I thought the Agincourt evening very cheery, didn't you?'

' "Oh, for he's a jolly good fellow and so say all of us." ' He sneer-sang this, made it sound empty, meaningless—even more empty and meaningless than it had been.

'Fun, wasn't it?'

'You, lead singer and conductor, but with the suspicion of him, no—outright distrust of him—yes, distrust of him like white hot rivets in your eyes.'

'Oh, I wouldn't say so.'

'No, I suppose you wouldn't, Ralph. *He* could feel it, though. He sits there, hardly a move in response. That tiny, formal quarter-smile. You both clearly had weapons aboard. And then, later, he's shouting something at you. I saw it, half heard it.'

No wonder Brown must hate and envy his brother's success. Joachim possessed terrific, sickening sharpness and fair spiel now he'd loosened up, yet here he was, in a measly, go-nowhere job: go-nowhere unless Ralph gave him something better. And that's what Ralph proposed, wasn't it, in a way? Hazardous, yes, but a step, and maybe a step with prospects if Turret could keep himself alive. Ember poured them both more Sauvignon. He needed it, and actually needed something stronger, say Kressmann armagnac.

'Of course, "that tiny formal quarter-smile" means Shale's as scared of you as you are of him,' Brown explained. 'Therefore, a handgun each in your bras. It's a typical business relationship—lovely cooperation and mateyness for as far as profit demands, and then, beyond this, the dread and certainty that the other one is really after the whole bloody caboodle, and has sly plans to get it.'

He found himself worth quoting, the smug serf. 'Manse and I have a genuine, long-lasting "mateyness", in your term,' Ralph replied. 'This has very considerable ramifications. For instance, he wants me as his best man.'

'Gesture.'

'I don't think that's—'

'What we have to sort out, Ralph, is the difference between gesture and the real, isn't it?' Brown said. 'One of life's eternal quests.'

Oh, a sodding philosopher now. And a cocky one: that 'we'. Any sorting out required, Ralph would do solo, thank you, sonny boy. Ember said: 'Admittedly, there are bound to be tensions in the kind of arrangement Manse and I—'

'You want me to get in there and see what the unholy shite is cooking up, do you, Ralph?'

'What I'd like is—'

'Sure, I can deal with that for you. You'll worry about the nickname, I expect—Turret.

76

Don't. It's no more correct about me than "Panicking Ralphy" is about you, Ralph. I can be subtle and watchful, as well as a blast.' He leaned forward, one hand on offer. Ember shook it. Brown said: 'There'd be due reward and progress in the firm, I take it. You've got quite a decent little set-up out here, haven't you?'

'Bare stone walls and exposed beams give a kind of motif, I like to think,' Ralph replied. 'Everything open, strong, authentic.'

'I heard a villain of villains had Low Pastures not long ago.'

'I—'

'This is absolutely no reflection on you, Ralph.'

'Reflection? On me? How could it be a reflection on me?'

'I said *no* reflection.'

'Yes, but—'

'I'd need £5K a week for the kind of work you have in mind, and certain definite assurances,' Brown replied.

It depressed Ember infinitely deeply to hear Turret name that pay, and name it with a defiant, no-arguments flourish, especially just after Ralph had referred to the marvellous quality of the Low Pastures structure. Of course, he had been thinking of offering more for this job, say eight a week, or even ten. Did Brown realize the kind of risk? Some naivety, here, despite all the flatulent talk? Or was all

77

the flatulent talk on *account* of the naivety—to camouflage it, compensate for it? His brother would be used to speaking concocted lines, many of them corny, full of attitude and not much else. Turret wanted to compete? Did he appreciate what type of difficult information he would be looking for?

Ember never bought cheap. The bare stone walls and exposed beams of Low Pastures had not come cheap. If you bought cut-price you almost always got cut-price results, or no fucking results at all. God, run-of-the-mill people like goalkeepers, barristers, poker pros, surgeons made £5000 a week and more. Ember had imagined he was picking talent when he picked Turret. Ralph felt let down by this miserable, penny-pinching modesty. And Brown had cut across something Ralph began to say—cut across in Ralph's own drawing room—cut across as if the demand for £5K were so bold it must come out at once. As a matter of fact, Ralph had an £8K cluster of twenties already elastic-banded in a desk drawer and another twenty in twenties alongside it in case Brown tried to bargain up.

Ember would not say Turret had actually besmirched Low Pastures by the sad pifflingness of his demand, but Ralph wondered whether he should have let him into the drawing room, especially as his manners in conversation seemed so rocky. Ember could have sited the interview somewhere less, such as the breakfast room or study. It would be amusing but tiresome now to bring out the eight wad and count off five. He'd look like some damn bookie. He wondered whether as Brown watched this procedure he'd realize he had comically underquoted. Ralph decided he would not show the other twenty also. Why be pointed? Let Brown go off with his five, uncertain if he'd done well or pathetically.

Maybe he'd ring up his parents as if to talk about the weather and so on and mention as something incidental that he'd just landed a business commission at five grand a week, so stuff whatever it was his brother earned poncing about on the stage—not five grand a week, definitely. And his parents might consider five grand a week quite a bit, even though they'd been brassy enough to call a kid Joachim, a British kid.

'When I say "certain assurances" I'm thinking of a decent post on the financial side of the firm,' Brown said.

Ralph could have guessed Brown was thinking of a decent post on the financial side, but to pick up five when it could have been eight or ten didn't seem much of a recommendation for someone thinking of a decent post on the financial side. Ember said: 'We're hoping to develop in several new directions. There will be openings.'

'You mean when Manse has been snuffed—deservedly snuffed?'

'It's in the nature of a vibrant company to find previously untried channels,' Ember replied.

'How are you going to do it, Ralph?'

'What?'

'See to Manse.'

'The purpose of this exercise is for you to get a working familiarity with the binary character, yet unity, of the companies,' Ember replied.

'It's not my sort of operation,' Brown said.

'You're backing out?' Ralph felt almost pleased. Did he want to hand over preparations for the possible slaughter of Mansel Shale to this half-baked big-mouth? Didn't Mansel merit a better angel of death than that, after all these years? Manse had a lot to be said for him, and Ralph wouldn't at all have minded saying it, even if Manse might have to be put down for inescapable commercial reasons.

'It's not my sort of operation to see to Manse,' Brown answered. 'I mean, actually to see to him personally. Listen, Ralph, have you got the wrong notion, because I'm called Turret?'

It enraged Ember to be addressed like that, 'Listen,' on his own property. 'What wrong notion, Joachim?'

'I don't do hits.'

'Hits?'

'Shooting in a street battle is fine, entirely

and efficiently fine. This is a matter of fighting for due territory, for respect, for security. But if you're telling me to look for the clever moment to do Manse personally, and do it personally while I'm in there—that's not on, Ralph.'

'What I have in mind is standard business practice at a certain upper level. Perhaps you're not familiar with it yet. Someone considered executive material—potential executive material—is seconded in a career-expanding move to another business to learn—to absorb—its ways, its *intricacies,* first hand. A widening process,' Ember explained.

'There's a basic difference between warfare and execution.'

Seminar time. 'Very much a matter of observing mood, tendencies, atmosphere, and reporting back,' Ember said. 'In some respects akin to an ambassadorial mission. That's how I'd like you to think of it. I'm puzzled by this talk of "hits".'

'If it comes to carnage around the territory, I'll be right there, sweetly with you, Ralph, my gun flair yours to count on. You'll see then where the Turret name comes from. But I'm not one to step up behind Manse and put a few rounds into the back of his head, however noble and necessary the cause.'

'Ambassadorial in the sense that these would be findings from someone embedded in the other, as it were, country—the other business, in this case—embedded and yet not entirely *of* it, and able to apply detachment, perceptiveness, judgement,' Ember added.

'Do you get the gap, the great gulf, I'm talking about, Ralphy? I'm a soldier, not an assassin. The trade unions would refer to this as a demarcation matter. Gunfire might be necessary in each role, but the application is different.

'It's Ralph. Or Ember.'

'I can chart his routine for you, if he's got one, so your people would know where and when to take him. I'd do notes and sketch maps. All that kind of thing is OK with me, within my ambit. I'm pretty good at graphics, clarity one of my watchwords. This would be an exhaustive guide to his habits and itinerary.'

'A thematic approach,' Ember replied. 'To get the as it were *tone* of the other, sibling operation and look at it against ours. This is what I have in mind. Yes, tone.'

'And I'll report back here,' Brown said. 'Phones are out. Insecure. And it wouldn't be a good idea to be seen talking together too often around the firm's buildings.'

'Here?'

'To your house.'

That was meant as a poke in the eye, of course—to dub the domain a 'house'. He could have said 'Low Pastures' or 'your home', or 'the property', but he said 'house' to make it sound nothing much, like a place in a street,

82

not its own acres—sound like the kind of place he lived in himself. Or he would be in *half* a house, or less, most likely, a so-called flat, 15A Singer Road. Brown wanted to try to bring Ralph down, make him sound manageable and only run-of-the-mill. And Brown's methods? To speak slightingly of Low Pastures, and to use the word 'panic'. Obviously, Ember would admit that Low Pastures could, technically, be regarded as a 'house', since it did provide what a family required from a 'house'—shelter, heat and light, domestic fitments. That ludicrously failed to catch the full undeniable nature of Low Pastures, though. In any case, Ralph didn't want him at the 'house' again. The one visit should do to let him see the Ember style. Brown might—might—be entitled to that. Anyway, he'd been allowed it. And this was enough. 'No, we'll fix some rendezvous points, discreet, secure,' Ralph said.

'I'd rather come here.'

'Not on, Joachim.'

'I'd be careful.'

'How can you be careful? You'd drive. Your car's a give-away.'

'I came in my car this afternoon. You must have expected that.'

'Once is all right. It could be anyone, anything. But not repeatedly.'

'Taxis.'

'Hardly, Joachim. Taxi drivers talk.'

'Best here,' Brown said. 'I don't want to be

clock-tied. It might not be easy to get away for an arranged meeting at a named time. I'd prefer to just drop in.'

'But I'm not always at Low Pastures.'

'I know your daily routine pretty well. Everyone in the firm does. In any case, it wouldn't matter. I could wait. It's a comfy billet.'

He'd 'drop in'. Again it was a way of insulting the property. Ralph didn't mind 'billet', an obvious bit of waggishness. But people did not 'drop in' at Low Pastures, and especially not people like Brown. Ralph's daughters might be here when he 'dropped in'. Venetia, the older girl, nearly fifteen, responded too enthusiastically to men, in Ember's view—probably only a phase, but troublesome. He had sent her to finishing schools run by nuns in Poitiers and Bordeaux, hoping they would show her the value of temperateness, though, given the news about some nuns, this had risk. She was back now. Ralph didn't feel sure she'd changed. He had the idea that Brown's bit of moustache and the chin whiskers would get to her, also his flashiness and cheerful insolence, plus a brother an actor. 'Yes, I'll drop in—as and when,' Brown said.

'We'll be flexible about times at these selected locations. I'll wait an hour at some pre-agreed place, say, and if you haven't come I'll assume it's awkward and leave it until the following day. I've got some reasonably anonymous places in mind—say a launderette or one of the old coastal defence blockhouses.'

'Yes, I'll drop in here—as and when,' Brown replied. 'I feel at ease. That plaque on the gate—the Cicero quote: "A man's mind is the man himself." I like this. It means fuck all, but he gets away with it because of all the nice q and s sounds in the Latin. It shows what can be done if you're smart enough.'

* * *

And he dropped in as and when at Low Pastures.

Drop-in 1
He came by hired VW on a Sunday afternoon. Ember and all the family were at home. Brown brought the bill for the day's use of the car and handed it to Ralph. When Ralph gave him the £5000 at the end of their meeting, he added £70 in tens. Brown said he'd do it the same way next time, but on a different day and in a different car, and not a VW. 'As you mentioned, Ralph, "it could be anyone, anything,"' Brown said. But it wasn't anyone, it was Turret. He had on what Ralph took to be skateboard gear—loose, threequarter-length beige trousers, a floppy brown V-necked sweater and trainers: another sad try at proving he wasn't stunned by the splendour of

Low Pastures, and wouldn't dress up for it. All right, all right. To Ember, Brown still looked like someone who would take £5000 for an eight or ten job, had to worry about hire car costs and who couldn't stomach his brother's success. Venetia was in one of the paddocks practising gymkhana jumps. Ember had been watching her from the drawing-room window when he heard the VW's approach. Venetia obviously heard it, too, and pulled the pony around so she could watch as the car stopped and Brown got out at the front door. She'd probably think those drooping clothes brilliant, especially on someone with a bit of beard.

Ember let Turret in and this time took him to the study. 'We'll be undisturbed here,' Ralph said. Brown carried a blue canvas document case.

'Welsh cob?' he said.

Ralph reckoned he could see right through that fucking cob reference. Brown would pretend he was more interested in the pony than in the girl on it. Well, if you picked someone sly enough for a snuggle-up-to-Manse project, you had to expect a helping of all-round slyness. He boasted of his subtlety, didn't he? Ralph would be watching, though. And it was not merely that he didn't want Venetia involved with a man of twenty-seven. He didn't want Venetia involved with a man of twenty-seven who'd taken on a very dangerous ploy that might kill him, or at least get him crippled/disfigured, and for undistinguished money. Taken it on at Ralph's invitation. Venetia could be daftly, wilfully teenage, but she also had the genuine feelings of a young girl. He knew she would be appallingly hurt if a man she'd fallen for were suddenly taken from her, or catastrophically injured. And Ralph dreaded what she might think of him should she discover he'd sent the man into such risk. He feared her hatred.

'How do you manage with the hire?' Ralph said.

'Manage?'

'Do you have to use your real name? You have to show them your licence?'

'I'll use a different hirer next time.'

'And do you keep an eye for tails?'

'There's the good straight, narrow road past farmland, isn't there, before the turning to Low Pastures? Not much traffic. I'd spot anyone behind me.' He looked around the study. As studies went, it was spacious and well furnished with Victorian and Edwardian pieces and a couple of red leather armchairs, also Edwardian in style, but re-covered many times. But Brown would be sure to see it as a downgrading. Never mind: he had to learn that entrance to the drawing room came to nobody as standard. What Ralph gave he could also take away. Perhaps he'd revert Brown to the drawing room on another visit, depending on how Ember judged his behaviour and attitude. Turret should feel lucky to be in Low Pastures at all. He had rejected Ember's suggestions for meetings outside. An advantage of the study over the drawing room was that it had no window looking out on to the paddock and Venetia, as she rode today.

Brown opened his case and spread two sheets of unlined foolscap on the rectangular mahogany table that served as desk. They'd been hinged together at three points with adhesive tape. The pages contained a street map, hand-drawn in pencil. Brown nodded down at it. 'This I've found is the best area for our operation, Ralph,' he said. Again that comical, sidling suggestion of equality. '*Our* operation.' (a) Who decided there should be an operation in the first place? He, Ralph Ember did. (b) Who selected from a barrelful of talent someone perhaps able to handle it? He, Ralph Ember, did. (c) Who finally briefed him and sent him in? He, Ralph Ember did. Ralph knew some history, and felt that for Brown to talk this way was as though a corporal on Utah beach claimed to run D-Day with Eisenhower. Brown—a hired hand, nothing more. But Ralph didn't correct him. Instead, he smiled interestedly, encouragingly, the kind of smile a leader might offer a hired hand, whether the hired hand knew Latin or not. Ralph unhesitatingly bent and studied the sketch map with Turret. He recognized the district. It was borderland ground between his and Manse Shale's territories in the north of the city. Brown pointed to his portrait of a big, square park, full of what he'd drawn as bushy-topped trees and an oval lake. He moved his finger down the left edge of the park. 'This side ours, the other, Shale's.'

'There's a clear division,' Ember said. 'No colonizing or trespassing. Never any trouble.'

'The opposite. And that's why it suits us, Ralph.' His enthusiasm crackled. 'I'm up there a lot, restocking dealers, occasionally debt netting, generally keeping an eye. And the same goes for Manse's couriers. We see one another at work, have a chat now and then, compare problems, conditions. It's amicable—because you and Manse have created and maintained an amicable mode at the top. Of course, the effect of that reaches everyone. It's part of your unique joint achievement.'

'What I meant when I spoke of the complicated binary nature of things.'

Brown pointed again, now to the southernmost part of the park. 'Occasionally, Manse Shale himself will turn up in the Jaguar here and watch his people trading and so on. He drives himself.'

'He lost a chauffeur. Before your time here, probably.'

'Lost?'

'Denzil Lake. Query suicide. Extremely query. Manse has a new driver now, but doesn't always use him. Eldon Something. Dane. Eldon Dane. Manse got used to doing without. Dane gets put on other work for spells.'

'Days and timings vary for Shale. I said I'd get an itinerary for him. Not possible at the park. Well, obviously. He's there to surprise check his team and doesn't want them forewarned.'

'Shale can sound more than usually retarded sometimes, but he's wily.'

'He'll call people over, talk to them through the car window. It's usually friendly.'

'He calls *you* over?'

'Not exactly. But this is why I said it suits us. If I'm talking to one of his people, and Manse calls him, it seems reasonably OK to go to the Jaguar together. That's part of the general friendliness, isn't it? Mind, I'm not pushy. I'll say hello to Shale and we might discuss a few nothing topics—football, cricket, Iran—but if I see he's got something private to say to his guy I'll move on, leave them to it. So, I'm getting a start of some contact with Manse, though never anything forced at present. Nothing stupidly rushed and noticeable.'

'And when you're talking to his people—couriers and so on—do you get any indicators?'

'Indicators as to what?'

'They might give hints of a change, or a forthcoming change, without being aware of it.'

'I'm listening all the time, Ralph, listening, listening, to them and to Manse himself.'

'And?'

'Maybe.'

'What?'

'It's vague—imprecise at present.'

'What is?'

'Just an undertow. Glimpses.'

'Of?'

'Like a longing—a longing that if they came out and spoke about it, spoke plainly about it, which, of course, they don't, a longing that says, "Wouldn't it be so much simpler, so much easier, so much more convenient, if we had the whole district here, not stuck on one side of the park?"'

'Monopoly?'

'Ralph, I've got to stress this is only an impression.'

'They want monopoly. Do you ever hear them use the word "rationalize"? That's what they call it in business. It means, get rid of the competition to make things more "rational"— rational from their point of view, of course: scooping the whole bloody lot in an easy, assured, comfortable, reasonable, rational way.'

'An impression only, and, of course, it's confined to one segment of the city trade.'

'For now. Perhaps it's typical. It forewarns of a general strategy. Hitler started his assault on most of Europe by marching into a small, apparently insignificant state, Czechoslovakia.'

Brown shrugged, as though wanting to tell Ralph that he, Turret, did not go in for perhapses, whatever Ralph did. And the shrug might also signify that Brown couldn't see sense in the comparison with Adolf. He, Turret, had to have current evidence, even if the evidence was only—stressed—an impression. Ralph read all this insolence into the shrug but decided not to retaliate, or not yet. He said: 'And your *impression*—which of them does it come from?'

'Several.'

'Other couriers and so on?'

'Right.'

'And what about from Manse himself?'

'I haven't talked to Manse all that much and then, as I said, mostly very ordinary, safe topics. But, yes, from Manse as well.'

'What about his eyes at these times—these moments when you think he's cosily dreaming of both sides of Willows Park—dreaming of *taking* both sides of Willows Park and regarding them as a template for—a first victory towards—a pattern for—total city-wide monopoly?'

'His eyes?' Brown said.

Someone knocked on the door and Ralph called, 'Come in,' knowing, of course, it would be Venetia. She still had on her riding clothes—jeans tucked into calf-high boots, and a yellow, fluorescent waterproof jacket. The hard hat she'd left somewhere, so her hair could be on show.

'I wondered if you and your guest would like some tea or coffee, dad,' she said at a gush. 'My father can forget about such things,' she told Brown. 'Sometimes you wouldn't think he was mine host at a social club, used to dealing with guests.' She stood in the doorway, her face cheery and hospitable, giving Turret a more thorough examination than she'd had time for outside.

'Welsh cob?' he said.

Venetia provided one of her large, instant smiles, which those French nuns, if they were worth any fucking thing at all, probably told her should not be aimed at men, except the helplessly sick and/or old. She'd ignore that. 'Oh, you recognized her, did you?'

'What's her name?' Brown said. You could more or less believe from his voice that he really longed to know. This lad had flair. Ember saw he had done well to pick him for the job, the sneaky bastard.

'Jasmine.'

'Lovely.'

'She's not always well behaved,' Venetia said.

'No, well perhaps we can't say that of anyone,' Brown replied.

Oh, let's play Hints. 'This is Venetia, my elder daughter,' Ralph said. 'This is Mr

Brown. Venetia has been living in France, in an educational sense, though with a religious element, also. We felt a broadening of the cultural base to be so long-term advantageous now things are increasingly, indeed irreversibly, global. I feel it is a kind of courtesy to familiarize oneself with at least one other language. Myself, I'm a bit old to learn, but Venetia does it as my representative, you might say!' He laughed briefly.

'Do you ride, Mr Brown?' Venetia said.

'A bike sometimes.'

'Oh, *moi aussi.* But horses?'

'I used to. Not much chance these days. No stabling at 15A Singer Road, I'm afraid.'

'Oh? We have several mounts here, haven't we, dad? Maybe you'd like to—'

'Tea or coffee?' Ember said. The way Brown slipped her his address infuriated Ralph. It might be just modesty—an understandable, unavoidable, admission that 15A Singer Road didn't rate with Low Pastures, and that he had to think bike not cob. Or . . . or it might be his way of telling her where to find him, the dirty schemer.

'Tea would be great,' Brown said.

'Two teas, then, Venetia. Yes, Mansel's eyes,' Ralph said, when she had gone. 'Can you read a yearning there, a policy, and a determination?'

'I haven't concentrated on his eyes.'

'Eyes convey, Joachim, especially with
94

someone otherwise hard to read and whose words come out as such a mess.'

'But it's his voice I notice. Not what he actually says, of course. An impression I have. I keep coming back to that word.'

'You can hear this yearning, this determination, in his voice, regardless of what he actually says?'

'There's *something* there. Intent is there—as if he has to fulfil a destiny, and cannot do other than aim for it.'

'And this "something". Does he try to involve you in that, Joachim?'

'Perhaps too early for such an approach. As I say, I don't push. He probably wouldn't see me at this moment as any more than a courier for you, who happens to bump into him during market times at the park. We have to bring him on, Ralph.'

'Bring him on', like fattening up a goose to give *foie gras*. Ember loathed to hear these cruel, purposeful words used about Mansel, but, yes, the scheming, ruthless sod had to be brought on. 'Does Shale speak of me?'

'Now and then.'

'In what terms?'

'Always friendly, admiring, at this stage. And I'm sure you'd speak of him in friendly, admiring terms, at this stage.'

'Which stage are we at, Joachim?'

'The game-playing stage. The best-man stage. The old buddies who'd never harm each other. It's the phoney war.'

Venetia reappeared with the teas on a tray. She'd brought a cup for herself. Ralph would have expected this. 'There are good rides here,' she said. 'Not just around the paddocks, but down towards Aspley's farm, Mr Brown— oh, but, look, I can't keep calling you Mr Brown, can I, if we're to ride together?'

'Joe.'

'What, like the actor in old TV movies, Joey Brown?'

'That was Joe E. Brown. No, not like an actor. Just Joe.'

'I like short names for men. Bold.'

'Venetia's a grand name,' Brown said.

'It's historical,' Venetia said. 'She was a Lady and very beautiful. A famous painting of her, by Van Dyck.'

Drop-in 2

'I think we have a change,' Brown said.

They spoke again in the study. Ralph made the tea. 'Change?'

'The kind we want. There's a sort of bond.'

'Between you and Manse?'

'This time he obviously wanted to talk to me in private, not to his own man. Manse sent him away.'

'You were out in the street, chatting through the Jag window?'

'It's jokey, light-hearted.'

'Manse? Jokey?'

96

'Relaxed. His words get a bit garbled, as you know, but what he's saying in his own style is, doesn't it seem strange that in one way we're rivals up there, although I hobnob with his people like mates. Punters move from one side of the park to the other, looking for the sweetest deal—best stuff, lowest price. He sees what he describes as "like a contradiction there". He wonders if it's "max efficient". He mentions that lately he heard about a terrific business school in one of the US universities. He asks, would this business school consider the trading arrangements around Willows Park sensible, if the professors did a deep study of drug pushing there? He means Harvard Business School. He couldn't get to that but did say he thought it began with an H or a V or a W. He asks me, don't I believe the experts in that business school would regard it as mad that two companies who are almost partners should at the same time waste effort and perhaps endanger good relations through local competition?'

'What do *you* say?'

'Not much. I let him go on. Of course, he doesn't—can't—put things as simply as I've just done, but that's what he means. Although Manse talks gibberish, there's a lot of nous behind it. Well, you wouldn't have an arrangement with him otherwise, would you, Ralph?'

'It stays like this—in the realm of theory?'

97

'Not a bit. In a while he asks, why don't I come over and look at how his operation works, look thoroughly, so I know from the inside what he's talking about? Just out of interest, to make it not all academic. However, he stresses, no neglecting of my duties for you—he's very strong on that. But when I have a few hours free, get in touch and he'll give me the tour of his firm.'

To Ralph, the invitation seemed damned quick. Damned? 'You'll do it?'

'This is how we hoped it would go, isn't it?'

'Along those lines, yes, but does it strike you as too pat? What about his eyes, his voice?'

'Nothing unusual. Not that I could make out. I watched his eyes especially, after what you said. Just steady, businesslike—as if he was offering work experience.'

'But what *is* he offering?'

'Oh, I'd say he wants to bring me over, so the balance at Willows shifts. He'd be stronger—got an extra body—me—plus, and much more important, he'll expect me to talk about *your*, *our*, operation and plans, won't he—reciprocity? It would look suspicious, otherwise. So, he thinks he'll have a spy—the way you wanted a spy, Ralph. I'll be double-agenting! He can make his initial move against your firm at the park. Then the rest of the city.'

'But if you went to him like that he must realize I'd guess something was up.'

98

'He'd act fast. It's like Hitler grabbing Czechoslovakia, isn't it? No Venetia today?'

'They're at school.'

'Ah, I should come Saturdays or Sundays if I want to talk horses.'

'On the whole, I think weekdays are the best.'

'But I enjoyed her company. I'll try for Sunday week, Ralph.'

Drop-in 3

It didn't happen.

Venetia said: 'I thought Joe might come back.'

'Why?' Ember said.

'That was just the feeling I had,' Venetia said. She'd cornered Ember in the Low Pastures library. He'd gone there to do an internet search on a London club he'd not previously heard of, the Oriental. Ralph constantly looked for metropolitan models to base the reshaped Monty on any time soon. Obviously, he was careful. He didn't believe *all* London clubs might give him a pattern. Good God, the papers had a story lately about someone shot in a London club for asking people not to smoke. That most probably would never happen at the Monty, even in its present shady state. But he didn't want to be entirely stuck with imitating exceptionally respectable clubs like the Athenaeum or the Garrick or White's, either. Limiting. These clubs certainly had their strengths and reputations, but might be over-conventional. The Oriental possibly offered something unusual, exotic, he could aim for at the new Monty.

'It was a bit of business previously with Brown,' Ember said. 'A one-off, really.'

'I wanted to show him around the stables.'

'He's a busy character. He handles a lot of work for the company.'

'What kind of work?'

'Specialized.'

'But specialized how?' Venetia said.

'It's just that he called by for an urgent briefing,' Ralph said. 'Exceptional. He needed my instant advice. That's what I'm here for.' But he, too, had expected Brown to show at Low Pastures today, the Sunday week he'd mentioned. He'd know Ember would be anxious following their last conversation. Following that, and as the result of Ralph's instructions, Brown meant to make his move, into the Shale operation for a look-around. Although Brown would decide tactics and timing himself, ultimately he was acting *as the result of Ralph's instructions.* Ember worried about that. Brown ought to realize this and get out to Low Pastures, if only to prove he still could. A turnaround. Ralph recognized it: he *wanted* Turret at Low Pastures now.

'Many a beard like his I saw in France,' Venetia remarked. 'Not those big bushy things like over here, but neat and distinguished on the end of someone's chin, often for what are referred to as intellectuals. Called an imperial because their emperor Napoleon III had one.'

CHAPTER FOUR

Harpur's mobile phone rang. Jack Lamb said from his car outside: 'Alert, Col.'

'What?'

'Possible bother.'

'What?' But Jack did not answer. Harpur stood still and waited until Lamb spoke again. The pause stretched. Harpur considered ringing him back. Then Lamb said: 'Sorry. I had to put the phone out of sight. It draws attention.'

'From?'

'Do you know what this reminds me of, Col?' Lamb replied.

'Should I?'

'*All the President's Men.*'

'All the what?'

'That film. It comes on the movie channel. About Watergate. The break-in at the Democratic Party HQ. The raiders' lookout man warns them by radio phone they've been rumbled. And so we're on the way to the end of Nixon.'

'Have I been rumbled, for fuck's sake, Jack?

Are we on the way to the end of Harpur?'

Another break. Then Lamb said: 'Repeat, please. I missed that. Had to hide the phone again.'

'Somebody's spotted you? Us?'

'This one's sharp.'

'Which one?'

'This kid. I worried that she'd see me. I'm noticeable, anyway, lurking in a car at night. The phone makes it worse.'

'She?'

'She.'

Lamb was on watchman duty for Harpur in the street. As he would expect from Jack, he seemed to be handling it conscientiously. Twenty minutes earlier, Harpur had broken into Joachim Bale Frederick Brown's place at 15A Singer Road for a quick look around. Now and then, Harpur regarded this kind of visit to someone's home as absolutely necessary—a proactive surge, though not one to win him the Queen's Police Medal if he got caught. He felt he could learn quite an amount about the occupier from the way the rooms were arranged and decorated, plus, occasionally, there might be some revealing find on the premises, not otherwise reachable. This could be true of tonight's search. He wondered if he might discover Brown dead in there, and dead a long time. *Joachim Brown's body lay a mouldering in 15A*? Harpur went quietly. Brown's flat occupied the ground floor

102

of a large old semi. Above it, on the first floor, was 15B, well-lit and obviously in use.

Harpur liked to make these intrusions solo. He could observe and think better then. Other officers moving about inside would distract him and possibly interfere with fittings or ornaments. Harpur wanted such items exactly as they should be: their situations might signify. Even the trivia could talk. Or, Harpur kidded himself it could. He suspected he actually fancied illegal break-ins because they excited him, and that kind of job excitement at his rank was rare.

'Perhaps she *has* seen me,' Lamb reported. 'Hold on, Col.' Jack went quiet again, presumably lowering the phone once more. Then he said: 'This is a girl about fourteen, fifteen, on a bike.'

'What about her?'

'I thought at first maybe your daughter. Hazel? I met her once at your house. I wondered if you'd told her you were coming here.'

'Of course I wouldn't tell her.' He told nobody—except Jack. But that was the wrong way to put it. More accurately: it had been Jack Lamb who suggested the break-in, with himself as flagman, and Harpur had said OK. If he'd done the entry with a police team there'd be all the worthy, dismal palaver about permission and a warrant. These were very admirably intended to safeguard ordinary people's important rights and privacy, but, plainly, Harpur couldn't always be arsed. Perhaps he should have been. He realized it now.

'Someone ought to take a look inside 15A Singer Road,' Lamb had said. This was at a second, urgent, Jack-called meeting with Harpur a couple of days ago.

'Which someone would that be, then?' Harpur replied.

'I'll watch, if you like, while you're at it. Make sure your mobile's working.'

And Harpur's mobile *was* working. Now, he waited again for Jack to come through on it. Harpur stood near a big wardrobe in the 15A bedroom. He had a thin-beam torch with him, off for the moment. The flat was ground-floor, half the house, self-contained with its own front door. As soon as he entered with his plastic card, he'd heard someone, perhaps more than one, moving about overhead, in 15B. Harpur had stood still in the small hallway and tried to decide the disposition of rooms. There were three closed doors near him, two on the left, one on the right. Also on the right, another door stood partly open. Briefly, he shone the torch there. He could see what seemed to be a breakfast bar and beyond that a fridge and stove. He reckoned a bedroom, a bathroom, a sitting room and the kitchen.

He did some big breathing, partly to quieten

himself, partly to take in the atmosphere of the flat: after all, Jack believed a body might have lain here for up to three weeks. 'The mind and the instincts of a burglar are of the same kind as the mind and instincts of a police officer.' This gem had fixed itself in Harpur's memory years ago, when his wife, Megan's, books still lined the walls of the big sitting room. Occasionally, among all the heavy, dismal stuff there, he'd find an interesting title, and one day he pulled out a volume called *The Secret Agent*. Glancing through it, he'd found that sentence. Harpur did not fully agree. No, not fully. Close, though. And he sometimes thought of the words, muttered them to himself. He thought of them again in 15A, muttered them again in 15A. They fitted pretty well, didn't they?

The dangers for a police officer on this kind of grossly lawless jaunt at Brown's flat also matched those faced by a burglar. Absolutely no entitlement. Absolutely no back-up. Brown could be alive but away for a while. He, or someone else with a key, might arrive and find Harpur here. He was unarmed, of course. Because the job did not officially exist—*could* not exist—he had no cause to ask for a weapon from the armoury. A bad drawback when dealing with somebody nicknamed Turret? All the same, the risk of discovery had seemed to Harpur just about acceptable—acceptable against the big, unavoidable need to get in and

105

do some gifted nosing. This was how he argued and re-argued the case to himself.

He needed to re-argue, and re-re-argue, because he didn't stay convinced. If he thought Brown's body might be here, shouldn't he organize a proper, authorized rummage, regardless of his mad, egomaniac, juvenile taste for going alone? Didn't a suspected death make that behaviour wrong—more wrong than usual: wrong from a police procedural point of view, obviously; and also wrong towards the dead man, if here, and his possible family—disrespectful? Yes, it did. But Harpur couldn't go public with his fears for Brown, because the tip-off behind the fears came from that important, second symposium with Jack Lamb. This meant, it was *only* a tip-off, not guaranteed fact, though Jack's tip-offs almost always turned out sound. More important: because Lamb gave the tip to Harpur privately, he, Harpur, must do nothing that might point to Jack as the source, or there would be no more tips from him. This followed the sacred, unvarying precept of all cop–informant deals. If Harpur announced that he wanted a police party to scour 15A Singer Road, he would naturally have to say why. And, however discreet and evasive he might be when answering, someone—say, Iles—say, especially Iles—someone would probably be able to work out where the original murmur came from. An informant might speak to a detective when *only* the informant could have known what he spoke about. Dicey. And, therefore, Harpur felt bound to do at least his first inquiry unsupported and on the quiet. Something precious, binding and very practical existed about an officer's obligation to a source, particularly a priceless source like Jack.

Soon after bringing his earlier item about Shale's drive for more important, more expensive, pictures, Lamb had telephoned Harpur at home, as usual, wanting another rendezvous. Not in the launderette. They'd talked this time at the remains of a Second World War anti-aircraft gun site on wooded high ground near the edge of the city. For some months they had abandoned this venue, afraid it might be known. But Lamb seemed to consider the spot safe again. Invariably, Harpur let him pick the location: it was Lamb's balls at risk in the mincer, not Harpur's. It was *always* the informant's balls at risk, except if the informant were female. Grassing—the unforgivable virtue. Jack liked military connections. When they met here, or in an old concrete defence pill-box on the foreshore, he'd generally come wearing army surplus gear, though not necessarily British or harmonious. Perhaps he could convince himself by the costume that this was someone else blowing the treacherous gaff.

This gun-site meeting would eventually—or,

actually, much quicker than eventually—lead to the disgraceful Harpur–Lamb operation at 15A Singer Road, and to this moment in 15A Singer Road when Harpur deep-breathed laboriously, more to keep himself steady now than to trace the possible remains of Joachim Brown. Harpur felt like—well, like a secret agent, and an agent who wanted to stay secret. Admittedly those words in the novel comparing detective and burglar were self-proving and vastly obvious: clichésville. When the police officer wanted to catch the burglar he had to try to think like the burglar, of course, so he, the police officer, could work out where the burglar would be, or had been, burglarizing. Harpur put up with the obvious, though, and how would writers fill a book as long as that without clichés? He'd read some of the tale and thought it pretty good. But he'd had most of the books taken away and never finished it. Books in bulk disturbed Harpur, and Megan had a lot. They'd seemed to disturb the children, too. Partly it might be the collection was associated with Megan only, and therefore continually reminded them of her absence. But he felt it was more than this. Books in such a number seemed to boast that life could be set down on the page and nicely presented between covers. This struck him as vain and presumptuous. Perhaps Hazel and Jill thought so, too. He'd never asked. The books were a sensitive topic. Neither girl objected when he had the majority of them taken away. Especially he'd hated books with gaudy gold or silver lettering on the spine. *The Secret Agent*'s title and author name appeared in ordinary black type, though. He liked the title, embraced it, enacted it now.

At their second get-together, Lamb had said: 'A youngster called Brown, Col—missing. One of Ralphy's. Courier type. Know him?'

'Missing? What's that mean?'

'Missing.'

'These people drift about, particularly low-level personnel. They go where they think the money's better. He might be in London, Manchester, San Francisco—not missing, questing.'

'He might.'

'Anywhere with what he'd regard as a bigger trade scene. Pushing is not like being a head teacher—stuck with one school.'

'Ember's worried.'

'Ember's always worried. He should have been somebody's mother.'

For their conference, Lamb wore a beautifully cut short grey overcoat, especially short on him at his height. Silver-coloured rank insignia decorated the epaulettes: a pair of crossed sabres and three narrow bars. In the meagre light at the gun site, the coat looked unmotheaten, inspection-standard, though it might date back to the French or Russian or Swedish cavalry, when cavalry meant horses, not tanks. They'd need a hefty mount for Jack. With the riding coat, he had on a large-peaked baseball-style—or American admiral-style—blue and yellow cap, a cerise cravat, and red-edged training shoes. 'This Brown from Ember's lot, Col—know him, or of him?'

'Brown?'

'Joachim Brown. Same first name as Hitler's foreign minister, Ribbentrop—and, of course, there's *Saint* Joachim apocryphally father of the Virgin Mary.'

'That's something to load a child with.'

'Which?'

'Both.'

'Also called Turret. He can shoot.'

'We'd probably have something on him,' Harpur said.

'You know Joachim Brown, do you? Brother an actor, Clement Porter Brown. Towards star status.'

'Ribbentrop was hanged, wasn't he?'

'This Brown, extremely close to Ralphy.'

'And only a courier?' Harpur said.

'Yet. My information is that Ember had, has, something very major lined up for him.'

'Information based on what, Jack?'

As a formality, Harpur always asked this kind of question, and, as a formality, Lamb always ignored it. Any informant would. A source's sources remained confidential, just as a source him/herself remained confidential. Tonight, though, Lamb had answered. 'You

110

know these Agincourt company get-togethers they have—his outfit and Shale's?'

'They still do that?'

'A very intimate—sensitive—chat between Ralph and Turret at the back of the hotel. The edge of the car park.'

'How do we know this?' Another disallowed question.

'*I* know it,' Lamb said.

'Ralph's gone gay?'

'Business.'

'Someone saw them?'

'Hurried. Furtive, you might say.'

'But seen all the same?'

'Obviously.'

'How—if it was intimate?'

'An accident. Someone going home early spotted them.'

'As I recall it, the Agincourt car park is badly lit.'

'No question—them. My source got under cover until they disappeared. A few minutes. Nothing more.' Lamb had climbed on to the low, concrete circular wall, marking the outer limit of the gun site. He looked down across the gleaming city. He probably felt protective, like one of those ack-ack gunners, ready to fight off Nazi bombers in the war, though the city would have been dark, blacked-out, then. A concrete slab road, originally laid for transporting supplies and ammunition and troops up to the emplacement, was part overgrown but still usable, and Harpur had driven halfway up, then walked. Lamb had left his car at the bottom of the hill and done all the rest of the climb on foot. Now, he didn't turn his head away from the sight below but spoke over his shoulder: 'Ah. *You* were at the Agincourt car park, were you, Col? You saw this encounter, too.'

'What are they supposed to have discussed?' Harpur replied. 'Not much, if they only stayed minutes.'

'And they did, didn't they, Col?'

'Perhaps a chance thing. Possibly they came out for a smoke.'

'They don't. Not fags in either sense—gays or ciggies. These were talks about talks. Plainly, what we have to ask, Col, is whether Ralph has started to wonder what Manse is up to?'

'Up to in what sense?'

'They like monopoly, these boys. Cartels are very nice, but they prefer total, unshared control. It's an imperative with them. Maybe Ralph has heard of the Manse search for pricey, big-name art. He—Ralph—wonders where the money's coming from. He suspects Manse hopes to boost his loot by emerging as the one-and-only. Possibly Ralph put Joachim into Manse's firm to read the signs. That's the sort of move natural to Ralph. He'd see he'd better do something, but wouldn't want to jump right in. Ralph is gradualism. Ralph is softly-softly. Ralph is keen to believe well of people, even Manse. He'd need evidence. Brown's courier job should give Brown a reasonable start.'

'Speculation, Jack.'

'And he's been at Low Pastures since the Agincourt. Briefing? Debriefing?'

'No. Ralph doesn't let his people into Low Pastures.'

'I know. That's why it matters.'

'And why it's unlikely.'

'Almost certainly Turret in a hire car, driving past the Aspley farm one Sunday. Where else would he be going? The road stops at Ember's place. Why a hire car? Disguise in case he's spotted driving past the Aspley farm to Low Pastures?'

'This Brown—young?'

'Late twenties.'

'Presentable?'

'A little beard and a moustache.'

Yes, Harpur knew all that. He didn't know Ember had let Brown into his house, though— if he had. 'Ralph isn't going to invite someone like that to Low Pastures. It's because of his daughter. She's a bit prone.'

'I believe my source. Unusual, I admit, for Ralphy to do this, but we're into crisis behaviour. Emergency, Col. Manse and Ralph might both regard it as crux time, king-pin time, monopoly time, fight time, grab time, taken-at-the-flood time, last chance time.

Ember's rules crumble. To me, that looks like the start of chaos. No good to any of us. I can't stand untidiness. We must have order. Iles and you have been able to deliver that so far. But from now on? Problematic, Col. So, I'm giving you the word. I don't grass for the sake of grassing—only when I feel the whole civic system under threat. Those two together have helped maintain that system. Take one away and we tilt towards destruction.'

'Have you checked what name he used to hire?'

'Joachim Brown. It has to chime with the licence.'

'And he's missing?'

'Brown's not around Ralph's outfit, nor Shale's, come to that. We're talking weeks, Col.'

'As I said, London, Manchester, San Francisco. You're building a hell of a lot on a mini-chat at the back of the Agincourt, Jack.'

Strangely, it looked as though Lamb and Iles had the same source about the Agincourt car-park meeting, Samuel Quint Aubrey Evox, from Manse Shale's Health, Pensions and Security (HPS) staff. And, naturally, S.Q.A. Evox would also talk to Manse. This lad must perform a lot of word-in-your-ear stuff. So, did Iles as well as Jack know that Brown was 'missing'? Did Manse know? Well, perhaps Manse knew it better than anybody. Possibly he'd actually arranged for Brown to be 'missing' after S.Q.A.

Evox of the HPS section described Ember and Turret in brief conversation—would-be unobserved conversation. After all, this was why Harpur had come for a look-around to 15A Singer Road tonight. Brown might be dead here. After hearing about that Agincourt incident, maybe Manse waited for Brown to try some sort of infiltration—or might even have offered him some sort of infiltration, as a come-on. And had Brown tried it, and suffered for it? People like Manse could be very hard on spies.

Conceivably, Manse was even aware of Brown's excursion or excursions to Low Pastures. This would really tell Shale that important schemes might be cooking. As far as Harpur knew, Manse himself had been invited to Low Pastures only once. Jack, as ever, most probably had it right: Brown's invitation signified. It must point to mightily sensitive, mightily root-and-branch plans. The prospect of these might have activated Shale. This thought, plus the disappearance of Brown, had pushed Jack Lamb towards that instructional, policy-forming remark: 'Someone ought to take a look inside 15A Singer Road.'

As a proper start to his search there and pre Jack's interruption on the cell phone, Harpur had stepped towards the door nearest him on the right. Except for the half-open kitchen door, this one was the least problematical. He knew it would take him into a bay-windowed living room at the front of the house. The curtains were open and, when doing his plastic card magic on the outer door, he'd been able to glance in from the porch and glimpsed easy chairs and a chiffonier. He realized he must use the torch very sparingly. The beam would be visible from the street, and could draw neighbourly attention, especially if there had been no lights in the flat for weeks. He would *look* like a burglar, as well as having the mind of one. A narrow light beam in a black room might do more to suggest something fishy than if he switched all the lights on. By being discreet, the beam told of furtiveness. Just the same, he wouldn't be putting all the lights on. Not yet. He gently turned the knob on the first door and pushed it back. He took one more step, which put him where he could see most of the room.

It was shadowy, though the large windows let in some light from the street. He went forward a few more paces and again briefly switched on the torch. He kept it pressed to his left trouser leg and pointed at the ground, to minimize spread. In any case, the ground—i.e. the fitted carpet—interested him above all. If Brown were lying here that's where he would most likely be. Harpur thought it improbable—improbable for this room, which could be examined through the windows from outside. The postman or Jehovah's Witnesses might have done a peep and seen anyone lying there, possibly for weeks. A fair quantity of post lay in the hall. Harpur intended to go through that later.

Besides the armchairs and chiffonier, the room contained a settee under blue velvet or velveteen loose covers, a knee-high, glass-fronted oak bookcase with a few paperbacks and hardcover volumes on two shelves, and a couple of round coffee tables, one with an old copy of the *Daily Mail* neatly folded on it. An oblong mirror hung over the fine, traditional-style, floral-tiled fireplace, and silver-framed technical drawings on grey backgrounds were grouped on the facing wall. Harpur used the torch to check the corners of the rooms, then switched off and moved back towards the door and hallway. No Turret. Harpur intended to go through the flat quickly and see whether Brown, or anyone else, were here. If not, he meant to carry out a more thorough and systematic search, including the mail. He couldn't really fashion a profile of Brown out of a chiffonier and blue loose covers. Harpur thought he'd risk pulling the curtains over in this room for a second examination, so he could switch on the lights and see properly—supposing the flat still had electricity.

He'd done a quick visit to the kitchen next, and found nothing there, either. Then he returned to the two closed doors to the left, giving on to rooms at the back of the house. He chose the first and eased it open. Not a bathroom. It must be the bedroom. The

117

curtains were across here, and the room very dark. Harpur did one of his breathing exercises again. Nothing bad reached him. He thought the torch would be safe now. He switched on and lifted it to chest height so he could light up the room reasonably well. He moved the beam slowly from left to right. He saw a double bed, properly, even neatly, made, with a fresh looking, flower-decorated duvet cover. A Victorian or Edwardian slatted back wooden armchair in its natural wood colour stood near a massive, his-and-hers mahogany wardrobe, which carried a long mirror on each of its doors. A couple could check their outfits for the day simultaneously. To the far right he saw an antique washstand adapted as a dressing table, with a hinged, satinwood toilet looking-glass on it, Victorian, possibly earlier, he guessed. Brown or his landlord liked antiques.

Harpur decided he'd better look inside the wardrobe. It was easily big enough to take a folded body. He moved forward and got a double image of himself and the lit torch in the two door mirrors. Because of the general darkness of the room he couldn't make out his face in much detail and felt glad of it: he might have been demoralized by the presentation of two lots of anxiety, both his. He'd been about to open the wardrobe when Lamb's call on the mobile came. Harpur had let the wardrobe wait and concentrated on Jack's warning.

Now, Lamb said: 'No, it's not Hazel. I've

been able to get a closer view. I don't recognize her. Very interested in 15A. She's been riding up and down Singer Road, as if just out on a spin. Yes, riding up and down, mock-casual. Now, though, she's focused.'

'Focused?'

'I think she's spotted me and decided, So what?'

'So what what, Jack?'

'She'll do what she wants, regardless,' Lamb said. Then, further silence, until: 'She's stopped outside, Col.'

Harpur turned away from the wardrobe and moved quietly back to the room doorway. He could look from there towards the flat's front door. It had a frosted glass panel. Harpur observed what might be the shape of someone holding a bicycle. Then that outline shifted, part dissolved, grew even less precise, broke into segments—the kind of effect frosted glass would bring sometimes. He thought the girl might have moved to put her bike against the outside railings.

'She's coming to 15A, Col,' Lamb said.

Did Brown have a daughter, or an underage girlfriend, and did she, whichever it might be, have a key? Or perhaps her 'focus' was actually on the door to 15B, which Harpur had noticed at the side of the house. He could hope. But, no, she wanted 15A. And, also no, she seemed to have no key. Two long rings on the 15A bell sounded. The flat did have

119

electricity, then. Harpur put the phone on to Silence and edged back a little further into the bedroom, so as to avoid her line of vision if the girl peered through the frosted glass. And, naturally, she would when no answer to the door bell came. She rang it twice more. He remained still. In a little while, he heard a click and, for a moment, thought she did have a key, or could do what he'd done with the plastic. Then he realized she must have pushed the letter box open. From his new standing point he could no longer see the front door but imagined she must be bending down to speak through the gap.

'Joe,' she said, 'are you there? Joe? Mr Joey Brown—you inside?'

She waited. Harpur waited. She said: 'I thought I saw a tiny bit of light, Joe. Well, I did. I know I did. Like a small torch, aimed down so as not to be noticed, but I noticed.'

Harpur wondered whether he could get out via the kitchen and the back garden if things grew really bad. What would be really bad? Say, if a police patrol car came down Singer Road and spotted her crouched against the front door like a burglar—or like a police officer, according to *The Secret Agent*, if the police officer were Harpur. There'd be some questions for the girl and then the patrol might decide they'd better arrange for a look inside the flat.

'I thought you'd come back one Sunday,

Joe. I wanted to show you the stables,' she said. 'But how many Sundays is it now—two, three? I like just *felt* you'd come back. You know?—when you *feel* something so strong it becomes the truth? I think dad expected you, too, although he says no. Well, he would. But he's worried, I'm sure of it. You can tell these things when you know someone really well, and I know dad really well, although I've been abroad a while. I biked down the road a few evenings last week and this week and the flat was always dark. And then that little gleam. It made me happy. It broke all that horrible, dead blackness.'

Not Harpur's daughter, then, but Ralph Ember's. Who else had stables? The older of Ralph's girls was sent to France for schooling, wasn't she—'abroad a while'—and to get her away from a man, or men? Harpur had mentioned that to Jack just now. Lamb said Brown had been at Low Pastures. On a Sunday? Lamb also said Ralph was a worrier, and the girl said her father worried. Yes, Ralph did worry. The girl had a fancy name, didn't she, almost as fancy as Joachim? Not Vanessa. Venetia?

She spoke more loudly, desperately. 'Are you frightened of something, Joe? Are you hiding, pretending nobody's in the flat, but really *you* are? So, you won't put any lights on? Have you been in there all the time? Who are you frightened of, Joe? Is it to do with why you came to our place? I think a big bloke in a car might be watching the place, Joe.' She increased her voice, made it urgent, as if afraid he was somewhere at the back of the flat now and unable to hear. 'He started talking on a mobile—I think when he saw me. But he's looking at 15A, too. He kept trying to hide the phone. So . . . so . . . what do you call it . . . so *vigilant.* Do you think he saw the torch beam, too? Has he called up some other people? That's what we've got to think, isn't it? He could be a what-you-call—a pathfinder. Will his gang come? Oh, Joe, will you be all right?'

Urgent footsteps sounded overhead in 15B, then came the clack-clack of someone descending stairs at speed. A man's voice reached Harpur through the open letter box. 'Hello.'

'Hello,' the girl said.

'I wonder would you mind telling me what you're doing there?' In 15B, he must have heard the shouting and hurried down to investigate. He'd have emerged from the upper flat's door at the side of the house, walked around and found Venetia crouched against 15A's letter box.

She probably straightened now. Her voice was more distant, but Harpur could still make out what she and the neighbour said: 'I wanted Mr Joachim Brown,' she told him calmly. 'So kind of you to come to help. I have an important message from an associate for him, a business message that brooks no delay, brooks no delay at all.'

'Who are you? Who *is* your associate?'

'We have been unable to reach Mr Joachim Brown by telephone—landline or mobile—and therefore my associate asked me to come and deliver a message in person, since it brooks no delay in a business situation,' she replied. 'My associate is unable to come himself personally, owing to commitments.'

'What business situation?'

'Timing is so important in a business situation,' she explained.

'I've seen you cycling up and down this road several times lately in the evening. I believe you're damn well casing the area.'

'Casing? What's that?'

'Don't come the innocent with me. Picking a place for you and your mates to break in at.'

'Some men look *really* interesting when they're angry,' she said, her voice softer, sweeter now.

'Which men?'

'It sort of lightens them up.'

'What does?'

'It shows they can be really emotional—not just angry but other feelings, too. Do you live here alone, I wonder?'

'What?'

'These flats—I should think they're very nice and comfortable, are they? Oh, my name's Venetia. But I don't know yours yet.'

A woman's voice was added now. She must be in slippers or stockinged feet. Harpur hadn't heard her move across 15B or come down the stairs. 'What is it, Graham?' she said.

'I have an urgent message for Mr Joachim Brown,' Venetia said. 'It brooks no delay.'

'He hasn't been in his flat for weeks,' the woman said. 'We heard the shouting but couldn't get the words.'

'She was talking into the letter box,' Graham said.

'Someone watched the flat from a car,' Venetia said.

'Which car?'

'He's gone,' Venetia replied. 'Drove away. I think he guessed I'd seen him. Someone big.'

'Oh, of course, of course. Eyewash! I don't know what's going on here, but it has to stop. Push off now. And if I see you in the street again—not just tonight—any time—I'm going to call the police.'

'I was telling Graham how fascinating some men look when they're cross,' Venetia replied.

'Please, go,' Graham said.

'I wonder if you have a piece of paper and a pencil?' Venetia said. 'I'd like to leave a note for Mr Joachim Brown, on behalf of my associate, since the matter is urgent and brooks no delay.'

'No,' the man said. 'This is ridiculous.'

'Oh, that can do no harm, Graham.'

'Thank you,' Venetia said.

After several minutes, Harpur heard something pushed through the letter box. 'Now, get lost and stay lost,' the man said.

'So grateful for all your help,' Venetia said.

Harpur gave it a quarter of an hour before moving or making any sound. Then he crossed the bedroom and looked quickly into the wardrobe. He did not find Brown. He rang Lamb. 'I'm coming out at once, Jack.'

'I'm in Cobalt Street. Left out of the house, then second left. I say again, this is a bright kid. She'd spotted me.'

'Ralphy's daughter.'

'Ah, so she *would* be bright.'

Harpur picked up Venetia's note and the mail and put it all into his pockets. He checked the road then let himself out, closed the front door and went to Cobalt Street. Jack drove him to Harpur's own car, parked a few more streets away. When Jack had gone, Harpur switched on the interior light in his Ford and read the sheet from Venetia: 'Mr Joachim Brown is invited to a Sunday with the Welsh cob and others. Coffee and/or wine will be served. RSVP ASAP.'

CHAPTER FIVE

Of course, Ralph Ember knew his anxieties about Turret Brown might be stupid, a kind of panic. People in the trade moved around, looking for the best scene—meaning where the money was bigger and easier. Free enterprise signified you could run free. Maybe Turret had heard tales of beautiful gains in London or Manchester or San Francisco. And so, 'Farewell!' Or not an actual 'Farewell!' No official leave-taking, no giving of notice. Just a flit, a sudden absence. And this would be especially true of anyone in a dogsbody job, with no real status or stake in the firm, no fully bought loyalty. By now he might have his own firm somewhere, using all the skills he'd been taught here, but using them for himself. Soon, there might be word of him and the scale of his new business from London or Manchester or San Francisco.

But Ralph couldn't totally believe this. For a start, Brown had started to emerge from a dogsbody job into something bigger and more promising. He'd sounded interested in a future with Ralph's outfit, and at once accepted a dangerous commitment to help make it secure. Yes, there'd been some cheek at Low Pastures, and some near-insolence, but a deal had resulted. And Brown did not appear money-driven—or not very efficiently money-driven: hadn't he settled for five a week, though he might have got eight, or even ten? There'd been real excitement in his voice when he described to Ralph how Shale began to show him special trust. Or seemed to.

Or seemed to. A ploy, a lure, a trap? Had Shale expected the approach, deliberately encouraged it, then acted? Did someone spot Ralph and Turret chatting behind the Agincourt? Was Brown identified driving to Low Pastures? Manse might sometimes sound untreatably thick, but he could join up hints and make a tale. He wouldn't own a company, otherwise. Shale didn't dawdle, and if he sensed a threat he'd pounce at once to eliminate it. Yes, eliminate it. Brown had reported that Manse more or less *invited* him to look over the Shale outfit. Didn't that sound bad? The constant darkness of Brown's flat at night troubled Ralph. Always that blackness on the ground floor, and, usually, lights upstairs in what Ralph assumed to be 15B. These past couple of weeks he'd detoured slowly through Singer Road a few times quite late to look at 15A from outside. Never any change. To go via Singer added only a mile to a trip Ember would have made, anyway: he generally went to the Monty for the last hour or two of the night, to make sure the wind-down stayed unviolent, put the takings safe, and check security at lock-up.

Tonight, Ralph went by the Singer route again. This time, though, he stopped and pulled into a space about 100 metres away from 15A. He decided he'd watch for ten minutes. He realized this would probably be as useless as simply passing through, but he'd give it a try. Ralph had an idea Venetia might occasionally come to look at 15A, too: perhaps even call there, some evenings, though earlier. This influenced him. Venetia would disappear for a couple of hours with her bike from Low Pastures and, if asked, say she'd gone to visit a school friend. He could tell she'd been a little wowed by Brown. She still wowed easily despite nuns. He'd mentioned his address while she was present.

Then, Ralph began to think that perhaps his daughter showed more guts than he did. He felt convinced she would not merely cycle past if she came to look for Brown. Almost certainly she'd go to the front door and ring or knock, no messing. Ember always reacted fiercely to a charge of cowardice, even one brought by himself. He knew about the harsh nickname some gave him—Panicking Ralph, or Panicking Ralphy—and he struggled to make this disgusting label look wrong. Surely he should at least match what his fourteen-year-old daughter did—or what he imagined she did. It might not be enough just to park here.

When Brown was around and working it

would have been mad for Ralph to go to his front door, even at this time of night—perhaps especially at this time of night, an unusual hour for visitors. Their connection had to remain as secret as it could be, regardless of Brown's insistence on coming to Low Pastures. But Turret Brown was *not* around and apparently *not* working. Different priorities took over. Top of these might be the question: did Brown's insistence on coming to Low Pastures in fact help get him slaughtered? Second question: had he been slaughtered at 15A and left there? Suppose he had little contact with his family, and no partner or regular sex life, he might lie unfound at home for . . . well, for as long as he had been missing. Ralph should try to find out the truth, shouldn't he? After all, he, personally, not his teenage daughter, sent Brown into those special, assured perils.

Duty niggled Ember, and the pressure began to nudge him towards one of his panics. It was the absence of choice that did it. To go to Brown's front door probably involved no particular danger. But Ralph always hated, resisted, any sense of compulsion. He wanted options, alternatives. Now, he couldn't see any, and he felt a line of sweat build across his shoulders. He feared that the old, long scar along his jaw had opened up and begun to seep something colourful but unattractive towards his collar. These were standard symptoms of an Ember panic. He put up a hand to touch the scar, and, of course, as ever, found it utterly intact. But this did not console him much. To *believe* a leakage was happening proved an attack. However, the fact that he could lift a hand to touch it showed full paralysis had not moved in yet. This amounted to something like a victory. But he wished he had parked nearer to 15A. He would not be able to rely on his legs for a while.

So, he waited for three minutes then left the car and began to walk towards 15A. And— another triumph!—his legs did it well enough. He reckoned anyone watching would regard this walk as confident and bonny. To his mind, it was plainly the walk of someone unafraid of approaching Brown's front door, or almost any front door; and of a man who had fathered a daughter unafraid of approaching Brown's front door, or almost any front door. These thoughts made his legs even more powerful, by a kind of compound interest. The sweat across his shoulders dried and did not resume. There had been a battle with himself and he had won it—that's to say, the part of himself which was not Panicking Ralph but rock-like Ralph had won it. He gave the bell two considerable, very unapologetic rings and waited. Ember felt that nobody more dauntless and determined had ever stood in this porch and rung the bell. Although he did not know the history of the house and flat, he believed this must be one of its most significant moments. He could look into the hallway through the door's frosted glass panel and see who might come to answer, if anyone did. It surprised him that no heap of post lay there. After three weeks, he would have expected at least a pile of junk mail.

Then he heard light footsteps and for a second imagined it must be Turret responding. Ember squinted hard into the hall and prepared a greeting, severe yet familiar: *Joachim, you undisciplined, dilettante sod, where the fuck have you been?* But he saw nobody. Then he realized the sound of those footsteps came from the stairs to 15B. The door of that flat opened and a man came around to the front porch. He wore a dressing gown and slippers. 'Can I help?' he asked. To Ember, it seemed the man had expected to find someone else here, and quickly adjusted what he meant to say, and its tone. Quickly but not altogether.

'I'm looking for Mr Joachim Brown, a colleague,' Ember said. 'He lives in 15A, I think.'

'A colleague? Excuse me, but may one ask where?'

'Yes, a colleague.'

'You see, we've had some . . . well . . . *activity* here tonight. My wife and I are rather on edge. We've been keeping an eye, as it were. And an ear! We heard you approach. It's very late. I thought I should come down.'

'Activity?'

'A caller—that is, *another* caller, before you.'

'Is it unusual for Mr Brown to have callers?'

'Well, he's not here, you know.'

'I thought I might catch him in.'

'As you see—no.'

'And the same for the previous visitor?'

'A young girl.'

'Called here?'

'On a bicycle. I've seen her in Singer Road before, sort of idling along, but obviously interested.'

'Obviously interested in what?'

'The flat. 15A.'

'Why?'

'Well, I don't know. But, to guess: perhaps because it looked unoccupied? I can't say.'

'Unoccupied and a potential break-in target, you mean?'

'One mustn't rush into suspicion, agreed. But that kind of thing makes one uneasy these days, you know. And nights. Excuse me, but perhaps you have another explanation. Possibly, I should not have spoken as I did—speculating without evidence. It's true, she did shout some messages through the letter box. Do you know this girl, I wonder?'

'Who is she? How can I tell?'

'She said she wanted to deliver a business message on behalf of "an associate". It would brook no delay. That was the phrase—"brook no delay". She said her associate could not

132

reach Mr Brown by telephone and was unable to come to Singer Road personally, because of business commitments. So, she'd been sent. We couldn't hear what she actually called through the letter box but it did not appear to be the communication that would "brook no delay". Only her attempt to reach Mr Brown. It sounded a bit quaint from a child—"an associate", "brook no delay".'

Venetia liked sending up jargon and fruity phrasing. Where had she come across 'brook no delay'? And she'd love the crazy pomp of 'associate' and 'commitments'. 'But she didn't say who the "associate" was?' Ember asked.

'I wondered, you see, if, in that case, *you* were the associate—the commitments now having been put on hold or concluded, so you could call in person, rather than sending her?'

'What is it, Graham?' A woman from 15B joined the man. She, also, wore a dressing gown and slippers.

'Another caller for Mr Brown, dear.'

'I'm afraid he's not here,' she told Ember.

'I mentioned the girl with the bike,' Graham said. 'And the way she said she was acting for someone else, and the business message she'd been sent to deliver.'

'Does this gentleman know her?' she said. 'It must be a very urgent matter—I mean, the time. Nothing wrong, I hope?'

'Urgency can certainly become an element in business, I'm aware of that. Deals, and so

133

on—the special moment may be crucial,' Graham said. 'Perhaps she *was* genuine.'

'Mr Brown hasn't been there to our knowledge for weeks,' she said.

'Sally is right,' Graham explained.

'We're perturbed by all this . . . all this interest in 15A,' Sally added. 'Mystified.'

'The girl said someone was watching the flat from a car across the street,' Graham added.

'Oh?' Ember said.

'But I don't know. I saw nobody like that. It *is* worrying, mind, this sudden rush of . . . well . . . activity.'

'She wrote a note for Mr Brown and put it through the letter box,' Sally said. 'I don't know what the message was, though.'

'Perhaps this was the one that would "brook no delay",' Graham said. 'She seemed to realize eventually that nobody would answer the door, and so the message had to be delivered differently, although this, in fact, might involve a delay. Obviously, *would*—even if, on the face of things, the message would not brook it.'

'Which kind of car?' Ember replied.

'Which kind of car what?' Graham said.

'Someone watching the flat from a car— which make of car?' Ember said.

'By the time she spoke of it the car had gone. That's what she said.'

'She didn't describe the car?' Ember asked.

'I don't think so.'

'Or the man?'

'Big,' Graham said. 'He had a mobile phone.'

'Hasn't everybody these days?' Sally said.

'And watching?' Ember asked.

'That's what she said,' Graham replied. He sounded constantly disbelieving, but wouldn't actually say so, presumably in case Ember knew her, had sent her.

'All this *is* worrying,' Sally said. 'I can see you're concerned about the car and the man watching. Is this something to do with your business?'

Well, yes. But Ralph said: 'It's all so baffling.'

'May I ask—what *is* your business, and, presumably, Mr Brown's?' Sally said.

'I wondered if the car might have been a Jaguar,' Ralph replied. Manse drove a Jaguar. He wasn't especially big, though.

'You think you know who this watcher might have been?' Graham asked.

'She said simply "a car", did she?' Ember answered.

'Did you send her, owing to commitments on your part?' Sally said. 'This would explain a lot—and be a comfort.'

'You're not the police, are you?' Graham said. 'I mean—the questions. Was it a colleague watching from the car? Many officers are big. Is something wrong? Is Mr Brown missing—not just not at home, but

135

missing? Or, then again, it wasn't *you*, personally, watching from the car, was it? You're . . . well . . . not small. Did you park elsewhere and come back? Don't mind my asking, will you? We'd like to understand what's happening. I think that's reasonable, in the circumstances.'

'It's funny, but I can't see any note in the hall,' Sally said, looking through the glass panel, 'or any mail at all.'

'Oh?' Ember said. 'The frosted glass makes it difficult.'

'There's nothing. She did put the piece of paper through, didn't she, Graham?' Sally said.

'It might flutter away a bit, Sal.' Graham did a session at the frosted glass, then turned back to Ember. 'In case Mr Brown reappears soon, should we give him a name, a number, so he can get in touch—I mean, if it really is a matter that brooks no delay? I feel this would be neighbourly.'

'And I'm sure I've seen the postman call here as I left for work—three or four times over the last few weeks,' Sally said.

'Suppose she was right about someone watching the flat, why would that be?' Graham said. 'I hope he realizes there are two flats here, and that 15B has nothing to do with 15A. One can be drawn into things inadvertently.'

'Entirely inadvertently,' Sally said.

'It's disquieting,' Graham said. 'We've had

hardly any contact with Mr Brown. You know that phrase people use on TV news when they find someone living next door is a mass murderer or serial rapist—"he kept himself to himself".'

'And likewise ourselves,' Sally said.

'What?' Ember said.

'Keep ourselves *to* ourselves,' Sally said. 'I don't mean standoffish, but respecting others' privacy, and expecting ours to be respected in its turn.'

'It's that kind of neighbourhood, and we like it so,' Graham said.

'Have you heard sounds from 15A, sounds you might not have taken much notice of at the time, but now, looking back, you wonder about them?' Ember replied.

'Sounds?' Graham said.

'Something beyond the normal,' Ember said. 'Possibly not seeming something beyond the normal at the time, but now, in hindsight, and in view of developments, perhaps different. There'll always be a certain amount of noise heard between flats in one property— that's routine. But, possibly in retrospect, significant, not routine at all.'

'When?' Graham asked.

'Say, just before he disappeared,' Ember said.

'*Has* he disappeared?' Sally said. 'He *is* missing?'

'In the sense that the flat seems unoccupied

for a longish period,' Ember said.

'And doesn't he turn up at your business, if you're a colleague, that is?' Graham said. 'So, he's not at home or at work.'

'*Violent* sounds, do you mean?' Sally said.

'Anything unusual,' Ember said. 'Raised voices. He lived alone, didn't he? Did you hear sounds of company at all?'

'We often wondered what business Mr Brown was in,' Graham said. 'He seemed to keep strange hours. And his beard. It didn't seem an ordinary office worker's type of beard, nor suitable in a manual job.'

'Just unusual sounds that, when you recall them now, you wonder what might have been happening in 15A,' Ember said, 'yet at the time you let it pass.'

'What *was* happening?' Graham said.

'This is scary,' Sally said. 'It's always been a trouble-free road. We're buying our flat, not just renting. It seemed a sound investment.'

'Is there a lot of travel in . . . well, in your kind of work, suppose you and he are colleagues?' Graham said. 'Perhaps there's an entirely simple explanation for his absence. If he were visiting clients elsewhere—possibly abroad.'

'These younger people think nothing of distance,' Sally said. 'Talking of phrases, there's one to sum this up, I feel—the world has become "a global village".'

'Ah,' Ember replied. He walked back to his

car. Neither leg gave trouble.

'Are you leaving on account of more commitments?' Sally called.

When Ralph arrived at the Monty, he saw Harpur standing near the bar with a drink—what looked like his usual, gin and cider mixed in a half-pint glass: a double or triple gin, the rest cider. A couple of people played pool. Not many members would hang about in the club once Harpur showed there, especially if they were evolving some project. They'd wonder what he wanted. They'd wonder what he knew. Ember wondered what he wanted. Ember wondered what he knew.

'I've been out and about, Ralph,' he said.

'I won't ask where.'

'Why not?'

'Where?'

'And now I thought I'd look in for a nightcap,' Harpur said.

'Excellent,' Ember said. Harpur was the sort who could guess from watching who talked together in the club the kind of job they might be planning. He knew people's individual flairs—safes, or hold-ups or driving or menaces, or sometimes a combination.

'How's everything generally, Ralph?' he said, in his grand, man-to-man, phoney fucking way, keeping matters vague and harmless so far, but then moving in on what he'd really come for. They had police courses in lulling.

'Good,' Ember said.

139

'Good. And Manse?'

'Good. You know Mansel! Always positive. And then there's his marriage coming up.'

'This will be a blessing for him. You're to star, I hear.'

'Not quite star. But, yes, Mansel has kindly invited me to be best man.'

'I suppose it's one way to help him feel reasonably secure.'

'Secure?'

'Your people won't be able to blast him when you're standing so close with the ring etcetera.'

'I feel gratitude bordering on pride that he asked me, you know, Mr Harpur. It's a testimonial.'

'The marriage should bring Mansel real happiness.'

'One does hope so.'

'In some ways, he deserves this,' Harpur said.

'Certainly.'

'Which ways especially would you say he deserves this?'

'Many.'

'The other women he's been knocking off on rota since his wife went—they'll understand he needs something settled as he gets older—Carmel, Lowri, Patricia. They'll resent the severance, yes, but shouldn't give him too much trouble. In any case, he might still have enough spare time for them.'

'Yes, something settled.'

'I'd hate to think of any of them yelling abuse outside an ex-rectory. Also, there's his first wife, Sybil. Temperamental. Ex-wives can turn unpleasant if their ex-husband remarries, even if it was the ex-wife who destroyed the marriage. It's a pride thing. And possessiveness. The house and so on,' Harpur said.

'I think Manse will be prepared for possible outbursts of stonking. And his fiancée is mature and understanding. She realizes that Mansel has lived, as it were, in the world. Naomi is very much to do with art, and therefore knows something of the bohemian lifestyle.'

'Do you see Manse as bohemian?'

'They enjoy the Pre-Raphaelites. This provides a happy bond.'

Harpur went even more genial. 'But then there's you and your family, Ralph. How are the daughters—Venetia, Fay?'

'Fine. All of us.'

'Wonderful,' Harpur said.

The barman brought a bottle of Kressmann armagnac and poured a drink for Ralph. Harpur stuck to gin and cider.

'Is Venetia settling after France?' Harpur said.

'No problems, thank you.'

'That will stand her in good stead.'

'What?'

'The experience over there.'

'Oh, yes.'

'Not just the language, but another way of looking at life.'

'Oh, yes.'

'I should think those schools are half full of crooks' kids. They're almost the only ones who can afford the fees,' Harpur said.

'Beautifully sited, some of the schools,' Ember replied. 'Former chateaux with orchards and moats.'

'Venetia will be a teenager by now, I suppose,' Harpur said.

'Fourteen.'

'They're developing a real personality at that age. I've watched it in my own elder daughter.'

'True,' Ember replied.

Harpur gazed about the club. 'It's looking great here, Ralph—the mahogany and so on.'

'I'm thinking about some changes.'

'Yes?'

'In due course.'

'Right.'

'Developments.'

'Right.'

'I see potential here,' Ember stated.

'Certainly.'

'I think of certain clubs in London as kind of models of what I might do: the Athenaeum. Often I read in *The Times* of meetings at the Athenaeum—the Ruskin Society, that sort of worthwhile gathering. This is what I have in mind for the Monty. Or another London club I like the sound of is the Garrick.'

'Theatrical connections there, I think.'

'What I plan is—'

'Someone was saying—don't recall who—someone was saying that one of your people—a lad with an odd first name—Joachim—or in that area—Joachim Brown has a brother who's doing pretty well on the West End stage,' Harpur said.

'Yes, I believe so.'

'Fascinating the way brothers can go in for such different careers,' Harpur said.

'Perhaps it's best we're not all the same, Mr Harpur. When I was doing my Foundation Year at the university I remember a lecturer talked about "the principle of plenitude". That is, the world's need for fullness, for variety, for a multitudinous creation. And so, there's a place for, say, wasps, though they might appear to us only a pest. It would be a different world without wasps, a lesser world. It came up in a book we studied, *A Passage to India*. A professor in this tale will not kill a wasp because it's entitled to a life as much as the professor is—Alec Guinness in the film—and as much a part of creation.'

'I don't have anything against universities,' Harpur replied.

'Your friend, Denise, is an undergraduate, isn't she?'

'What would you say were his main abilities?'

'Whose?'

'Joachim Brown's.'

'Oh, yes, he's a valuable part of the firm,' Ember said.

'I wonder—is the acting flair present in him, also, though less obviously, obviously?'

'We don't have a company Christmas panto, so I couldn't say on that one.' God, 'less obviously, obviously'. But Ralph saw why Harpur's conversation might get clumsy: trying not to sound nosy, he skated around so many dicey topics that his words fell over themselves. Ralph went back to those basic questions—what did Harpur know, or think he knew, about Turret Brown? What did he know, or think he knew, about Venetia? And *how* did he know it, or think he knew it?

'And Venetia rides?' Harpur asked.

'Oh, yes.'

'Horses and ponies, I mean, not a bike.'

'Very keen on the equestrian side. There's plenty of ground for her up at Low Pastures, you know. Paddocks. Convenient. Do *your* daughters ride, Mr Harpur? I'm always conscious of a kind of parallel in our situations, yours and mine—both with two daughters around the same age. But do you still live down in Arthur Street? Are there stables in that area, I wonder.'

'Which would be her favourite type of pony

or horse?' Harpur said.

'A whole range. If it's got four legs she'll ride it. That principle of plenitude again. Across the boardism, as it were.'

'They can get themselves into attachments,' Harpur said.

'Who?'

'Girls in their early teens. Or *imagine* attachments.'

'I've heard of that kind of thing. And then there are Romeo and Juliet. Kids, really.'

'Yet genuinely powerful emotions,' Harpur said. 'Such girls would suffer if something dark happened to the man in one of these attachments—possibly imagined attachments. I call them *possibly* imagined, because the man might be hardly aware of it.'

'On the other hand, Mr Iles was certainly aware of it when he started buzzing around your elder daughter, wouldn't you say?'

'But, then, we must all try to avert dark happenings,' Harpur said.

'Indeed. Anyway, I gather Mr Iles might have given up on your daughter at last. I've always said he's got some decency in him, though kept well buried most of the time. After all, he's made it to Assistant Chief, so we shouldn't expect an excess of morality. It must be a relief to you he's backed off. Was it a kind of revenge thing because of you and Mrs Iles? Is your daughter upset, though?'

A couple of men both carrying leather

holdalls came a few steps into the club but saw Harpur, paused, then turned around and disappeared. 'Will you keep the Monty name when you relaunch, Ralph, or go for something, say, classical—like the Athenaeum?'

'I feel the Monty must always be the Monty. It's part of the city. Many see it as . . . well as a fulcrum.'

'Often I hear it described so, and in remarkably far-flung locations. Someone will ask a new acquaintance whether he/she knows the Monty, and the reply will instantly come, "Ah, such a social fulcrum!"'

Naturally, Ralph realized this was Harpur taking the piss in his lumbering, oafish, vox-cop fashion. You learned to put up with that kind of crude, envious tease. He would never have heard anyone refer to the Monty as a fulcrum. Ralph himself had never thought of the Monty as a fulcrum until just now. The word popped from his mouth, more or less unplanned. How the fuck could a club be a fulcrum? He had wanted an out-of-the-ordinary, daft sort of term that would take Harpur's mind off the two men who vamoosed a minute or two ago when they saw him at the bar, Shane Gordon Wilkes and Matt Bolcombe. Ralph knew them, of course. They were club members. In fact, there'd been a seven-hour Monty champagne acquittal party for Shane not long ago, when the prosecution collapsed because witnesses would not testify,

146

despite lots of attention and encouragement from police investigative assistants. Probably, the pair had meant to come to the Monty late tonight and do a share-out over drinks, after some sortie. This would be tactless with Harpur present, though.

Ember felt glad they'd gone. But he did not want Harpur's main Monty impression now to be of a hotbed where villains arrived to share loot—and a hotbed they fled from because of him, the law. Ralph longed to get the Monty on the path to transformation. Shane and Matt's abrupt, scuttling exit knocked that hope. And so Ralph had come out with 'fulcrum', simply to waylay Harpur's attention. Ember delighted in the two u's and the rich jostle of consonants. He spoke them with gorgeous thoroughness.

Ralph had guessed Harpur would need to activate his creaking, clichéd mockery at such a ripe slice of gibberish. So, have your little giggle, you CID sod, and spin your comic fantasy of a worldwide holy chorus of 'fulcrums' whenever the Monty was mentioned—in Belize, Djibouti, Jerusalem, Hobart, Blackpool. Fine if it pushes Shane Gordon Wilkes and Matt Bolcombe out of the reckoning, and leaves the Monty image without further injury. Probably few Athenaeum members would have to bolt if they noticed a detective in the club.

'This brother thing between the two Browns

147

still fascinates me,' Harpur said. 'I imagine you'd have to take that into account?'

'Take it into account in which way?'

'Personnel selection.'

'For what?'

'As I said earlier, Ralph: suppose you were looking for someone who could pass himself/herself off—the way actors have to pass themselves off as characters in a play. Might you wonder whether that kind of skill dwelt in the blood, a family trait—like brothers, Edward and James Fox, or Vanessa Redgrave and her daddy, Michael.'

'Pass himself off how, where?'

'If you wanted someone to pass himself/herself off—no, not as you so humorously remarked, in the firm's panto, but to . . . well, pass himself/herself off as a loyal follower of someone he's not actually a follower of, and, in fact, whose destruction he might be helping with.'

'I think I'm more a cinema person than a theatre person,' Ember replied. 'It's probably a generational matter.'

'But, of course, an actor on the stage—suppose he/she makes a mistake with his/her lines, he/she's got a prompter to put him/her right. Catastrophe averted. However, that would definitely—disastrously—not be true for someone trying to pass him/herself off in a snooping role if he/she made a mistake. Early curtain.'

Ember said: 'I suppose what appeals to me about cinema is its range—it can show us so much, and the more so as technology advances. Like reality. But in the theatre, you can hear their feet banging about on the boards. When King Richard III calls out, "A horse, a horse, my kingdom for a horse," he's actually complaining about being in a play, because, obviously, a horse can't be brought on to the stage.'

'As a kid I used to think it was an ad for Mike Ingdom's stables,' Harpur said.

God. Ember kept his face blank.

'I realize Joachim Brown is only a low-level member of the firm, but would you have much personal contact with him, Ralph?'

'I try to know all our people on an individual basis, as I expect you do with your workforce, Mr Harpur. That's an essential of leadership, isn't it? We have a lot in common. I mean, besides two daughters each. Yes, I try to maintain worthwhile links with all members of my staffs, whether in my companies' general commercial divisions or here at the club.'

'Anyone can see the Monty benefits magnificently from that.'

'Thank you, Mr Harpur. The club is dear to me.'

'A fulcrum.'

'One word for it.' As a matter of fact, Ralph had recently read the obituary in the *Daily Telegraph* of someone called Mark Birley, creator of one of the smartest clubs in London, Annabel's. This was a different kind of place from the Athenaeum or the Garrick—more a nightclub. But it did interest Ember as another possible prestige model for the new Monty. Rich and famous people went to Annabel's, including Royalty. Birley ran the club with renowned courtesy and taste, his shoes and even his socks custom-made, apparently. Ralph thought he might be able to manage something similar to Annabel's with the Monty one day. He liked the idea of custom-made shoes, though socks seemed less important. Shoes mattered because the kind of people he wanted to attract would spot at once if the footwear were only ordinary—OK but made for just anyone of his size. He did not mention his Annabel's project to Harpur, though, because the prole slob would probably have turned even more fucking satiric and sneering.

*   *   *

Next day there was a rehearsal for Mansel's wedding at St James's. Although people wore their ordinary clothes, the rest of the run-through tried to imitate accurately how the service would be. Ralph did not often go into churches, but when he did he always found a few absolutely plus points. The materials generally looked so honest—stone walls in an old building like St James's, slate plaques to honour dead benefactors, the pulpit of fine, genuine wood, and set above the congregation like a crow's nest on a whaling ship, though lower than that, of course. When the vicar climbed those few steps to preach you could see him seeming to grow, until he stood there very much on top and able to give the people some decent topic to think about, like kindness or thrift, if they wanted to. Although Ralph didn't know many vicars, or any at all currently, he would accept that some might be valid. Also, flagstone floors seemed so right to him for a church. They were usually grey or black yet had a kind of glow to them from years, even centuries, of buffing by devout shoes, though none, probably, custom-made.

Ember could tell that Margaret, his wife, felt a real thrill at the thought of the wedding, and Ralph's role. It would be crude to tell her Shale had probably picked him as best man so there'd be less chance of Ember's people salvoing Manse at the service. Of course, Harpur *had* mentioned this to Ralph. From Harpur, he'd expect such unpleasant, truthful, sourness. Margaret used to worry about the way Shale invited a series of women into his home for spells. She'd thought he deserved something more continuous. Ralph wondered how the hell he got any woman to spend time close to him, continuous or not, including Naomi.

'Although this is only a practice, Mansel, I

151

already feel some of the joy and fulfilment we'll all experience on the actual day,' Ember said.

'Your presence contributes to that joy and fulfilment, Ralph, contributes great and unique. I thank you.'

'I'm proud to participate.' What's happened to Turret Brown, you fucking marital sod? But this was not the kind of question that could be asked here. Ralph and Shale sat together in the front pew on the right, as laid down for wedding procedure, Shale nearer the aisle, so he could get out to be alongside Naomi at the altar. Manse and Ralph had been told to arrive at least half an hour before the bride. The vicar said timing was crucial, and placement— that is, where everyone sat or stood. He meant weddings generally, not just Manse's and the possibility of trouble. Ralph felt pretty certain Manse had not wised him up about that. After all, few vicars agreed to marry anybody divorced, and Manse would hardly want to give this one extra stress after he'd been so helpful. In some ways it struck Ember as vilely insulting and even farcical that Shale could imagine Ralph ordering a hit on a church wedding, whether or not he was best man. Wouldn't it be barbaric to misuse such a holy and blessed occasion in this fashion? There was a term sometimes applied to Church of England weddings which Ralph especially cherished: the 'solemnization' of marriage.

That word really caught the seriousness and glory of what took place. How gross to turn a sacred event into an execution yard. Ralph more or less discarded any thought of having Manse riddled during solemnization.

In any case, there were big impracticalities. Like many churches, St James's had a lot of wide stone pillars to prop up that huge, vaulted ceiling, and these could make lines of fire difficult. If he *did* decide to do Manse in that setting, he'd have to hire exceptionally good people from London or Manchester and brief them thoroughly with pictures of Manse. But there could be mistakes because of the very close grouping in a wedding service— what the parson called 'placement'—and ricochets off the tough stonework. Ralph certainly did not want the vicar or possibly rector shot. That was sure to niggle many in the city, and the police would have to get serious about nailing those responsible. A priest blasted in his own church must strike some as symbolic of a general decline of behaviour, and they would demand reprisals. Iles himself probably didn't give a fish's tit about church things, but even he would feel pressured.

Then, again, someone at the back of the church during the fusillade might turn holy hero and slam the heavy doors shut, trapping the assailants. Their response, almost certainly, must be to blast off without much thought of where the bullets went, as long as they got out: these would be professional people, with a professional and profound sense of urgency and self-preservation. Ralph desired no massacre, particularly not in a church, but probably not anywhere, nor ruined stained glass depicting saints, possibly haloed.

Manse said: 'Me and Naomi chose the service from the Book of Common Prayer, going right back—1662, not none of the modern ones. We agreed instant on that. I would of bet on it, this agreement. It's because we are so much in tune with each other. I never had that with Syb, my first. I'd say something and she'd come out with the fucking opposite, just to irritate. As I see it, Ralph, if you got all them couples married by it since 1662, it *must* be right and strong. This date stuck in my head, because it's important. Oh, I know not every marriage that used the 1662 lasted and was good. Maybe some of them royals who split up used the 1662. Most probably they did, because it was handed down and historic. But we like it, all the same. This is not something fly-by-night and trendy. It's tradition, Ralph. It's Britishness. We want to be part of that.'

'So like you, Manse.'

Naomi's mother was shown into the front pew to the left. This officially signalled that the bride had arrived and would soon move up the aisle from the church door, to take her place alongside Mansel in front of the vicar. Even then she'd be able to tell herself nothing was finalized. A rehearsal only. She could still get out. Although she'd know the procedure in advance, the actual moment when she encountered Manse's face in a sanctified building might come as a foul shock.

The organist began the Wedding March. Everyone stood. In a few seconds, Manse must take a step out from the pew to greet Naomi. Suppose Ralph, on balance, decided to get Manse finished at his wedding, despite quibbles, this could offer the obvious chance. For several seconds the bridegroom had to be completely solo in the aisle waiting for his bride. Ralph thought it should be pretty straightforward to pick him off then, and no pillar gave protection at this point. Obviously, the architects who designed the nave would not have been thinking mainly about how to protect a bridegroom from gunfire when they sited the pillars. The triumphant organ music might half drown the sound of shots, making it unclear what was happening, and the gunmen could get out and escape before anyone had time to shut the doors or interfere in some other troublesome way. True, that meant the bride would never make it to being a wife, which could lead to difficulties over getting at Manse's money and other property. Ember saw this as regrettable, yet he felt unable to worry too much about the finances of someone dim enough voluntarily to marry Shale. In any case, the bride might herself get hit—not deliberately, but because she would be lining herself up in the aisle with Manse. Although, clearly, Ralph did not want that, a woman willing to put herself in this situation must surely expect snags.

Ralph experienced a large, natural gratitude to the vicar for running this rehearsal and showing the possibilities, without knowing it. Although Ralph still considered a church wedding as holy and blessed, and still felt hugely disgusted that Shale might believe him willing to lay on a barrage here, he did see potential opportunities. Ralph began to wonder whether, after all, it was foolishly extravagant and exaggerated to regard the wedding as a sacramental event and to let himself get softened up by this notion. During his Foundation Year at the university, he'd read some history and remembered a quotation from Admiral of the Fleet, Lord Fisher: 'The essence of war is violence, and moderation in war is an imbecility.' Ralph saw that this might be the kind of uncompromising war he and Manse were destined to fight. Shouldn't Ralph get pre-emptive and have Shale done at St James's? Would it be an imbecility not to?

Ember glanced back at Naomi, approaching up the aisle on her stepfather's right arm. Ralph wanted to gauge how long it took her to progress from the door to the spot where she joined Manse. Luckily, Ralph had brought a stopwatch and set it going now, though hidden in his trouser pocket. During nearly all that time Shale was certain to be a beautifully exposed, unmoving, smiling target, his head or chest absolutely still in the sights. The experts Ralph hired would need only an extremely basic briefing, plus pictures of the prat.

'This is your marvellous future, Manse,' Ember whispered.

'So true, but I'm still scared that miserable bitch, Syb, will get in on the day and ruin everything.' Manse moved out from the pew.

And what about Turret, and *his* future, and present? Another silent question. Ember stopped the watch.

CHAPTER SIX

Now and then, Iles would talk like a really heavy thinker, although an Assistant Chief. This could be a fucking pain, of course, but— also of course—Harpur usually put up with it for at least a while because Iles had the big rank and knew how to turn unpleasant with anyone lower who seemed to forget he had the big rank, especially Harpur. And when Iles turned unpleasant it was not a middling or sane thing, as others might turn unpleasant, but a Desmond Iles, crash-ball thing.

'What was it Karl Marx said about this sort of topic, Col?' he asked.

'Which sort of topic would that be, sir?' Harpur said.

'This sort, twat.' Iles was crouched very low, going through the suit pockets, and actually spoke down towards the corpse, rather than up to Harpur, who stood behind him, not needing, not wishing, to get near the victim again. But Harpur heard it all OK. In any case, along the way, there'd probably be familiar items he'd listened to before from Iles, though not previously while the ACC trawled a body. They both wore white sterile dungarees and face masks. 'Yes, I'm pretty sure it's a chapter or two in Marx, Col.'

Harpur said: 'Karl came out with quite a bit over the years, sir, no denying. Oh, yes. Statements of rich significance. And extremely famous volumes running to many a page. But I don't need to tell you.'

'As a youngster I continually had my head stuck in a book,' Iles replied, easing his fingers right under on the ground, to plumb the trousers' back pocket. Not even Iles would have the gall to turn him over. 'That's how my mother used to describe it—"forever your head stuck in a book, Desmond," as though a book were the village stocks, or a permanent waver. Not just Marx. I read all sorts, consuming the printed page. Oh, yes, consuming. "Omnivorous", "voracious"—these are terms that would hardly have been off key for my youthful attitude to reading, the one being a pre-condition of the other, you'll agree.'

'This is the point about mothers,' Harpur said.

'What?'

'Occasionally they'll produce a dismal old phrase or two, imagining these are witty and sharp. They're trying to help. Some mothers are quite interested in their children, regardless.'

Iles pulled his hand back, empty. Naturally, empty. 'But I'm certainly not one who has the arrogance to think of himself as precocious when young, Col.'

Harpur laughed mildly for a while, as at the inane, thunderous modesty of this. 'Well, I'm afraid I might not be able to believe that, sir.' Iles often purported to deny his boy-genius status. Harpur constantly had the prolonged, doubting, overwhelmingly smarmy laugh on call, the way petrol stations kept a fire extinguisher prominent. His disbelieving response would be expected. It was compulsory. *Contradict me fast, Harpur, you sodding, snide, subordinate jerk.*

'I will admit, though, to an early, obsessive fascination with words when written down,' Iles said.

The dead man's mouth was part open. Iles

brought a pencil-style torch from somewhere, switched it on and spent a few focused minutes examining and most likely mentally charting teeth, tongue condition and dimensions, fillings, plaque and tonsils, if any. Iles did not make notes. He'd accurately recall everything he thought important.

Harpur said: 'Written words are certainly items books can't do without, and, therefore, if you were/are interested in books, it would follow that you gave/give attention to words, sir.'

'I mean their sequence . . . yes, the way words fall into . . . well, a sequence—their mutual cheek-by-jowling.' Some of the ACC's sentences became slightly broken up for a while because of his concentrated mouth delve. 'You ever get enthralled by printed matter as a kid, Col? Did they encourage . . . did they encourage reading in that school for muggers and the retarded you won an uncontested scholarship to? Myself, I enjoyed . . . I really enjoyed many hours of almost sensual experience noting the way conjoined letters seemed to vie with and complement or compromise one another.'

'You can say that again, sir!' But, for fuck's sake, don't.

Iles said: 'An interesting example—take the intriguingly angled z in the word "zoo". This intrigued me, from my childhood on.'

'Ah, I've always thought the zoo z a
160

remarkable z even among other z's,' Harpur happily commented. 'A tremor would go over me whenever I came upon the word "zoo".'

'The z pushes forever against those damn smug double o's in "zoo", exactly as a gloriously sinuous caged panther might push against the bars in an *actual, real* zoo, you see.'

'Ah.' Harpur thought this gloriously sinuous panther and the z and smug o's might be new. He couldn't immediately recall earlier references to them by Iles, during other long, brain-dazing sessions on the anatomy of words. But Harpur's memory was often merciful to him and would bury some of Iles's maddest crap, as cats buried all theirs— domestic cats, anyway: maybe not panthers. The ACC withdrew his torch and wiped it thoroughly on the lower part of Harpur's left dungaree leg before replacing it in his pocket. Iles loved system, unless it was a system devised by someone else: this he would tend to see as no system at all, but a mess. He put a middle finger into the dead mouth now, apparently to rock one or more teeth as a test of gum hold or overall mandible state. Things told Iles things. There'd be some eventual point to the jabber and search activities. Watch and wait. Things told Iles things, but, of course, he didn't always or even often tell others what things things told him. Harpur could reciprocate this kind of editing. He said: 'Obviously, that might have affected your subconscious, sir.'

'What might have, Col?'

' "Zoo".'

'In what respect, Harpur?'

'Perhaps without realizing it properly—you being comparatively immature at that age—perhaps, you saw yourself as like the bold, vigorous, engagingly sharp-lined zigzag z *of* "zoo", or, alternatively, and more likely, the cruelly confined, graceful, padding panther *in* that actual zoo. You had an urge—possibly deep and undefined—to escape the restrictions of childhood—i.e. the zoo cage bars—and reach your true, fully emerged, unique, panther-quality, Ilesian self, a self we're all fortunate enough to see and proudly serve under now, sir.'

'And to revere and love, Col?'

'The subconscious is quite a thing,' Harpur replied. 'Most agree on that. It's not like a chin or an elbow—obvious, tangible, able to jut. But it's there all right. Think of Freud, or *The Manchurian Candidate*, both versions.'

'For all of you to see and proudly serve under *and* to revere and love, Col?'

'The panther's one of the best animal runners there is, and caged it would be really fed up.'

'Also, I'd analyse the progress of a paragraph,' Iles said. 'Its strategy of persuasion. Again, not only Karl Marx. Oh, no! Others.'

162

'Others are a lot.'

'Hegel. Descartes. Longfellow. Plato, naturally. Sartre.'

'Between them, people like that can certainly sum up many aspects of life, although foreign,' Harpur declared.

Iles withdrew the finger and made a fanning movement under his nose with that hand: 'God, he's been here quite a time, Col.' The other hand rechecked a side pocket, uselessly, as Harpur knew. 'Talking of Descartes, "I stink therefore I am, or was."'

'I don't think you'll find anything, sir. The Scenes of Crime people did their search and said he had nothing on him, not even an arm tattoo.'

'But I expect you were here early-birding and cleaned him out for your own slimy get-ahead-Harpur purposes. Right?' Iles took a lump of the fair, curly hair and pulled the dead man's head up off the ground, then, with his free hand, loosened the jacket around the shoulders for a squint at any name tag or maker's label. Harpur knew there wasn't one. He hadn't needed that kind of indicator, anyway. He'd recognized the man at first sight on the ground, despite the mutilation: Joachim Bale Frederick Brown. Harpur suspected the ACC recognized him, too—perhaps had already tragically fitted Brown into his theory about Ralph Ember's need for a spy in Shale's firm. Iles liked to act dumb now and then.

Perhaps he needed to sample, to mock-up, the symptoms of stupidity, empty-headedness and general intellectual blankness that afflicted folk who were so piteously not himself. It reminded Harpur of those children's tales where a prince dresses down as a pauper and goes out disguised among his subjects to find what things are like for them. Harpur had often heard Iles quote that guru he'd mentioned, Sartre, who said, 'Hell is other people,' though that, apparently, didn't stop him shagging oodles of them. Naturally, Iles said it in French first, and then generously translated for Harpur. And sometimes Harpur would think, Yes, hell *is* other people, such as Iles. The ACC didn't really need anyone to tell him hell was other people, but he needed to chart what exactly made these others so *wholeheartedly* hellish. Occasionally, therefore, he would pretend to be as half-baked as he thought they were. He wanted to feel like them, *be* them, temporarily, actorly. Did they *know* how hellish they were? Did they enjoy it? Iles would not expect these others to be images of him, but it amazed him—perhaps distressed him—that they might not *want* to be images of him. Also, Iles's pretence at ignorance meant he could come out eventually with a shock revelation of what he knew. Harpur considered it only kindly to play along. He owed the ACC an occasional minor kindness.

Iles let the head fall back to the ground. He went to the other end, removed both Brown's shoes and socks, and methodically eased the toes apart to peer between. He hummed and half sang what Harpur took to be a First World War chorus about packing up your troubles in your old kit bag. He had folded the socks neatly and placed each on top of the shoe from the due foot. 'And yet, for all this devotion to written words, Col, I'm worryingly sceptical about them, worryingly and worriedly.'

'Is that so, sir?' Harpur got some fellow feeling into his voice, though not quite a sob.

'If we can't trust words, Col, what *can* we trust?'

'Words *are* useful, sir. That's from the communicating point of view. They come into their own then. When you think about it, even Morse code, which seems to be only dots and dashes, is actually dots and dashes signifying letters, and letters that go to make words. I don't know where we'd be without them. For instance, I wouldn't be able to say "I don't know where we'd be without them" if we *were* without them.'

The foot examination took a while. Iles gave each interface about twenty seconds. Now and then he'd run a finger against the side of a toe, as if tracing a Braille-type message in the wrinkled flesh, on its way to decomposition. 'What do words actually *mean*?' Iles said. 'Can they—words—always come up to scratch?

What we obviously have to ask is, Are they themselves or their opposites? Do we scent chaos, Col?'

'This *is* a question,' Harpur replied. 'But, for myself, I admit I find words quite handy, especially during, for instance, speech or writing. Yes, I think I'd find both of those tricky without words. And I can usually see a large difference between opposites, say, "up" and "down". And "dead" and "alive". For instance, *we* are alive—on our feet, chatting, breathing—but *this* lad is well dead. This is an obvious distinction. In my view.'

'Take that formula you see on the back of commercial vans,' Iles replied: "No tools kept in this vehicle overnight." Supposed to deter pilferers.'

'Our security people recommend some statement like that printed at the rear.'

'Oh, yes, the intention is good. Idiotically, naively good. But let's think of it another way, Col: what if the notice said: *"Plenty* of tools kept in this vehicle overnight"?'

'I've never seen that one,' Harpur said.

'You won't, unless I buy a van myself.'

'Are you into vans?' Perhaps during an earlier part of the ACC's career, toe gaps of someone had turned out crucial and he'd learned from this. Harpur tried to recall any case where a deceased's toes figured interestingly.

'Which would be the more effective,

though?' Iles said.

'Which what, sir?'

'The notice saying "No tools", or the one saying "Plenty"?'

'Well, I—'

'May I suggest the second, Harpur?'

'The second? All right, if you really—'

'Why the second, you'll ask.'

'Why the second, sir?'

'Because no bugger would believe it. Any thief must think this a ploy or a trap and assume there were *no* tools in there although the notice says "Plenty", only some mechanical, toothed grab to take his balls off once he jemmied the door, plus a CCTV camera. The thief probably wouldn't believe the first notice, either, and would break in because he thought the words declaring there were *no* tools inside overnight were meant to disguise the fact that there *were* tools inside overnight. What we have here, Harpur, are words doing the reverse of what they aim for. Can civilization endure on such a shaky footing? All right, all right, I know this is not a totally original thought. Obviously, you're eager to point me to philosopher Ludwig Wittgenstein's warning against seduction by language, aren't you?'

'Ah, I have to remind you, respectfully, sir, of Ludwig Wittgenstein's warning against seduction by language.'

'Fucking touché, Col. You're exceptionally

sharp today.' Iles replaced the socks and shoes, relacing these carefully. He had respect for feet.

'And *will* there be tools inside the van overnight?' Harpur replied.

'In which case?'

'Either—in the "No tools" van or the "Plenty" van. And if you do get a van yourself will you leave tools in it overnight, no matter what you've had written on the back?'

Iles stood, and with both hands smoothed down his white protective suit. Against all procedural rules, he had not worn gloves and Harpur saw tan dirt under the nails of his right hand from when he worked it beneath the body to investigate the rear pocket. 'I reckon I should be looking through *your* clobber to find what he had on him, Harpur, not his.'

'John Staley ran the Scenes of Crime group. He's exceptionally thorough,' Harpur said.

'When I refer to Karl Marx, I'm most probably thinking of *Das Kapital*, but it could be some other work, Col,' Iles answered.

'You'll unquestionably have read many. The moment you mentioned his name, I told myself, "Clearly, Mr Iles will have in mind *Das Kapital*, or possibly a different Marx source, as applied to this deceased." In a way it's funny that you should adore books although you're not happy with words—or, at least, words on the back of vans.'

'Now, of course, you see the relevance to

our decaying, butchered friend here, don't you?' Iles said.

'Not easy to recognize in the present state but I think he's from Ralphy Ember's outfit,' Harpur replied.

'Because, deceitful, intrusive, rapid bastard, you've been through his cards and papers.'

'Some type of courier who'd take replacement crack or E to designated street and disco dealers,' Harpur explained. 'Also an enforcer-minder-chauffeur. Not much more elevated than that. I believe I've seen him about. We'll get identification from The Squad. His curls are distinctive and one side of the face still all rightish for identification.'

'Monopoly, Col,' Iles remarked.

'Ah.'

'Oh, yes, monopoly, Harpur.'

'In what sense, sir?'

'Marx.'

'He covered many a theme. As I gather. One thing he was never short of—a theme.'

'His reputation's shaky now, but hc gave us several abiding truths. I don't dismiss him. No, no, no.'

'In London, there's a graveyard statue of Karl looking damn thoughtful and constructive posthumously,' Harpur said.

'Col, I keep returning to the one central idea.'

'Which?'

'Monopoly.'

'That *is* a prime area.'

'Bringing us back to this bonny item.' Iles gave the corpse a couple of kicks in the pelvis, but with no genuine, Iles-type commitment— token kicks, only, not enough to mark the skin, almost leather caresses or tributes, as if to thank him for so plainly and definitely establishing the link with Karl Marx, whatever it might eventually turn out to be, or never. Even these minor impacts of Iles's magnificent black slip-on, though, released a notable mortality waft that reminded Harpur of something. Something? Oaf: plainly it matched the first time he'd caught it when doing his original quick frisk of Brown alone.

They were at the edge of hillside woodland to the north of the city, not far from that old anti-aircraft gun site where Harpur and Lamb sometimes met. A rabbit hunter's terrier had found the body well hidden in undergrowth. Harpur naturally heard of it before Iles, a due and convenient spell before Iles. The system routinely and properly worked like that. Harpur, as Detective Chief Superintendent, ran the Criminal Investigation Department. He would be told at once if a phone caller reported this sort of discovery. And, also in line with the system, Harpur would then correctly inform Iles, Assistant Chief (Operations). A dead male with what could be bullet wounds and carving of the features clearly called for a full police operation and therefore came into the Operations ambit of an Assistant Chief (Operations), if he got to know of it. Harpur made sure the ACC did get to know of it, of course, at the proper stage.

So, this trip to the hill. Iles loved to attend personally at the scene of major cases: what he called 'an indomitable demand within me, Col, for the concrete, for the flintiness of the nitty-gritty.' Always there was a fine flintiness and indomitable nitty-grittyness to the way he said 'nitty-gritty'. The wish to get himself to the actual location could be a tic taken from a previous Chief Constable here, Mark Lane, whom Iles had despised, pitied, loyally half-propped, cheerfully lampooned into mental breakdown, and frequently copied. Lane used to visit such sites fearing they signalled final collapse of order, beginning on his patch, spreading nationally, then globally, then throughout the cosmos, all of it his clear, catastrophic fault. Lane had repeatedly read Revelation, the Bible's prophetic book about the end of the world, in case he was coded in there as a dragon or serpent responsible for the overall muck-up.

Iles said: 'We have to grant that, post Berlin Wall, most of Marx's stuff looks risibly weak. "Risibly" in the sense of laughably, Col.' The ACC fingered hard both the shoulder pads of Brown's jacket. Occasionally, people did try to hide items there. Iles seemed to detect nothing exceptional. Well, of course he detected nothing exceptional. Staley would have had a previous feel, and Harpur a feel previous to Staley's. Negative.

'But did you spot this early on—ahead of the others, sir?' Harpur said.

'Spot what?'

'That Marx's ideas are risibly weak in the sense of laughably.'

'How early on?'

'While the Wall was still there—during your reading stints as an infant: e.g., when your mother said, "Forever your head stuck in a book, Desmond," did you answer, "Maybe so, as in the village stocks or a permanent waver, ma, but this *Das Kapital* is risibly weak in the sense of laughably"? That would *certainly* be precocious, if I may say—to rumble him so young. Some thought his teaching very cuspish then. Only time rubbished him. This happens to many. Think of Bishop Ussher, who thought the world only 4004 years old.'

'One of Ralph Ember's people, you say, Harpur?'

'I think so. An impression only at this stage.'

'You *know* it. You've got his damn name and blood-type.'

'Such impressions are strange and mysterious, aren't they, sir? Who . . . yes, indeed . . . who can say where this one comes from?' Harpur replied.

'*I* fucking can,' Iles said. 'His pockets. Or you recognized him right off.'

172

'But it's real and strong, this impression. Yes, I'd speculate a hanger-on with Ralphy.'

'All right, let's *speculate*, shall we? Suppose this mysterious *impression* of yours is correct. Where does it take us?'

'Well, sir, I imagine—'

'I'll tell you where it takes us, Col. This body takes us instantly to *Das Kapital*.'

'Ah.'

'Direct.'

'This is remarkable.'

'You see the connection, of course.'

'It's amazing how things tie up.'

'It is, it is, Col.'

'But many of us need somebody to point out these links, somebody with your insights, sir.'

'And am I widely revered and loved for this flair, Harpur, among people of your in many ways estimable type?'

'Then we wonder why we couldn't locate these affinities for ourselves, they are so apparent and unarguable,' Harpur said.

'What *is* the connection, then, of this body with *Das Kapital*, Harpur? Tell me the links? List them.'

'They'll be able to remove the remains now you've seen him *in situ*, sir,' he answered. 'We can stand down the guard officers.'

A small square tent about five feet high had been erected over the corpse for fear of media intrusion and motorized sightseeing troops from the town. Inside, both of them bent over

173

slightly, near the body. Harpur didn't like having to stand so close to Iles. And Harpur knew the ACC would dislike more having to stand so close to *him*. It was a matter of one's personal space, the territorial imperative, not necessarily hygiene. 'He's Joachim Bale Frederick Brown, isn't he, Col?' Iles said. 'The one they call "Turret". As you mentioned, he couriers and brutalizes for Ralphy Ember. Did.'

'It *could* be Turret.'

'It's Turret, you shifty git.'

'It's Turret,' Harpur said. 'Should we go outside now, sir?'

'Yes, you don't look too good with a yellowy tent-canvas background, Col.'

'Not too good in which ways?'

'People with your sort of complexion should be careful about backgrounds,' Iles said. 'You can't afford more handicaps.'

'Which background would suit me best?'

'You'll ask how I know it's Turret,' Iles replied.

'No, I won't, sir. You know most things.'

'Oh, come now, come now, Col, I can't claim that! But it's a fact my mother used to cry out when I was, say, eleven or twelve, "Desmond, you're an encyclopedia!" She meant the *Britannica*, not that old Arthur Mee thing for kids.'

'Mothers worry about the brain overheating.'

'Not yours.'

'You heard about the meeting with Ember, did you? Or saw it?'

'Which meeting, Col?'

'So you've been expecting the hit.'

'Which meeting with Ember?'

'You know someone called Evox, sir?'

They came out and talked near a police ribbon strung around the trees to keep people at a distance. Chief Inspector Francis Garland, who would run the investigation, went into the tent. 'Dossier pix. You recognized Brown at once, the way I did, yes, Col?' Iles said. 'Even without whatever you found on him and illegally lifted in your fashion. But what do you care about legality? After all, you're only a police officer.'

'Almost certainly carved and killed elsewhere. Dumped. The road's not far. He could be carried from a car.'

'As well as Marx, I think of Hobbes, Col.'

'Hobbes. I wondered if you had them in mind.'

'Thomas Hobbes, another thinker.'

'One of the best.'

'He believed human beings were all pretty much of a muchness in ability, and that they'd always be fighting to get on top, because the gap between the top and the next looked small and easy. In other words, a hotbed struggle for monopoly, Col. So, Hobbes an iffy royalist at times, considered there had to be someone

175

strong and tough to rule and stop these squabbles.' He paused.

'You wouldn't need a screen test for that part, sir.'

'My role, indeed.' Iles worked at it and dredged a little humility from somewhere. 'And you and the rest of the Service come into the picture as well, to some degree. Certainly. To some degree. Brown, straight, I believe. But no steady woman or kids. He liked to ramble. You'll sympathize with that kind of prick twitch, won't you, Harpur?' The ACC began to wail and stamp one of his grand shoes on the soft ground. 'I have a wife, as you know. Oh, yes, you know all right and—'

'Turret lived alone.'

'Number 15A Singer Road,' Iles said. 'Calling a British child Joachim might suggest cosmopolitan, in-your-fucking-face, professional-class parents.'

'We don't have much on family.'

'I aim to keep on top of things, Harpur,' Iles replied. 'My mind? Active. My memory? Active. My work rate? Beyond anything you can visualize, however much you would wish to visualize it.'

'Considerably wish.'

'Not within your reach, I'm afraid, Col.'

'I've heard one or two people speak of your work rate, sir. Speak amazedly of it.'

'Which?'

'Which what?'

176

'Is it one or two?' Iles said.

'*Very* amazedly,' Harpur said.

'Reverentially?'

'Unprompted.'

'Now, you'll see plainly why I mentioned *Das Kapital* and monopoly,' Iles said.

'Ah.'

'Turret dead hints at it all, doesn't he, Col? A symbol.'

'Right, sir.'

'Turret—his death and mutilation—tells us clearly, emphatically of a fight for total dominance.'

'Ah.'

'Now, having spent more time with the dead Brown, just remind yourself briefly how *Das Kapital* treats monopoly.'

'Yes! That's unquestionably a work covering a multitude of aspects, sir,' Harpur replied instantly.

'What does Marx see as the central, driving life-force in all capitalist ventures, Col? Plainly, this provides *such* a window on to our situation here now with dead, chivved chummy.'

'Marx is someone who gets right to the basics, although he might see them all wrong. If you stop a stranger in the street and ask him, "What about Karl Marx, then?" this is what he's almost sure to answer—"He gets right to the basics, gets right to them and gets them wrong."'

177

'Marx believes that every private business—
every private business—he believes every
private business strives to eliminate all
competition from every other private business.
So, Joachim Bale Frederick Brown, dead. The
message shrieks at us, doesn't it, Harpur?'

'Ah. This would be like Shell trying to—?'

'And so, having won a domineering,
unchallenged, *monopoly* position, the
victorious business can mercilessly screw and
milk the customers, or—his words—"exploit
the proletariat". By then, you see, the
customers have nowhere else to go. Hence the
need for public ownership, as he saw things.
He wanted the annihilation of capitalistic
competition because, in his view, competition
was inefficient—from the proles' standpoint.
It's a simple and simple-minded theory.'

'Is this—?'

'You ask, is this, in fact, relevant to us? So
right it is! I'm glad you appreciate that, Col.
We watch it working here, now. Marx believed
competition must ultimately become so
intense it would push capitalism into crisis and
collapse. Therefore, consider Turret on the
ground in there, teeth probably good for
another thirty years with care, yet rendered
useless by events.'

'Joachim Bale Frederick Brown destroyed
signifies the end of capitalism, does he, sir?'

'You'd be a member of that, Col,' Iles
replied.

'What?'

'The proletariat. Very much so. And you'll understand it all from the viewpoint of the screwed and milked. In that particular sense, you're all of a sudden quite valuable, the way rats and mice are in some scientific experiments. Incidentally, "quite" is another word that can mean one thing or its almost opposite: "quite drunk"—a little bit drunk or "quite drunk", utterly rat-arsed. If you'd met Marx and he hadn't at that stage come to fix on the word "proletariat" he would after seeing and hearing you talk at any length because you're so exactly it. Quite it. Marx doesn't merely suggest private companies would *like* to wipe out the opposition, as just one of their various ambitions. His argument is they *cannot* behave otherwise. Absolutely cannot. It is their essence. They *have* to expand. They must obliterate or be obliterated. This is their nature, as automatic as breathing.' Iles put a commanding hand on Harpur's shoulder, like an arrest or a very belated paedophilia start-up. Harpur did not want to be touched, even through his jacket, by fingers that had been in Brown's mouth, and/or among his toes. Although Iles was not someone you shrugged off, Harpur tried to shrink his body away from the contact by willpower and muscle-tightening. '*Now*, then, you finally see what Turret signifies, Col.'

'Ah.'

179

'But you'll say Turret is *not* breathing, automatically or otherwise.'

'No, I don't say that. It would be cheap and inane.'

'Sorry. I'd never suggest the cheap and inane are what appeal to you. Or I'd hardly ever suggest it.'

'Thank you, sir.'

'We are watching a typical battle for commercial dictatorship, Harpur. Hence this death.' They began to walk towards their car. The green, windowless, mortuary van arrived, bumping slowly over rough ground. Harpur glanced at its rear to see if it had 'No tools kept in this vehicle overnight' printed there. He felt troubled that, if it did, Iles might go to the crew while they were carrying Brown out and start a rowdy argument across the long bag about whether 'No tools' should be changed to 'Plenty of tools'. In the days of Burke and Hare, the bodysnatchers, mortuary vans might have had 'No corpses kept in this vehicle overnight', or, if the thinking then was like Iles's, 'Plenty of corpses kept in this vehicle overnight', so Burke and Hare would suspect a ruse, a trap, and leave the van alone, although, in fact there *were* corpses kept in the vehicle overnight. This vehicle today had nothing printed on the rear, though. Garland reappeared from the tent and went to meet it.

'Drugs trade monopoly?' Harpur said. 'You mean someone's trying to destroy Ralphy

Ember's firm by killing his people? And ultimately perhaps killing Ralph himself?'

'Not simply killing his people, Col—killing someone who's been told to find out how Mansc plans to make himself trade Supremo, trade One-and-only.'

'So this shows Manse *does* plan to make himself Supremo and One-and-only, and doesn't want Ember to know how he's going to do it?'

'Col, no better example of raw capitalism exists than major traffic in unlawful powders,' Iles replicd. 'It's a perfect model, a paradigm. Perhaps they use it to illustrate lectures in business schools. Consider, would you, the core features?

'(a) An eager, hooked, eternally expanding market, with enough disposable income. Even when there isn't enough disposable income, people who can't live without the stuff will burgle, con and/or mug their way to enough disposable income.

'(b) Price classically tied to competition rates and to levels of supply—abundance or scarcity.

'(c) Vaunted—though dubious—quality control based on purity and mix levels.

'(d) Attempts to establish a so-called "territory", a "niche" and forcefully and perhaps forcibly to annex the territory and niches of rivals—that is, of pusher enemies— and so move towards monopoly and ruthless price fixing, which customers can't fight because there's no alternative and—in the special instance of drugs—because of their habit.

'(e) Compare nineteenth-century "Tommy Shops" run by factory proprietors and pit owners where work people *had* to buy their necessaries and were shamelessly and irresistibly ripped off.

'(f) Luxury, prestige, possibly out-of-town living for the directors/barons. Consider Ralphy Ember in his manor house, Low Pastures: I've heard of stables, paddocks, park, a studded front door in not wood-type wood but authentic oak, daughters sent to private schools, including one at leg-and-arm places in Poitiers and Bordeaux for a decent spell, club ownership, even if the club is only the Monty—and it *is* only the Monty.'

'And Mansel Shale with his priceless collection of Pre-Raphaelite art, and his house a vast ex-rectory.'

'I knew you'd get to see it, Harpur.'

'Yes, but I'm not sure I—'

'Of course, you'll say, Ralphy Ember and Mansel Shale used to be . . . used to be . . . well, not exactly partners but through-and-through allies. And apparently still are. Yes, apparently. They split the local drugs business between them in a happy, civilized, sensible, enormously profitable pact, earning what—half a mill a year each?'

'Six hundred grand.'

'All right. So, you'll ask how could one of them consider wiping out the other when they're so friendly and interdependent? And, perhaps, vice versa.'

'Yes, I *would* say that. And you blind-eyed them and their businesses, despite the old Chief, as long as they maintained peace on the streets.'

'There've been some changes made, Harpur.'

'Yes, but—'

'Note: (a) relaxation of the drugs laws, resulting in (b) new firms, several from abroad, decide they can have a go here. (c) A growing trickle of customers transfer to them. (d) Turnover and profits for Ralphy and Manse slip accordingly, and might slip more. (e) Frantic alarm. We've already witnessed stray symptoms of trouble—regrettable, small-scale outbursts of turf violence.'

'That was only Ember and Shale as virtual partners, mates, allies, trying to see off invasive minor firms, small-scale, would-be rivals,' Harpur said.

'There've been some changes made. They'll tear at each other instead now. Have to. A new era, Col. As I see it, Mansel Shale is very aware of present business trends, and scared. Manse might sound thick, but isn't. He caters for the future. He observes his firm start to dwindle. The decline might accelerate,

183

exponentially. You'll find that in the dictionary, Col, under "e". Meaning rapidly, and then *more* rapidly. Manse is due to remarry, isn't he, after his first swine wife, Sybil, ditched him and the son and daughter? He wants stability. He demands continuing status not only for himself but to satisfy this new, rather smartarse fiancée, I'm told. Naomi Gage.'

'Told by whom?' Harpur said

'And so, suddenly, those standard, crucial, animal-like aggressive survival impulses described in Marx take charge. They've been unnaturally suppressed for the last few years during the spell of comfy co-operation. Now, they re-emerge, refreshed and grown powerful in their idleness, irrepressible. But this is Darwin as much as Marx, Col. Survival of the richest and only the richest. Shale craves that autocrat position. He realizes it's beside the point to fight the small, novice, Johnny-come-lately companies. He has to squash mighty Ralph Ember and his utterly established firm. We see big-hitter against big-hitter. Once he's disposed of Ralph, he'll be super-strong, and to smash the upstarts a doddle. He'll have what Marx would tell him he's programmed to seek and strive for. In fact, *doomed* to seek and strive for. That is, total trade control.'

They changed back into their ordinary clothes in the Volvo. Iles said: 'Is that one of those £19, fit-anyone suits from Asda?'

184

'A Shale–Ember war?' Harpur said. 'Those long-term confederates? Turret dead indicates all that? We don't know—*know*—provably know—Manse or his people killed him. For instance, it might have been somebody from one of those small-time firms, niggled or terrorized by Turret. He *did* niggle and terrorize.'

'Well, yes, it might. But my instincts are otherwise. No tattoos, perhaps, but I see *Das Kapital*, or some comparable treatise, written all over Turret in there. At my rank, Harpur, one learns to value one's instincts, submit to them, as it were. You'll find the same, should you ever get promotion to this level, which, of course, you never fucking will, and not just on account of your clothes.'

CHAPTER SEVEN

When it came to Joachim Balc Frederick Brown's funeral, Harpur's daughter, Hazel, told him she and her sister thought they'd get along to see the procession. It was half term and they had the time. The three of them—Hazel, Jill, Harpur—often pow-wowed here at home in the big Arthur Street sitting room. Now, Jill seemed sorry things had been put so head-on and curt by her sister. Jill said: 'You see, dad, there'll be a terrific crowd. Real grotty atmos! Great! What's known as "a cross-section" of people, meaning heavies, junkies, jailbirds and their ladies on sky-high heels. The hearse to be drawn by four black horses with tall, bobbing bunches of black plumes on their heads for mourning, like in earlier times. It will be . . . well . . . well, like . . . like terrific. Such a sight!'

'I don't know,' Harpur said.

'It will, dad, honestly,' Jill said. 'There was a piece about it in the press. And many terrific floral tributes coming—maybe spelling out his names in lilies or roses, "Joachim" and the rest. "Joachim Whatsit Brown—never to be forgotten."'

'No, I meant I'm not sure it's a good idea to go and stand around there,' Harpur said.

'Why not?' Hazel said. 'There *will* be lots of very interesting lowlife on show.'

'Yes, so it would be wise to stay away,' Harpur said.

'I think it's positive for us,' Hazel said. 'Like an eye-opener. Of social importance. A glimpse of a parallel culture. "Terrific," as Jill says, and says again. Narrow, even snobbish, to ignore it.'

'Best stay away,' Harpur said.

'But, look, dad, you and Desmond Iles go to the funerals of people who've been murdered,' Hazel said.

'When appropriate,' Harpur said.

'Why isn't this one appropriate?' Hazel said.

186

She was fifteen, dogged, tireless, frequently right, or almost, and pestilential.

'Well, we do know why, *really*, don't we, Haze?' Jill said.

'No, we don't,' Hazel said. 'Or, *I* don't.'

'Joachim Whatsit was a crook, wasn't he?' Jill said.

'And?' Hazel said.

'*We* can go to the funeral, or look at it near the church, but dad can't go,' Jill said. 'The funerals he and Mr Iles turn up at are of blameless people, victims. It's to show the family official police sympathy. What's known as "public relations", like a Health Minister with patients, asking about their cough.'

'But now it would be *in*appropriate, would it?' Hazel said.

'Dad thinks it would be lining up as a villain's buddies,' Jill said.

'How do you know what he thinks?' Hazel snarled. '*He* hasn't said that. You, a thirteen-year-old nobody, can see into his head? Anyway, someone's dead—killed and cut about. I should think sympathy would be all right.'

'But maybe not from dad. Not from police,' Jill said. 'It's gang war. This is what I hear. That's the word.'

'What *word*?' Hazel said.

'The word on the street,' Jill said. 'It's an absolutely new kind of war because it's between the main men, Ralphy and Shale.'

'And who speaks this word on the street?' Hazel said.

'It's around,' Jill said. 'Maybe you're not in the loop, Haze.'

'Oh, thanks, thanks so much, Madam Big,' Hazel said. She was curled up on one of the long settees. Harpur had an armchair. Jill sat very straight on the other settee. They all held mugs of tea, prepared by Jill. Hazel looked as though she might not drink hers *because* it had been prepared by Jill. Hazel unfolded herself a little, bent forward and made a big thing of putting the mug on the floor.

Although he liked the room now, it used to unnerve Harpur and give him colic. His wife, Megan, had kept her books on shelves around the walls, most of the many volumes lumpy, with off-putting titles. He struggled to disremember all of these because of the depression and nausea factors, but a few dogged him just the same—one called *Edwin Drood*, another, *Old Fortunatus*, another, *The Virtues of Sid Hamet the Magician's Rod*. Quite a tactful time after Megan's death he'd felt able to pull down the shelves and ditch most of the books. Jill decided to keep two she was fond of: the playwright, Joe Orton's *Diaries* and *The Sweet Science*, about boxing.

Harpur saw Jill's tactics for today. She'd obviously sensed from the outset that he might not want them to join a mob-gawp at the funeral, and so tried to make him see how

188

exciting and unique it would be. She'd attempt to win him, convince him. He suspected Jill almost always understood him better than Hazel did. Often, Jill would defend him from her sister. Or perhaps Hazel didn't *want* to understand him all that well: she was the elder and meant to go her own way, think and act in her own style. He believed that, up to a point, Hazel didn't mind listening to him. If she liked what she heard, fine. If not, she'd ignore him.

'Monopoly,' Jill replied. 'We were talking about it the other day. Remember, Haze?'

'I remember,' Harpur said. It helped send him to the Agincourt.

'What about it?' Hazel said.

'They're after monopoly,' Jill said.

'Who?' Hazel said.

'All of them. The firms,' Jill said. 'They can't help themselves. It's like built in. That's exactly what we were saying. Karl Marx worked out a theory on it. I know a bit more about it now. One of the boys has studied all this, in Politics. Or it could be Economics.'

'Which boy?' Hazel said.

'A boy I know,' Jill said. 'A bit older.'

'Which boy? *How* old?' Harpur said.

'Yes, a boy I know,' Jill replied. 'Firms are like sort of almost helpless. They are just caught up in the, like, theory.'

'No need for the "likes",' Harpur said.

'Firms are programmed, so they *have* to behave a certain way,' Jill said. 'All of them,

189

not just druggy firms. All businesses everywhere. They try to wipe out the opposition. Then they can shaft the customers because the customers got no choice.'

'*Have* no choice,' Harpur said. 'Not a theory I've ever heard.'

'Such as supermarkets crushing small shops. Juggernauts. That's what he called them, the supermarkets,' Jill said.

'Who?' Hazel said.

'This boy I met,' Jill said. 'A bit older.'

'*How* old?' Harpur said. Now and then, since Megan's murder, Harpur found single-parenting two teen daughters a worry.

'I don't know if you ever came across this word, "juggernauts", at all,' Jill said. 'It means really huge. Tramplers.'

'Educate us, do,' Hazel said.

'His idea is, the two big drugs kings that everybody knows of—Ralphy Ember and Manse Shale—want to destroy each other, because trade is very tough,' Jill said. 'Suddenly, not enough to go round. They're afraid. Too much competition. So, they lash out. Or one of them does. Then, the other will have to defend himself and fight back. The word says this Joachim is called Turret, owing to gunfire, and worked for Ralph Ember. Also, the word says Ember might have sent him into Shale's lot as a spy, because Ralph knows about monopoly and thinks Manse might try for it. This is the beginning. It's like shooting the Archduke Francis Ferdinand at Sarajevo started the Great 1914–18 War in History. Ember and Shale used to be total comrades, yes, but not now. And then the word also says Desmond Iles looked after Ralph and Mansel as long as they stayed peaceful, but he can't do it no more, because there's too many at it and a new Chief. The word says Brown has a brother who's an actor—not just TV— theatres. Maybe it's the sort of brother you'd expect someone called Joachim to have. A play called *The Duchess and Alfie*, or something like that.'

'*Any* more,' Harpur said.

'Any more what?' Jill said. 'Tea?'

'Any more, not "no more",' Harpur said.

'This is all tripe, isn't it, dad?' Hazel said.

'One of our best detectives is handling the Joachim Bale Frederick Brown murder,' Harpur replied.

'But, dad, I'd still like to go to see the funeral—the horses with black feathers and that,' Jill said. 'Terrific! Please!'

'Well, I suppose it *might* be a sight,' Harpur said.

'This boy I know says to check who's there. It could be a sign. Ralphy will be, yes, because Turret worked for him and that's the way things are—the chief goes to the funeral of one of his people and sends top notch flowers. And the knees-up after will be at Ralph Ember's club, the Monty, I bet. But will Manse

Shale go to the funeral, too? Maybe he caused it, or even did it himself, and would he have the cheek to come and do public sorrow? The boy I met says this will be the thing to watch.'

'How did you get to know this boy?' Harpur said.

'So far, Manse Shale and Ember still behave like true friends, you see,' Jill said. 'They got to for now. Sorry, *have* to for now. The buzz says Manse is going to marry again and Ralph Ember will even be best man. But all that's just show. This is definitely the word, isn't it, dad— that it was Manse or one of his people who did Turret? The boy I know heard it from three different people, which is what's called confirmation.'

'It's the first time you've spoken about this boy, isn't it?' Harpur said.

'He's older. He's in touch with many.'

'Many what?' Harpur said.

'Many,' Jill said.

'How much older?' Harpur said.

'It'll be on telly news because of the horses and plumes and flowers,' Jill replied. 'What's known as visual.'

'*We* can't be restricted because of *your* job, dad,' Hazel said. 'This would be unfair, like the sins of the father visited on his children in the Bible.'

' "Expotential",' Jill said. 'That's another word. This boy says it's expotential.'

'Isn't it "expo*nential*"?' Harpur said.

'Of course it is,' Hazel said. 'But she wouldn't get it right, would she?'

'Dad, how do *you* know a word like that?' Jill said.

'It's around,' Harpur said.

'Meaning, swift and getting swifter, like feeding on its own swiftness to get swifter,' Jill said. 'This boy thinks Ralphy and Manse Shale could lose customers in an expo*nential* way because the trade has become so tricky. "Exponential" is from Economics. His lecturer mentions it a lot. That's her nickname, "Exponential".'

'Whose lecturer?' Hazel said.

'This boy's. He's a bit older.'

'How much older?' Harpur replied. 'Why are you talking to him so much lately?'

*   *   *

As Jill said, it would have been wrong for Iles and Harpur to attend Turret's actual villain funeral, but the ACC decided they could and, in fact, *must* look in on the après crem evening drinks session at the Monty club, owned by Ralph Ember: about this venue Jill had been correct , too. Harpur was at home when the girls returned from the funeral and he gave them their tea-supper before setting out to join Iles at the club. As a single parent he regarded the preparation of their meals as important. When they grew up and looked back on these days he wanted them to recall him as a conscientious, capable father. Denise would probably have helped him with the meal, but she was playing lacrosse for the university this evening. The funeral had thrilled Hazel and Jill as much as they'd expected, and they watched the local news coverage of it on television.

'Both there, you see, dad,' Jill said, pointing at the screen. 'Ralphy Ember and Manse Shale. I would of recognized Ralph Ember anyway, because the word's around that he looks like Charlton Heston on the movie channel in old films.'

'Would *have* recognized,' Harpur said.

'And Shaley—someone in the crowd says "There's Shaley with his new bird." He's getting married again soon. She looks too good for him. Auburn. He's a bit ferrety.'

'Who in the crowd?' Harpur said.

'A lot of drugs scene people spectating,' Hazel said.

'How could you tell they were drugs scene?' Harpur said.

'Because they recognized everybody, of course,' Hazel said.

Jill said: 'I told you, dad, this boy I know said we should look to see if only one of them came, Ralphy or Manse, because this would be interesting.'

'Which boy?' Harpur replied. 'Was he in the crowd?'

'But both turn up,' Jill said.

'And a lot of very heavy-looking people. I mean, *very* heavy,' Hazel said.

'One called Unhinged Humphrey,' Jill said. 'But really dressed for a funeral. Black jacket, silver-striped trousers, bowler. That's not his real name. It's just how he can be sometimes. Humphrey Maidment-Fane, known as Unhinged, someone in the crowd said.'

'Who?' Harpur said.

'He goes to all the funerals. That's why he's got the gear,' Jill said. 'He's not mad or anything, just . . . well, unhinged sometimes. Nobody gives him a job because . . . because he can be unhinged. So, he's like what's known as a freelance. But he went to the funeral all the same.'

'And the parents there, of course, and his brother, who's the actor Clement Porter Brown,' Hazel said. 'I recognized him from pictures in the Sunday supplements, even though he had glasses on, which he doesn't wear on the stage in dramas from back in history, obviously. Some plays he's in are old.'

'His mother and father looked like they thought the whole thing—the horses and these thug people everywhere—they looked like . . . well, like they were uncomfortable. They looked like they couldn't believe their son could be in this kind of funeral, with this sort of people. His parents wanted it over as soon as poss,' Jill said. 'This was not their kind of thing. Anyone could tell. I didn't recognize him—the actor—but you could see he probably had something to do with plays or films. The way they move—like the way they move this way or that shows what they're thinking, so it helps out their lines.'

'What did he look as if he was thinking?' Harpur said.

'And someone else there—a surprise,' Hazel said.

'This girl—really crying in the crowd, dad,' Jill said. 'And holding two flowers, two carnations, like she wanted to put them on the coffin but couldn't. Like it wouldn't be allowed.'

'Venetia Ember,' Hazel said.

'How do you know?' Harpur said.

'We sort of half recognized her. I think she came to judo once or twice. A friend of hers from school does judo and Venetia came to see what it was like. Maybe she didn't like it. She gave it up. At the funeral, we went to talk to her,' Hazel said. 'She had a bike.'

'To give comfort,' Jill said. 'It seemed right.'

'Yes,' Harpur said, 'I can see that.'

'I asked her did she know Mr Joachim Brown, the deceased, seeing she was so upset,' Jill said. 'I didn't do it in a nosy way or anything like that, not pushy at all, honest, dad, but just so we could understand what was what and how to comfort her. She said, "Indeed, yes." It was like a really big

196

statement—"Indeed, yes." Sort of dramatic. Old-type dramatic. Corny dramatic, maybe like some of those plays Joachim's brother is in. I mean, she's only about fourteen, but she's saying things like "Indeed". What it seemed to me was, she didn't mind being asked if she knew this deceased because it gave her the chance to come out with this terrific "Indeed". She *wanted* to be asked, so she could do a bit more than the weeping.'

They ate fish cakes, boiled potatoes and peas. Harpur also had a pudding for them, rhubarb tart with custard. The girls were both good at eating and talking at the same time and, in fact, at talking most of the time. He regarded this meal as nutritious. It pleased him, but if he could have devised a meal which kept them quieter he would have served that.

'She stayed far back in the crowd. She told us she didn't want her father to see her there. And she was scared she might be on TV news,' Hazel said.

'Like she was some celebrity, but wanting to go anon for once,' Jill said. 'You know—what d'you call it?'

'Incognito,' Harpur said.

'Yes, that sort of thing. But this was how we found out her name for definite,' Jill said. 'We asked her if her father was there in the funeral and, if so, who was he and she replied, Mr Ralph W. Ember of Low Pastures. She didn't say also of the Monty club, like she didn't

197

think the Monty was much of a place, or not much compared with Low Pastures. She said her father was a "principal mourner"—those were the words, a "principal mourner", owing to Mr Joachim Brown's employment. Everyone knows Ralphy Ember got two daughters, one about fourteen, Venetia and Fay. But I didn't say, "You must be Venetia, then." I didn't want her to think everyone had heard about her because her father runs a drugs empire, as well as the Monty dump. "He'd hate it if he found I'd come," she said. "Who? Your dad?" I asked. "He's against all that kind of thing," she said. I didn't say "Which kind of thing?" because I could tell what she was getting at. This was to do with . . . well . . . relationships . . . sex. She's only about fourteen, and in the paper it said Mr Joachim Brown was twenty-seven, but—'

'It might all be in her imagination,' Hazel said.

'We didn't give *our* name—I mean, Harpur,' Jill said. 'We thought it was better like that. "Oh, many's the time he came to Low Pastures," she said. "Our interests, you see—they made a link. We were both very much horse people." I didn't say he'd have liked to know the hearse was pulled by four of them, then.'

'No,' Harpur said. 'Good.' He washed up and left soon afterwards. The Monty often hosted these significant get-togethers—almost invariably hosted them. The club had that sort of warm, very solid community role. For now. Harpur knew Ralph yearned to kick out permanently most of the present clientele and lift the Monty to the social level of, say, distinguished London clubs like the Athenaeum or the Garrick, where surgeons, professors, national newspaper editors, judges, media people and Secretaries of State belonged. But this transformation would take at least a while yet—yes, at least—so the present membership could go on using the Monty for many important kinds of traditional celebration:

(a) wedding, divorce and christening parties,

(b) jail releases,

(c) helpful parole or bail decisions,

(d) enemy deaths or major disablings, and turf battle triumphs in general,

(e) charity cabarets and strip shows,

(f) acquittals, like that of Shane Gordon Wilkes,

(g) successful Appeal Court judgements,

(h) knockabout comics,

(i) loot share-outs after extremely unnamed jobs,

(j) suspended sentences due to full prisons,

(k) births,

(l) and, as tonight, the traditional drinks session following a funeral, especially when, as with Turret, he'd been an associate of Ralph and deserved a full, affectionate, prestige

Monty send-off.

'Ralph!' Iles cried. 'Here's a lovely, large, clean-linened, bustling, deserved turn-out for Joachim.'

'*So* deserved,' Ember said. 'This community had taken him very much to its heart.'

'Obviously, a fucking dangerous spot,' Iles said.

'On these occasions—not frequent, thank heaven—on these occasions I feel one can enjoy the strength and genuineness of human fellowship, Mr Iles,' Ralph said.

'Some people here might fit into that category,' Iles said.

'Which?' Ember said.

'Human,' Iles said. He did an inventory gaze. 'Everyone's on parade, in tribute to Joachim. That is, everyone not locked up. Old faithfuls—Rex Sallis, Bart Haverson, Unhinged Humph—but Unhinged Humph? Should he be out yet? How's his unhingedness these days? Then, Teddy Brinscombe, Icon Watkins, all cosy and peaceable in your hotbed, Ralph. You, and you only, can occasionally manage this epic, vile, post-funeral synthesis for a few hours. We salute you. I include Harpur in this.'

'The full range of age groups, women as well as men,' Ember said. 'Across the as-it-were board. Such a tribute to the club. It makes me very humble, Mr Iles.'

Tonight, Ralph had come out from behind

200

the Monty bar and stood in the crowd with Harpur and Iles near one of the pool tables. 'Joachim will be severely missed in our company policy meetings,' Ember said. 'He could be wonderfully succinct. A remarkable gift for administration. This was entirely natural to him.'

'How *is* policy, Ralph?' Harpur said.

'Who paid for the hearse nags?' Iles said.

'Joachim had the manner and looks of someone assured of a splendid future,' Ember said, 'someone who could inspire others to share that splendid future with him, and to work for it.'

'This was a man with almost all his own teeth, notwithstanding,' Iles replied. 'Harpur will bear me out.'

'Now this,' Ember said. 'Who, who, could have wished such an all-round likeable, talented, gracious man dead?' Ember said. 'Continually I ask myself that.'

'What answer do you get?' Harpur said.

'And is Manse with us?' Iles said. 'Did he and his grand cohort make it to the funeral, regardless?'

'This was, undoubtedly, a funeral, yet I prefer to think of it as the celebration of a life, Mr Iles,' Ember said.

'Which bit of Turret's life should be celebrated most, Ralph?' Iles said.

'Mansel present?' Ember replied. 'Yes, of course. How would he, as it were, not be? This was what I meant by human fellowship, as blazoned by a Monty occasion of this type. Manse would naturally share the general affectionate esteem for Joachim among business colleagues and wish to affirm it today, though sadly.'

Iles said: 'Good. Harpur will be glad because he and some others with his kind of dark, unforgiving mind might wonder whether, in view of—'

'Manse and protocol—linked unbreakably,' Ember said.

Iles said: 'And do I see Alec Maximilian Misk over there with some rather grown-up ladies?'

'Alec, a regular,' Ralph said. 'And his family.'

'Today, trailing clouds of rumour about his splendid cut from the International Corporate Diverse Securities tickle in London,' Iles said. 'Who'd have thought it of dear, stunted Articulate Alec? Graduated to top-level loot from a bank job.'

'That's what I mean about community, you see, Mr Iles,' Ralph replied.

'What?' Iles said.

'Alec with not just his mother but great aunt Edna,' Ralph said. 'Cross-generational, inter-gender support of the club.' Ember sounded almost genuinely delighted, though Harpur thought the Misks would be among the first to get the membership heave-ho from a

202

relaunched, upmarket Monty. Ralph wanted a fine future for the club, and also felt a debt to its past. Twenty years ago, the Monty operated as a select meeting place for local commercial and professional people, and some of the handsome brass fittings and mahogany panelling remained. Ember had taste and believed thoroughly in conservation. Harpur could tell Ralph hungered for true quality. He had begun a mature student Humanities degree at the university up the road and, although he'd suspended this for now because of a sudden need to provide hands-on protection of his charlie, H, skunk and crack territories from intruders, the original turn towards higher education proved his seriousness. Apparently, he'd read quite a few books for the courses. His letters to the local press about the environment always showed weight and judgement. The pollution of rivers and state of the ozone layer gave Ralph a lot of agitation.

'And the rumour goes further,' Iles said.

'You listen to rumour, Mr Iles? I thought police needed absolute evidence, insisted on absolute evidence to such an inflexible degree they often make it up.'

'I hear the Misks want to use some of the gains by buying into redevelopment of the Monty,' Iles replied.

'That's shit,' Ember said. He seemed startled, though.

'They might think now's just the time to propose it—you being shaken and weakened by the death of Joachim, one of your best people, Ralph.'

'That's shit,' Ember said.

Harpur wondered. Iles heard a lot.

'Investment of the big sudden funds in a worthy enterprise—the brilliantly salvaged, prestige Monty,' Iles said.

'That's shit,' Ember said.

'Why are they all here, then, Ralph, and looking businesslike?' the ACC said. 'Expect an approach. Things mesh, things interlock—Alec's massive new boodle, Joachim's death, your known dissatisfaction with the social rating of the Monty—a minus. I'm used to taking the overview. One sees that everything is of a piece. Remember that E.M. Forster plea, Ralph—"Only connect"?'

Anything that seemed to menace the club would shock Ralph into momentary robotism. He cherished the Monty. It went beyond conservation. He also applied creativeness, and signs of this could clearly be seen at the club. Ralph bought the Monty from trade profits, and since then the tone had altered. He'd added several notable new features to the furnishings and decor, features entirely special to Ralph and chosen by him, some with a cultural quality. For instance, a thick metal slab two metres square and bolted to a support pillar would block any fusillade from a marksman who came blazing through the main club entrance hoping to take out Ralph quickly at his little desk behind the bar with a burst of good chest shots. But, so that this bullet-proof barrier would not look too starkly, vulgarly, a bullet-proof barrier, it was covered with a collage of interesting, prestige illustrations. Ralph had explained to Harpur they came from a collection called *The Marriage of Heaven and Hell*, by the well-known poet and artist, William Blake, who did *Tiger, Tiger, burning bright.* Ember most likely heard of him at the university. If asked about the steel screen he always said it came as part of the ventilation system, to improve ducting. He must have sensed that the Athenaeum and the Garrick probably didn't need this sort of precaution against contracted hit men, and was ashamed for the Monty and its screen, despite the classy drawings.

'The club is proud to act as venue for a general, spontaneous welling-up of affection for one of its own at these times, you see, Mr Iles,' Ember said.

He had mentioned once to Harpur that at the university he'd been asked to read a novel by the Victorian author, Anthony Trollope, in which its hero, happening to walk down Pall Mall, sees a famous statesman and a bishop chatting on the steps of the Athenaeum. This moment stayed vivid in Ember's memory. He visualized something like it for the Monty steps in Shield Terrace ultimately. If Ember had recounted that to Iles the ACC would probably have replied, 'Very fucking ultimately,' but Harpur had only nodded and smiled. He liked to hear of people seeking betterment, no matter how hopelessly. Ember had said that, in his view, the British gentlemen's club was unique to this country—unmatched in Europe or even the United States. He wanted the Monty to become a notable part of the tradition, though for both sexes.

'Well, and here's Mansel now, as it happens,' Ember remarked, fondly beaming, 'and with his lovely fiancée.'

Shale and a tall, auburn-haired, mid-thirtyish, undocile-looking woman Harpur did not know edged forward through a knot of people and joined them. She seemed wary in the club crowd, but Harpur would expect this of anyone possibly used to a different sort of company, and most other company *would* be different. Both she and Shale wore very good dark suits. The cut of Mansel's jacket looked so right that Harpur felt more or less sure he had no shoulder holster and piece aboard, or only a small, low-calibre Saturday night special. The similarity of these suits might have helped bring her and him together if they wore them to art galleries. Those clothes would stand out among more relaxed, even bohemian, outfits favoured by many paintings fans. 'Manse!' Iles said. 'Splendid! Ralph was just speaking about the community as community. And you undeniably and justifiably figure in that at some level.'

'Naomi, this is Mr Iles and Mr Harpur,' Ember said.

'We felt it only respectful to look in,' Iles said. 'Well, actually, Harpur is a bit of an old-style purist, but I don't necessarily see him as obsolete on that account. No, not necessarily on that account. He objected, didn't want to come. His words: "Those people can do without us." I at once objected, as you'd expect. I cited his word "us". What made up that "us"? Did he mean us a unit? Or us as two separate entities, yet joined for the sake of his argument? In neither case should he presume to speak for me. "These are our neighbours, Colin, just as we are theirs," I said. "At such a time, they are entitled to our backing. This is a resonant, indeed, touchstone event. Turrets don't grow on trees."'

'Ah, that's puzzling—I saw they called him Turret in one of the papers, too,' Naomi said 'Why?' From her appearance, she had struck Harpur as the questioning sort. 'Obviously, I know what a turret is in say an aircraft or tank, but was Joachim Brown given that name because—'

'Sorry,' Iles said,'I'm mixing my metaphors a bit. Turrets aren't the sort of things that don't not grow on trees. But you'll see what I'm getting at.'

'Turret, why?' Naomi said.

'Welcome, indeed, to the . . . well, yes, to the community,' Iles said. He lightened his voice, grew congratulatory: 'This is very fine of you, Naomi.'

'What?' she said.

'To attend in support of Mansel at such a distressing time. You are, I think, new to the scene here, and yet you so readily make yourself a part of it, for his sake. Manse and Ralph naturally feel in equal measure such time-honoured bonds to someone like Joachim. They will put on a brave show because it is in their characters to put on a brave show, yet the grief, the shared grief, is inevitably there. And you, Naomi, splendidly help Manse bear his.' Iles leaned forward suddenly and shook Shale's hand. 'But I must congratulate you on the engagement, Manse!'

'Thank you, Mr Iles,' Shale said.

'I hope that much-travelled bitch, Sybil, doesn't come and mess it all up on the day,' Iles said. 'Have you provided against this foul possibility, Manse? She has the balls. Excuse me, do, Naomi, but one must speak of these things. In the long run, it's for the best. We all set great store on this wedding, want it to avoid farce and/or carnage. It is a wedding that will, perhaps, in due course, chase away at least some of the sadness of today's proceedings and what led to them.' The ACC released Shale.

'True, Mr Iles,' he said. 'Life goes on.'

'Tell Joachim,' Harpur said.

'Many of us who've known Manse for long felt it would be marvellous, therapeutic, if he could find somebody who'd permanently bring joy and warmth to his home,' Iles replied, 'providing a new mother for those sweet children, Matilda and Laurent. Manse has needed and deserved a loving, established environment, and now . . . well, now, here you are, Naomi! Oh, yes, birds flit in and out of the ex-rectory at Manse's invitation, but without any real, satisfying continuity. Mansel deserved better—and, in due time, he has gloriously got it, via you, Naomi. Bravo!'

'You're police, aren't you?' she said. 'Why so concerned about Mansel's family life?'

'Oh, dear, we're rumbled! Yes, I'm police,' Iles said. 'And Harpur. Manse mentioned us, did he? I'd like to have heard how he put it. Or would I? Perhaps, though, it isn't necessary to say Harpur is police, given the diameter of his neck and total appearance. But I—well, you can imagine that many are surprised to learn *I* am police! Utterly disbelieving! People who guess at my profession simply from how I look and dress and so on—my demeanour—suggest I must be someone very highly placed in the British Medical Association secretariat, though completely over any drink problem. Or they wonder if I'm the definitcly straight

Master of one of the bigger, mixed Oxford colleges, yet with no hint of scandal involving girl undergrads. However—sorry, sorry, you ask, why so caring re Manse? Harpur, I know, worried about him acutely. Unrelentingly. He visualized Mansel quite often sleeping entirely alone in his vast ex-rectory. Oh, yes, quite often. But, then, Harpur *does* worry.' Iles's tone darkened: 'Mind you, talking of beds, I don't say he worried too much about me or my feelings when infiltrating my wife and—'

'Let me congratulate you, too, Manse,' Harpur said, taking his hand.

'Thanks, Mr Harpur,' Shale said.

Iles said: 'If it's not anxiety about Manse— and perhaps it won't be now he's so happily at one with you, Naomi—if it's not Manse that Harpur frets over it will be Ralph here. For instance, I'm sure Harpur looks at this death of Joachim and wonders. Wonders what? you'll say. Well, I gather from Harpur that this was someone—Joachim, I mean—someone very close to Ralph, in the sense of being a prized workmate, involved in most of Ralph's main dealership ventures. What concerns Harpur, with his sort of quite valid mind, is that, if someone like Joachim gets his head half blown off, and his face given the blade, or blades, before being pitched into brambles, who's to say Ralph in person won't be next? This is the kind of step-by-step thinking Harpur can manage and is, in fact, not too bad

210

at. If anyone is banging on re the indispensable requirement of a good education, I always say to them, "But what about Harpur?" They are silenced. You see what he means, Naomi, Mansel? Yes, he would ask, who, who, is to say that Ralph in person won't follow—Turret as an opening shot, then his boss? Would, for example, *you* say it, Manse, if, entirely at random, oh, yes, entirely, if entirely at random you were asked—would you say that Ralph is in no similar peril—would *you* say it, Manse, knowing the local conditions as you do?'

'Shock—bad, deep shock, that's what come over me immediate on hearing of a death and abuse like that,' Shale said. 'Well, it's bound to, for sure, isn't it?'

'How *did* you hear of it?' Harpur said.

'And lying there undiscovered for so long,' Shale replied. 'This is sure to add to the grief, in my view. A wood up a hill like that. Weather. Like you said, Mr Iles, brambles. This is a total wild scene. Animals nosing into him willy-nilly. Don't tell me there's no foxes or stoats and that sort up there. And Turr . . . And Joachim just laid out for them. I'm not against Nature as Nature. No. It's obviously truly environmental in some aspects, such as the sea joining up five continents, but is this dignity for Joachim, dumped without consideration of any sort in foliage?'

Ember must have signalled to a barman who now came out with drinks on a tray. The staff

211

knew Iles's and Harpur's tastes. There was a port and lemon for the Assistant Chief—what he called 'the old whores' drink', the mixed cider and gin in a half-pint mug for Harpur, and a black-labelled bottle of Kressmann's armagnac and three brandy glasses for the others. Ember almost always took Kressmann's.

'Was Joachim done elsewhere, then relocated?' Harpur said.

'"Done elsewhere"?' Naomi asked. 'What does that mean?'

'Done somewhere else,' Harpur said.

'"Done"?' Naomi said.

'Harpur's into low speak,' Iles said.

'Killed?' Naomi said.

'Then transported and ditched,' Harpur said.

'How would Mansel know?' Naomi said.

'That's a point,' Harpur replied. He was aware of Ember listening hard to this conversation, but pretending not to— pretending to give all his concentration to the armagnac.

'This will be such a positive, wholesome local occasion,' Iles said. 'How good it is that in the midst of death today we can talk so affirmatively about joy and love. This Turret was a spy and total shoot-first menace, wasn't he, Manse, a peril to many, including you?'

'Was *what*?' Naomi said.

'Joachim—such a flair for . . . well, for

people,' Ember replied. 'Flair. No other term will do. An almost mystical power. Innate. His ability to get on with all sorts. His kindness and good humour. I do hope your wife is well, Mr Iles, able to settle better, perhaps, these days and nights.'

'And what's that about, for God's sake?' Naomi said.

But Ember didn't reply, once more gave the armagnac attention. He loved to project his profile while sipping this high-grade West France tot. He seemed to feel that the armagnac plus his features and physique together helped create much of his image—his features and physique recalling the young Heston's. Ember was married, with a family, but also did pretty well alternatively. He had that obvious scar along one side of his jaw and this could intrigue admirers, with its suggestion of a rough, brave, hazardous, ultimately triumphant past. They would speculate on the kind of all-out, hand-to-hand battles he must have been in, possibly—most probably?—as leader. Wasn't El Cid, as famously played by Heston, a leader, even when dead and strapped on to a charger, to inspire his men still?

Once, Harpur had watched a woman busily finger Ember's scar as though convinced that if only she could hit the right code combination the blemish would open like a door, and give special access to the inner rich Ralphnesses of

Ralph. Naturally, Ember's enemies said the wound came from no noble passage of arms. Some maintained he'd fallen forward when drunk on to an open tin of baked beans, the lid still fixed to the can and sticking up like a circular saw, not a moving circular saw but jagged and able to give a hearty wound. This version said he was afraid to go to Accident and Emergency in case they thought he'd been in a gang fight and reported it to the police— the kind of gang fight some women decided he *had* been in when they noticed his scar. He'd done first aid on himself and, so the tale went, then ate the baked beans cold although they were awash in blood as well as tomato sauce. The scar remained more noticeable than it should have been because he'd failed to get it stitched and treated properly at the time.

'And the ring?' Iles said. 'May we see the ring?'

Naomi held out her hand and showed the large single, square diamond in a silver claw.

'That is so typically Manse!' Iles said. 'The uncluttered excellence. Many, if they were asked to sum up Mansel in a couple of words, would say "uncluttered excellence". That's even without having seen the diamond.'

'Why was he called Turret?' Naomi said.

'Tell us about the wedding? Where?' Iles said.

'St James's,' Shale said.

'But, of course! Perfect,' Iles said. 'You live

214

in what was once the St James's rectory, don't you?'

'I felt it sort of right to do it this way,' Shale answered. 'Such as continuity.'

'Yes, yes, plus a symmetry to it,' Iles said. 'Already you have a link with the church through your property. But now this link will express itself through a further link, that between you and Naomi celebrated in that same church.'

'I thought of it like a responsibility,' Shale said.

'Yet, not a burdensome responsibility but a joyous one,' Iles said.

'So joyous,' Shale stated.

'And need one ask who is to be your best man? Could it be other than Ralph? Doesn't this give a wonderful new dimension to a relationship already of memorably brilliant quality? Perhaps one could even say it sanctifies that relationship.'

'Yes, Ralph has generously agreed,' Manse said.

'Some would argue Turret Brown, an intelligencer, only got what he'd been asking for,' Iles replied.

'Who?' Naomi said.

'Who what?' Iles said.

'*Who* would argue that?' Naomi said.

'Some,' Iles said.

'But which some?' Naomi said. '*Why* would they argue it? How come a name like

215

Joachim?'

'You'll have stimulating times with Naomi, Manse,' Iles said. 'The questions etcetera.'

On the other side of the club, three or four women and a couple of men started a sing-song, accompanied on a comb wrapped in what was probably two sheets of low-grade lav paper, and blown on by one of the men, like a kazoo, a shallow, buzzing, unmelodious din. The numbers seemed mainly old: 'You Always Hurt the One You Love', 'Roll a Silver Dollar', 'Jealousy', 'Run Rabbit Run', 'Who's Afraid of the Big Bad Wolf', 'There'll Always Be an England'. One of the women conducted with two arms, both a beat behind the singers. Harpur thought Ralph would detest this—not just the paper-and-comb, and the age of the music, but any maudlin pleb noisiness. It was out of tune with what he wanted for the club. He'd realize this was another Monty feature not likely to be met with in the Athenaeum or the Garrick. That kind of membership was never going to perform some number like 'You Always Hurt the One You Love', accompanied or not, and the lavatory paper would be of higher, softer quality, unable to vibrate. As the singing began, Ralph looked angry for a few moments, but then must have decided to put up with it for now. Ralph had a doctrine. He wanted the club different but while it was *not* different, such as now, he must tolerate the Monty as presently existing. In any case, if he

216

intervened they might defy him and he and staff would have to eject them. It would embarrass Ralph to have scrapping and breakages while Harpur and Iles watched, particularly rough stuff on women. Violence was even less the kind of behaviour he wanted for the Monty, particularly on a funeral occasion. Harpur had often heard Ember speak of decorum, as a quality he demanded at the club, or, at least, desired. A long time ago, Ralph told Harpur that one of the most dismal sights he'd ever had to encounter was a ginger wig—man's or woman's—discarded on the floor, under a radiator, after a fist fight at the Monty.

Harpur guessed Ralph would let the singing continue unless the choir climbed on to pool tables or the bar and performed. He always reacted to that. But it was people who leapt up and dangled from *The Marriage of Heaven and Hell* that could make him most furious. This hadn't happened yet this evening. He'd know it couldn't ever happen in the Athenaeum or the Garrick—even less so than the lavatory paper music—because there'd be no hanging bulwark there and, even if there were, the membership would probably not include the sort to monkey-swing from it. Ember treated that kind of behaviour as an insult not only to himself, but also to William Blake and artists generally.

'And Joachim, so versatile,' Ralph said. He'd

217

want to get attention off the damn demeaning singers.

'I've heard that,' Iles said.

'In what ways?' Naomi said.

'Several,' Iles said.

'Yes, there *would* be several if he was versatile,' Naomi said. 'That's what versatile means. But which several?'

'Various roles,' Iles replied.

'Which?' Naomi said.

'Manse must have noted his various roles, I'm sure, although Joachim didn't work for him but for Ralph,' Iles said. 'Important to distinguish. I say, Manse, what would have been the first word to come into your mind in one of those free association tests if someone mentioned the name of Joachim Brown? Don't tell me! Don't! I know it would be "versatile".'

Shale said: 'Well, I—'

'Oh, yes, "versatile" would be your instant reaction,' Iles replied. 'But that's when he was alive. Clearly now your first word to describe him would be "dead".'

Naomi stared for a few moments at Iles. 'I'm trying to work out why you're only an Assistant Chief, not Chief,' she said. 'So much aplomb and disdain.'

Harpur knew this could be a bad sort of thing to bring up with Iles. There were times when the ACC would speak that word 'Assistant' with its insistent, snivelling 's' sounds, as if it were a dirty, immovable curse, placed in his title by those ranking above Iles, and full of hatred, envy, and wise fear—fear that if they did not keep him at Assistant he would soar past them in the hierarchy and make it his main and expertly managed task to fuck them up good and continuous.

'Mr Iles is not obsessed by crude ambition, as some officers might admittedly be,' Harpur said. He thought it best to get in fast and do the answering for the Assistant Chief on this.

'You mean like Skule in Ibsen's drama, *The Pretenders*?' she said.

'Ah!' Harpur replied at once.

'Ibsen's a Norwegian writer, Col,' the ACC said.

'Skule—ultimately lacking what Ibsen refers to as "the great kingly thought",' Naomi said.

'Mr Iles loves theatre,' Harpur said. 'Many's the play he knows, in his own right.' Harpur moved away before Iles could talk for himself. In any case, Harpur wanted to look at some other sections of the crowd, do a bit of an inventory, remind himself of who was in circulation these days. For instance, like Iles, he'd thought Humphrey Maidment-Fane—familiarly, and aptly, Unhinged Humphrey—had still some time to do inside, but he was here, over near the door, chatting with Matt Bolcombe and a few others, apparently coherent.

When Harpur had taken a few steps, a man

of about thirty with fair, curly hair, middle-height, thin, wearing heavy spectacles and a black tie on a very white shirt touched his arm and said: 'You're Harpur, yes?' A grand voice, totally audible and precise above the club din. A presence. Something familiar about him? 'I'm Joachim's brother. C.P. Brown.'

'Yes, a resemblance. Hair. Build.' Had Jill, or 'the word' to those in 'the loop', said actor?

'My parents went straight back to London after the service. They both have evening surgeries. But I wanted to see people here. It seemed necessary. In fact, no more than courteous.'

'Which people?' Harpur asked.

'On my parents' behalf as well as my own. Someone said you were head of detectives, pointed you out. And he mentioned there's another top officer in the club tonight, also. It seems . . . it seems . . . unusual?'

'I'm sorry about what happened.'

'We'd all more or less lost touch with him,' Brown said. 'I gather he worked for the man who owns the Monty—Ralphy Ember. But doing what? Ember has another business, besides the club?'

'If you meet him, don't call him Ralphy. He thinks it makes him sound like somebody's moronic cousin, not allowed out alone, "Our Ralphy". Make it "Ralph" or "Ember". He's there, by the bar, talking to friends.'

'What *kind* of work?'

220

'Various roles,' Harpur said. 'Joachim had versatility. Many noted that.'

Brown looked across at the singers and then at the crowd generally: 'God, though, some club.' The singers began, *She was only a bird in a gilded cage, a beautiful sight to see.* Alec Maximilian Misk's mother and great aunt, if that's who they were, joined in, swaying on their chairs to the rhythm. This spread would irritate Ralph more. He'd visualize the whole club at the crummy tunes soon, like a soccer crowd.

'It's a good turn-out, isn't it?' Harpur remarked. 'Someone truly remarked just now that the community had taken your brother to its heart.'

'Which?'

'Which what?'

'Which community?' Brown said.

'This one.'

'But what kind of community is it?'

'The Monty draws folk of many careers,' Harpur said.

'Occasionally, my parents would get a call. Then, nothing for months,' Brown said, 'no idea where he might be, how he might be living—even whether there was a girlfriend or that kind of thing.'

'A bad shock.'

'I looked around a bit in the funeral for a woman on her own, perhaps, and especially stricken. But too big a crowd. And why should

I imagine she would be on her own? She'd have pals, probably. Would someone like that come on here, to this sort of party? It's hard to associate it with grief and a death.'

'This is the living,' Harpur said. 'Think of those New Orleans funerals—solemn music en route to the graveyard, then "When the Saints Go Marching In"—swinging and cheery—for the return.'

'Is there a woman?'

Harpur had nothing on that—nothing beyond Venetia Ember's fascination, which might mean . . . nothing. He said: 'Apparently, he—'

'Look, the fact is, I need to talk to anybody who knew a bit about him lately,' Brown said.

'Well, I—'

'You seemed the right sort of person.'

'Well, I—'

'Had Joachim turned crook?'

'We're at only an early stage in the investigation.'

'Drugs?'

'We have some leads,' Harpur said.

'It sounded like a gang execution. The sudden disappearance. Then discovery of the body, probably at a spot very distant from where the death took place. One reads about such things—London, Manchester. And the torture. Those murderous families. You have people like that here? This place—the club— it's . . . it's . . . I don't know . . . it reeks of

222

villainy. A hotbed.'

'A *very* early stage,' Harpur explained.

'But there *will* be a proper, thorough investigation?'

'That goes without saying, Mr Brown.'

'I think in a way I'd prefer it to be said. I'd like to hear the promise, the commitment.'

'You're big on the spoken word? Well, you would be. Some are dubious about what words can actually do.'

'It's strange to see senior police at a place like this,' Brown replied. He nodded towards the singers and then pointed upwards. They were standing under *The Marriage of Heaven and Hell*.

'The Monty's an institution,' Harpur said. 'Ralph would tell you it's in flux.'

Pause. Then Brown said: 'You see . . . excuse me . . . but I heard . . . this is slightly ticklish . . . I heard there might be some kind of . . . some kind of, well, *arrangement* between the people my brother seemed to work among and the police.'

Yes, that *was* ticklish. 'Arrangement?' Harpur said.

'Yes, a sort of . . . a sort of, well, *arrangement*. An accommodation.'

'Heard where?' Harpur said.

'A local press girl collared me for information about Joachim post funeral. She seemed to know the scene.'

'Oh, press. They pretend to be in on so

much.'

'She said you'd probably be here despite . . . It's confusing. I'm uneasy. Did Joachim have enemies? . . . But isn't that absurd? Forgive! Of course he had enemies or he wouldn't be dead and gouged. Enemies why, though? Did the man he was working for have enemies? Ember? Is he a baron? *Was* it a gang thing? Joachim—he started and stopped in a lot of jobs. Did he try to pile up money too fast?'

Iles joined them. Harpur made the introductions. Iles carried out some very thrilled staring. 'C.P. ?' he said. 'Clement Porter Brown, the actor? Played Bosola in the West End not long ago?'

'Well, yes,' Brown said.

'Initials would fool Harpur, of course. Did you ever get round to Webster's *The Duchess of Malfi*, Col? It's a play. Bosola! A character. Not so much *im*moral as *a*moral. Some performance that.'

'Mr Brown is worried there might not be a really committed investigation,' Harpur said. 'He's picked up hints of a supposed police understanding with Ralphy and Manse. Would you know anything about that, sir? I think Mr Brown feels we shouldn't be here at the club.'

'I'm a sucker for all the Jacobean plays,' Iles replied, hearty fandom in his face and voice. 'The fun they have with evil. A sort of mischievous exuberance. Congratulations on the way you played it! Oh, yes. But I've always

224

been in love with the Duchess, so devilishly treated by Bosola. I'm awed by him and at the same time hate him. You really got those divided reactions going in me. Thank you.'

'The family had lost contact with Joachim,' Harpur said.

'Perhaps he felt left behind,' Iles said. 'Brother a stage star, after all. Parents?'

'Docs,' Harpur said.

'Well, there you are—those farcically fat salaries handed out by the Government to GPs,' Iles said. 'Joachim had to do catch-up. Competition is a terrible foreman. Why we're all here today.'

'I don't follow that,' Brown said.

'*Das Kapital*,' Harpur replied, 'or something else.'

'You're doing Hirst in Harold Pinter's *No Man's Land* next, I gather,' Iles said. 'I've seen Ralph Richardson and Pinter himself take the part, also Gambon. But you'll transcend! Sure of it. Sarah, my wife, and I will get to that, believe me. We can leave the baby with her mother overnight. Sarah's into drama, modern *and* Jacobean. In some ways we are very much on the same wavelength.' Now, Iles's voice became high and agonized. 'Listen, Brown, that's a fact—Sarah and I have a hell of a lot to bind us together. I don't know what you may have heard about my wife and Harpur when talking to people in a place like this but—'

'Yes, which other people will you want to meet, Mr Brown?' Harpur said.

'Some called Joachim "Turret", I gather,' Brown said. 'This sets up uncomfortable thoughts about . . . about, well, a gun-happy lout.'

'Bang, bang, bang. He had to make a show,' Iles explained. 'He couldn't let you take all the spotlight, could he? Brothers try to race each other.'

'One of Mr Iles's interests is competition,' Harpur said. 'And then, also, the back of vans, of course.'

CHAPTER EIGHT

Unhinged Humphrey eased his way with delicate politeness through the crowd to talk to Naomi, Manse and Ralph near the bar. Always when Ralph drew up in his head a list of people who'd get their Monty membership forever ashed once the transformation began, Unhinged appeared at sixth or equal seventh with Dean Knighton, who was also somewhere around the club now, getting down to a degree of post-mourning.

Ember reckoned Humphrey's personality had three ways of expressing itself, and only three: (a) Extreme violence, (b) Violence, (c) Mingled courtesy and tearfulness. Today,

226

Ralph guessed Humph would try to get in line with the occasion and go for (c), though you could not be certain this would last, and at any time he might tumble suddenly into (a) or (b), particularly during afternoons or evenings. People said that before midday he quite often had hours of total, safe, near-normality. It was afternoon now. He wore a formal morning suit—black jacket, black, silver-striped trousers, black shoes—and a black tie plus stiff white collar. When Humph attended funerals he always came in perfect turn-out. Off and on, propriety could be quite a thing with Unhinged. He reminded Ralph of Iles: both dressed with splendid care, both possessed hellishly seesaw, hacksaw, chainsaw minds. But Ember never pointed out this resemblance to Iles.

Although Ralph hadn't checked on the Monty computer, he thought Humphrey should have been still locked up on a menaces or bodily harm sentence for seventeen more days yet. Lately, however, jail overcrowding meant some people got early release. It surprised Ralph that Humph with his known tendencies should qualify, but Home Office policy produced weird decisions. Ralph regarded accuracy on dates as vital because, under a remarkably civilized clause in Monty rules, anyone jailed had his/her membership put on hold, giving him/her a holiday from subscriptions until he/she returned to the club.

He doubted whether the Athenaeum had any such humane regulation.

Because he was so often the way he was, nobody would work with Unhinged, and he did solo freelance protection, occasional racecourse and stables spying, and debt collecting on a percentage. His business cards, which had some sort of silver, yellow and puce armorial escutcheon at the top, said: 'Humphrey Maidment-Fane, Confidential Security and Recovery Services, established 1997.' During some of the years since then he had not been available to give security and recovery to clients, though. Now, Ember saw that, yes, Unhinged was weeping and mannerly, his big, bulbous face slack, moist, pitiable, chaotically pained. 'Here's a loss, Ralph,' he said. A tremor about his lips made talk dodgy for the moment. The double 's' was stretched, like tyre deflation. Unhinged had no drink with him, and Ralph considered it wisest not to offer.

'A loss indeed, Humphrey,' he said.

'I don't know when I felt a loss more,' Maidment-Fane said.

'Such a loss,' Shale said.

Ember introduced Naomi and Humph. 'You were at the funeral, so you'll know we've undergone a loss,' Maidment-Fane said, giving her a wonderfully respectful, small, slow, mournful bow: Ember saw that, on account of the suit, this had true, pallbearer quality.

Unhinged wiped around his eyes with a handkerchief, and almost at once had to repeat the movement. 'As if a part of myself gone. You'll recall those words, Naomi, "Never send to know for whom the bell tolls; it tolls for thee."'

'Ridiculous, really,' Naomi said. 'If it was tolling for thee, thou wouldn't hear it and couldn't send to know for whom it was tolling.'

Ember wished Naomi knew Unhinged better. She might be more careful about pissing on his quotes then.

'The vicar did it just right: "To every thing there is a season, and a time to every purpose under the heaven." Crucial, to know your purpose under the heaven,' Maidment-Fane said. 'I try to keep my aim on that at all times. Turret was always sure of his purpose under the heaven. You could feel it. People like Turret are *so* rare.'

'They don't grow on trees,' Naomi said. 'Why was he called Turret?'

'I wanted you to realize you have my full condolences, Ralph,' Maidment-Fane said. 'He used to operate for you, didn't he?'

Ralph said: 'Thank you, Humphrey. Yes, it was my firm's privilege to have Joachim as—'

Maidment-Fane twitched along his body-length. Ember remembered making a note on Humphrey's club data profile about this twitch type as a warning symptom in Unhinged. 'I couldn't be sure because I've been away and pre that, of course, you'd never give me a steady position in your fucking fine outfit, would you, Ralphy?' Maidment-Fane replied. But then, magnificently, deftly, unreliably, he got himself back to politesse. 'However, I admit the closeness would make his death, and such a death, all the more painful for you.' He wiped his face again.

'Thank you,' Ember said. He decided he'd let the 'Ralphy' go for now. The situation was dangerously balanced. It would not take much to push Unhinged into bad, really unhinged unhingedness. In fact, Unhinged could reach a state where 'unhinged' ceased to be adequate as a description. At these times it was as if he had totally lost touch with everything sane and solid so that, even if his hinges had been OK, there existed nothing for him to be hinged *to*.

'And you, also, Manse—no matter what they say, and keep on saying, I know you'll regard Joachim's passing with almost unbearable sorrow,' Maidment-Fane remarked. 'Definitely almost unbearable. Sensitivity is one of your main outgoings, famous for it among the firms on a nationwide basis.'

'What *do* they say and keep on saying?' Naomi asked. 'Which "they"?'

'A tragedy,' Shale said. 'Such a future beckoned for Joachim and yet he finishes like that. Again I remark, don't tell me there wouldn't be no foxes and stoats up that hill nosing at him in their totally wild, busy way. To them, he would be a strange item, lying there, and they can't be blamed for interest and nuzzling. It's their nature. But this was someone whose mother and father obviously regarded as special, so they give him the unusual foreign name, most likely German, although Joachim wasn't. The point about "Brown" as a name is it's common or garden. But if you stick "Joachim" in front of it this is all the difference, especially if it was not shortened to Joe. And then he's found by a dog in nettles. That got to seem untoward to anyone right-thinking.'

'I'd guess from the tributes I hear he was through and through a team man,' Naomi said. 'Did people in general love him? I expect he could take his place with aplomb in any group. Such a strength.'

Ralph wished she had not said this, either. Remarks like Naomi's might unsettle Unhinged. Ember saw now not just the body-twitch, but a serious tightening of Maidment-Fane's features. Then a frown started and quickly dominated. Humph did not like teams, because he never got into one. 'Joachim could act damned arrogant and stand-offish,' he said. 'That stupid fucking kraut name gave him swagger. They got it from some big Nazi. "Joachim", for God's sake! Where's the fucking jackboots? I offered a share in quite a tidy little job needing a duo once, takings assured, next to no outright gunfire peril from their security or police armed response cars, as long as we were quick—flak jacket only a formal precaution. But would he look at the project? "Thank you kindly, Humphrey, but not exactly my line, you know." What I'd call a fucking put-down, wouldn't you? That's the sort he was.'

Then, for a moment—and to his credit, in Ralph's opinion—Unhinged softened and seemed determined once more to repel anger and truth today in the RIP circumstances, no matter how much she provoked him. The raving sod tried to get his bulging, malevolent, balloon face back to intolerable sadness. Ember would admit the struggle had its own low-level poignancy: in fits and starts Humph wished to seem human. 'But still a loss. Oh, yes, beyond description this loss.'

'What sort of tidy little job?' Naomi said.

And his tone kept its edge. Maybe he felt hounded by her, serial questioned. 'All Turret thought about was staying this side of the wall,' Maidment-Fane said. 'Cautious. Jittery.'

'Most people want to stay this side of that wall, don't they?' Naomi said.

'Timid. And then, for instance, look at those two,' Humph replied.

' "For instance" meaning what?' Naomi said.

'Which two, Humphrey?' Ember said.

'Harpur and Iles,' Maidment-Fane said, and Ember saw he'd fully and hopelessly reverted now to universal hate, his default mode.

Sometimes Humphrey's fury took in everyone and everything: there was himself and there were his enemies, and this made the entire world picture. His resentments blasted a huge target arc. Transform and backdate his rage into depth charges and he could have won the Battle of the Atlantic solo.

'Oh, they'll often turn up at our functions, Humph, especially after funerals,' Ember replied. 'It's nothing much. They like to crow when it's one of our people dead from violence. After all, they're police. Standard behaviour. Iles got the Queen's Police Medal for gloating.'

'They talk,' Maidment-Fane said.

'Well, people do talk in clubs,' Naomi said. 'Conviviality. I'm sure there's a great deal of that at the Monty.'

'Unquestionably,' Ember said. 'Its very purpose, and a worthwhile one, I contend. Interaction. Civilized. A social duty, indeed.'

'Those two, rabbiting to someone I don't know at all. Do you like that sort of thing, then, Ralph?' Maidment-Fane said.

'Which sort of thing, Humphrey?' Naomi said.

'Confidential,' Maidment-Fane said.

'How can you tell it's confidential?' Naomi said.

'Look at them, for God's sake,' Humphrey said. 'They're not on about the weather.'

'Just a harmless chinwag,' Ember replied.

233

'There's whispers come out of this club, Ralph,' Maidment-Fane said.

'What sort of whispers?' Naomi asked.

'Those three, talking like that non-stop,' Maidment-Fane said. 'You could fucking *weigh* the whispers.'

'Whispers?' Ember asked. He took the bottle of Kressmann armagnac from off the bar as if to do some top-ups, gripping it hard around the neck and keeping it against his right leg at arm's length.

'Oh, fair enough, fair enough, we're here for a tribute to Turret and I wouldn't say a thing against that,' Maidment-Fane admitted. But his voice stayed hard and vindictive. 'I'd say he was definitely . . . definitely . . . well, a loss. That's the word I find I come up with finally. But there's other matters.'

'Which other matters?' Naomi said.

'You think this club gives the police insider whispers, Humphrey?' Ember said.

'That's the type of comment Ralph is not going to like, Humph,' Shale said. 'This is deep. You mean grassing. This is poisonous. This taints a great club, and its great proprietor.'

'Whispers about what?' Naomi said.

'I'll write you a script, shall I?' Maidment-Fane said. 'Yes? Shall I? You bet!' He put on a snivelling, slavish, piping voice, though easily audible above the songs: ' "Oh, have a free drink, Mr Iles, Mr Harpur—a port and lemon

234

as usual for you, sir, and Mr Harpur's gin and cider cocktail." Crawl, crawl. "Pray, is there any further way I can help you, gentlemen? Shall I put you in touch with someone who might have useful insights into certain folk frequenting the Shield Terrace area and arena? I'm only here to help." Yes, like that. As I see it, all Ralph Ember bothers about is this bloody club and its supposed glorious future. Somebody's dead—one of his staffers—but does that really count to him? Would he be chatting to Manse here so friendly and peaceful now if it really counted? I mean, *actually* chatting to Manse Shale after what happened to Turret!'

'Why not?' Naomi said.

'Why not? Why fucking not? Are you joking?'

'I don't see that. Why not "friendly and peaceful"? You've got a down on talking? What's Turret to do with it?'

'You're shagging Manse, so of *course* you don't see it,' Maidment-Fane said. 'But never mind about Turret, let's think of me for two minutes, right? Right?'

'In what sense?' Naomi said.

'In *this* sense: I wonder to myself—and I had a lot of wondering hours—I wonder to myself, how did they find out all that stuff about me for the trial last time?'

'How did who?' Naomi said.

'Harpur. Iles,' Maidment-Fane said. 'These

235

two put people away. They're not here just for the conviviality and free drinks.' He stopped suddenly and mimed panic, his eyes aglow with false apology. 'Oh, dear! I should have asked, am I allowed to bring up this sort of matter—*jail* matter—on your lovely, sacred property, Ralph?'

'They found out all the stuff used against you at trial because you're so fucking careless, stupid, clumsy and unhinged, Unhinged,' Ember said.

'"Unhinged"?' Naomi said. 'He's called "Unhinged"?'

'Those two had been briefed,' Maidment-Fane said.

'What trial stuff?' Naomi said. 'Information? Evidence?'

'The cloakroom's over there showing "Unoccupied". He ought to go and wash his mouth out,' Ember said.

'Some comments are certainly not helpful,' Shale said.

'Is this one a plant?' Maidment-Fane asked.

'Which one?' Naomi said.

'The one they're talking to,' Maidment-Fane said. 'Look at those glasses he's got on. Ever seen glasses like that before? Last time I saw glasses like that it was a TV clip about Callaghan as Prime Minister in the '70s, and think what happened to him. A cover? Has he been spying about for them, now making the report and taking his fee?'

236

' "A plant"? How d'you mean, "a plant"? Planted by whom and for what?' Naomi said.

'Oh, hark at her with her "whom",' Maidment-Fane said. 'We've been to school, have we?'

'You started it,' Naomi said.

'What?' Maidment-Fane said.

' "Whom",' Naomi said.

'How?' Maidment-Fane replied.

' "For *whom* the bell tolls." '

Maidment-Fane bent suddenly forward, both hands raised as though to grab Naomi by the throat to silence her. Maybe, after all, it might have been better if he were carrying a drink because then he'd have only one hand available. 'So, who is this skinny slag, anyway, with her snotty niggles and questions?' he said. She stepped back fast, but he reached her. Uselessly she beat at his fingers with her fist. 'Whom do you think you can insult and attack?' he yelled. 'Fucking whom?'

Invariably, when Unhinged was about, regardless of the time of day, Ralph kept himself ready for an extravagance of this sort and intelligently had the three-quarters-full Kressmann still in his hand, as if hospitably ready to pour for guests, but really to do Humphrey if he turned vigorous. Unhinged had several excellent aspects, such as the dignified tone he and his clothes could bring to a funeral, but it was always wisest to keep something ready to floor him with. Ralph swung the bottle nicely across and back, hitting Maidment-Fane each time on the side of the head in the temple region, good, measured, very well-earned blows, enough to fell him, though without breaking the bottle. Naturally, from previous scuffles at the club, Ember knew what the Kressmann could take, and temples. Effectiveness varied according to how much was in the bottle to add poundage. As Maidment-Fane slumped, eyes half open, still not quite completely out, Shale crouched quickly and managed to get him with one knuckledustered left on the eye and nose top, just before Unhinged reached the ground. Manse clearly knew that, for this thump to be honourable, it must get to Unhinged in good time. Although Manse would be disgusted by Humph's attitude to Naomi in a social setting post funeral, he would hate to be noted striking with irons someone already blottoed by a blow from, say, a bottle. Manse believed in gentlemanliness to quite a degree, and he achieved it now by iron-belting Humphrey when, technically, he was still on his feet and able to defend himself.

Shale would have realized, like Ralph, that Unhinged could go badly temperamental, especially p.m. Manse probably slipped the finger armour on in his pocket during that dodgy, roundabout, bar-side conversation. Possibly he always took metal aids to funerals, especially as it seemed obvious to Ralph from the fine fit of Mansel's jacket that he had no handgun aboard. Like Ralph himself, Manse would most probably regard it as off-colour to bring a loaded piece in chest trappings to someone's obsequies, even Turret's. In these circumstances, Shale's knuckleduster compromise seemed inspired. Ralph considered that to shun guns helped with the Monty image. Almost certainly, no Athenaeum member carried a pistol in the club, post funeral or not, unless the head of MI5 belonged. Naturally, Ralph had to recognize that, most likely, no Athenaeum member wore a knuckleduster to clobber other members with, either. But Ralph knew the Monty could not hope to resemble the Athenaeum totally, yet. Since the Joachim death, Ralph's doubts about Shale, and what he might be up to strategically, had of course grown, but Ralph could still accept they had many outlook similarities, despite Shale's grammar. These had helped bind them together in the past. And now?

The singing continued and had spread. The new number was 'Land of Hope and Glory'. Normally, Ralph loved this anthem for its methodical, confident rhythm and forthright words, but today he became resentful. For a minute he wondered whether they picked the song to make a sarcastic comment on the recent degraded incident. *Look what our grand and noble land of hope and glory adds up to*

these days at the charming Monty club, prop.
R. Ember: attempted throttling of the soon-to-be-
bride, a vicious brawl, head blood drenching a
stiff white collar and dark lapels. 'How shall we
extol thee?' the song asked, meaning Britain.
Like this—with a brutal floor show? But, no,
no, he decided they'd have got to 'Land of
Hope and Glory', anyway. Patriotism could be
strong in the Monty. Many members felt
especially fond of the line, 'mother of the free',
as description of GB. The fact that they were
here, in the Monty, singing it, showed, didn't
it, that they *were* free for now and not locked
up? They could exult.

And this was exactly the filthy, depressing
point, wasn't it? An utterly roughhouse
episode such as the one with Unhinged—
somebody half strangled, and somebody else
clobbered by a black-labelled foreign shorts
bottle, and then by finger-fittings—that sort of
violence seemed regarded by people here as
mere par for the course at the Monty: no
funeral aftermath satisfactory without. The
singing and everything else around went on
uninterrupted and jolly. Yet to see someone in
full, proper mourning uniform laid out on the
floor concussed, thunder-snoring, two wounds
obvious, appeared to Ralph an undoubtedly
worrying come-down. Unseemly. So often his
hopes for the club suffered a harsh knock. He
tried to conceal his disappointment at these
times, but it was there. Occasionally, he felt

the fight had begun to slip away from him: not the *actual* fight or fights—he could deal with those—but the overall fight, the grail mission, to transform the club into a prestige, sedate haven. That suspicion pummelled Ralph's soul and brought long moments of despair.

Now, he noticed Harpur and Iles and the man in spectacles coming this way. Oh, God. Iles accurately stepped over Unhinged without breaking his stride and said: 'I bring a really grand surprise for you, Ralph.'

'Humphrey had a little turn, blacked out and seems to have struck his head,' Ember said.

'On both sides,' Iles said.

'The grief of the day burdened him rather,' Ember explained. 'He's known to be acutely susceptible to stress, yet continues to attend funerals, possibly because he's invested in the regalia. Of course, Humphrey wasn't really close to anyone, and nobody was close to him, but Humph liked to think he *was* close to some, and Joachim and other deads would be those he'd behave as if close to, knowing the deads, being dead, can't deny it.'

'Did you ever get up to London's theatreland and see *The Duchess of Malfi*, Ralph?' Iles replied.

'Not of late to my recollection,' Ember said.

'This is quite a play, Ralph,' Harpur said. 'I know you're sorry you missed it.'

'My God, it's Bosola,' Naomi said.

241

A couple of barmen put a pad on Unhinged Humphrey's head and fixed it in place with two bandage strips knotted under his chin, like a bonnet. Then they dragged him away by the legs. Although his head bumped about on the floor, the pad stayed in place. It was blood-soaked. Near the entrance to the club kitchen the barmen stood Humph up and took one of his arms each around their shoulders. They walked him through the door, his proper black shoes trailing and bobbing like a drunken tap-dancer's. They went out of sight.

'Ralph, you'll ask, "So what's your surprise, Mr Iles?"' Iles said. 'Well, *voilà*. Here's Clement Porter Brown in person. *Clement Porter Brown*, Ralph. And he's present and actual, in your club. Actor. Bosola *inter alia*. Naturally, he wanted to meet you, as My Lord Monty and general source of light and wisdom, and I told him he was fortunate because I have access.'

'Delighted,' Ralph said.

'I'm Joachim's brother, Mr Ember,' Brown said.

'Joachim's such a loss,' Shale said. 'We've just been saying what a loss, Mr Brown. This is a word we've agreed on, like spontaneous.'

One of the barmen came back with a bucket of water and mop and swabbed the floor around their feet. The paper and comb was attempting solo—no singers—'The Flight of the Bumblebee', in that notorious, soaring

242

Harry James arrangement, but for trumpet.

'You see, we've no indication, Mr Ember, of what exactly Joachim's life had become here,' Brown said. 'We feel a need to find out, my parents and I. This is natural, I think. It would give us a kind of contact with him again. When we last spoke he was thinking of Holy Orders.'

'He could have done that very nicely,' Shale said. 'He had the voice for it. I can imagine him in a cassock.'

'What *was* Joachim's career?' Brown said.

'Very various,' Ember said. 'He had aptitudes in so many directions.'

'Versatile,' Naomi said.

'An all-rounder outstanding among all-rounders,' Shale said.

'Why "Turret", for instance?' Brown said.

'I wondered about that,' Naomi said.

Now, Ember did top up her and Shale from the armagnac bottle. The other barman had come back from disposing of Unhinged and Ember asked him for a glass for Brown and new drinks for Harpur and Iles. When these arrived, Ember gave Brown some Kressmann's.

'And the terrible manner of his death,' Brown said. 'This is such a mystery to us.'

'To us, also,' Shale commented at once, 'all of us, believe me. Oh, yes, believe me. I may have already mentioned a certain thought: but you can't tell me there's no foxes or stoats up there behaving in their wild, busy way. They can't help this, the nuzzling. Nature made them like it. All the same . . . A death is bad, but there ought to be a dignity to it. I've always said this.'

'You're in the *Oxford Book of Quotations* with that one, Manse,' Harpur said.

'As if a punishment killing,' Brown said. 'Or a foretaste of others.'

'We hope neither,' Ember said.

'Indeed, yes,' Shale said.

'Why do you see the death of your brother like that, Mr Brown?' Naomi said.

'Can you suggest how else I should see it?' Brown said. 'To me, it seems more than a single, isolated act of violence, terrible though the act of violence might be. I feel the death of my brother signals the start of a war here. If it were so, the war itself would be of no concern to me, but I would like to know how Joachim became involved. This is not the Joachim my parents and I knew.'

'War?' Ember said. 'Oh, no. But I expect you're used to putting things in a very dramatic way.'

'Who would be the leaders in such a war?' Naomi said.

'Do you belong to a club in London, Mr Brown?' Ember replied. 'I like to hear how they're run up there. At the Monty we feel a sort of . . . well, a sort of companionship with them, a parallelism, fellow feeling.'

'The Garrick,' Brown said.

'Ah, for media people, actors, artists,' Ember said. 'Our emphasis here is not altogether in that direction quite yet but I don't see why we shouldn't admit some from such backgrounds in due course. Acting can be regarded as a profession.'

'And I wonder whether there's anyone who was especially dear to Joachim and vice versa and is dragged down by grief now,' Brown said.

'We're all dragged down by grief,' Ember said.

'Right down,' Shale said. 'The Flight of the Bumblebee' had finished and the singing was on to 'Mares Eat Oats and Does Eat Oats and Little Lambs Eat Ivy'.

'Anyone can see Manse is profoundly stricken,' Iles said. 'Such a change from his usual sunniness and poise.'

'You mean a girlfriend, or boyfriend, Mr Brown?' Naomi said. The jacket of her dark suit had a thin sprayed line of Maidment-Fane's blood across the bust.

'Of course, the Garrick club is named after a famous actor, David Garrick, in the eighteenth century,' Ember said, 'so would be bound to attract theatre men and that sort. The Monty's name doesn't go so far back, I believe. Probably after Field Marshal Montgomery in World War II, often known as Monty. But this doesn't mean the Monty is noticeably military, as is, say, the Cavalry and Guards club.'

'Yes,' Iles said, 'perhaps indications of approaching war. Your instincts might be right on that, Clement—if I may. One's own instincts say the same. I've come to rely on them.'

'But a war between . . . well, *whom*?' Naomi said.

'Mr Iles has read a lot of Marx,' Harpur replied. 'And many another work. As a child his head was often in a book.'

'And the awful defacement of my brother,' Brown said, '—perhaps meant to terrorize enemies, so they're demoralized, frightened, well before the war starts. Possibly, it's even an attempt to force them to surrender, sue for peace, without the war needing to begin. But this would make Joachim's death seem so cruel, so cold, not really to do with him at all: he was needed to send a signal, merely that.' Ralph detected a sort of rhythm in the way Brown spoke. Probably he'd been trained at the Royal Academy of Dramatic Art. Ember felt pleased to hear such management of the language by someone in his club. This could almost compensate for Manse. Brown went on: 'As far as I can make out, no real attempt to hide his body. It was meant to be found eventually. It carried a threat and therefore needed to be known of. My brother Joachim was only a token. Then, the manner of discovery—a rabbit hunter's dog. Who was this hunter? Could he have been part of things?'

Humphrey Maidment-Fane returned to the bar through the kitchen door walking unsupported. He didn't look too bad. The pad and bandages had been removed and his collar and jacket. Someone had lent him an old blue sweat shirt with 'Phi Beta Kappa, University of Life' printed in white capitals across it. His hair seemed to have been rinsed. The cuts had stopped gushing and Ember saw no blood anywhere on him, but his cheekbone under one eye was blue-bruised, though maybe not broken. Ralph called for another brandy glass and poured Unhinged a good measure from the Kressmann bottle. Ralph considered this gave a pleasant circular nature to things. Unhinged had been hammered by the Kressmann armagnac bottle and now, to help him recover from that hammering, accepted a drink from the same Kressman armagnac bottle. Ralph loved to find patterns in life. They helped him believe in a divine scheme, and in a divinity who schemed that scheme. As the hymn said, 'God moves in a mysterious way', and this could include via the Kressmann. 'Humphrey, here's Joachim's brother. He's a member of the Garrick where there's a six-year waiting list, so you'd better get your name down and tout for sponsors.'

'Joachim, such a loss,' Maidment-Fane said and took a mouthful of the armagnac. 'I think your type of spectacles are coming back in, Mr Brown, and understandably.'

'Did you know my brother?' Brown said.

'Remarkable versatility,' Maidment-Fane said. 'Many have mentioned this. If you spoke his name to someone, that's what they would respond with: "Joachim? Remarkable versatility."'

'But in what area? I don't ask for detail, just the ballpark,' Brown said.

'Where do these fucking spasms come from, Unhinged?' Naomi said.

'The fact I'm dressed like this now, Mr Brown, does not indicate in any way disrespect for the memory of Joachim,' Maidment-Fane replied. 'This was a man who knew the value of caution.'

'At the Garrick I believe it's a rule that everyone wears a suit, even given the slightly racy, bohemian character of the club,' Ember remarked. 'I'd most likely stipulate the same dress code in due course, but probably only as a request at first. Guidance. Denim, see-through garb, combat camouflage outfits and apache gear I'd definitely like to ban as soon as possible. Although clothing could never convey the whole personality of a club, it *is* a gauge.'

Iles said: 'Necks mark easily, as witness love-bites. But yours looks untrammelled, Naomi. Although Humphrey does turn savage now and then, he's generally useless, all curses and thumbs. And now and then I think about breaking them. Now, for instance.'

Ember noticed Alec Maximilian Misk's mother beckon excitedly to him from across the room, her smile touched by rampant friendship or something akin. My God, did Iles have it right about this scum family's ambitions, Monty ambitions? The Assistant Chief's words came back and battered Ralph: 'Things mesh, things interlock—Alec's massive new boodle, Joachim's death, your known dissatisfaction with the social rating of the Monty. I'm used to taking the overview. One sees that everything is of a piece.'

'Joachim might possibly have a child, children,' Brown said. 'This we are entitled to know about, and, in fact, duty bound to know about. They're possibly needy following his death.'

'I offered to bring him into a project of mine once, good profits, very minor personal risk,' Maidment-Fane said, 'but he declined in wholly polite and reasonable terms. He was someone who so clearly knew what he wanted. I, of course, bore him not the slightest grudge. On the contrary, I admired his clarity of mind.'

'Which project?' Naomi said.

'We have all kinds of enterprises here,' Iles said.

Ralph decided there was not much for him in this slippery, pry-pry conversation and went to find out what Mrs Misk did want, leaving Maidment-Fane, Naomi, Brown and the others to their chatter. He saw a spare chair at the

249

Misk table and calculated that, if he took it, the singing might not spread again, because the two women would surely lack the gall to take part while Ember sat with them. For now, the music remained stilled after 'Mares Eat Oats'. He wanted to keep it at least ghettoed in a corner of the Monty or, preferably, silent altogether: the silence of the little lambs, happily poisoned by that fucking ivy. If the singing did get to be a severe nuisance he'd drown it with disco numbers over the club sound system. He took the Kressmann bottle with him.

Even without those semaphored invitations from Mrs Misk and the mad speculation put forward by Iles, Ralph would have looked for chance of a talk. To update Monty records, he especially wanted a word with Alec Maximilian Misk—Articulate Alec, as he was cruelly known. His data might need adjusting. True, a week or two ago murmurs had gone around the Monty that somehow Alec had wangled himself into the team who did that copycat bank raid on International Corporate Diverse Securities, and came away with a very delightful, individual share in untraceables. Ralph needed confirmation of this gossip. Never would he put unsubstantiated matter on members' dossiers, even encrypted.

It was the press, not Ember, who gave the International Corporate Diverse Securities raid the 'copycat' title, because it seemed so accurately modelled on that huge loot-suction job done at the Northern Bank in Belfast, maybe by the IRA, in December 2004. Although the takings from ICDS in Kelita Street, Holborn, London, were not up to the Belfast haul of £26 million, the methodology looked similar: basically, get among the bank executives' families and keep them hostage until the managers coughed the codes and let the money go. Ralph thought the idea came from a Robert Mitchum film, *The Friends of Eddie Coyle.*

'Perhaps this setting for what we'd like to discuss will strike you as strange, Ralph,' Mrs Misk said, as soon as he joined them. 'I mean, a funeral occasion, and the all-round grief for Joachim Brown.' Although that seemed half-apologetic, to Ember her voice sounded as if she knew she had something immense and brilliant to tell him, and didn't really give a monkey's about the setting, nor about Brown.

So, should Ember smell ICDS takings? Or was he influenced by the Iles rubbish? Ralph said: 'Life goes on and—'

'But, as it happens, we've recently been brought into touch with death and grief ourselves, though an unviolent death—a full-of-years relative on my side of the family,' Mrs Misk said.

'Ah,' Ralph said. Money? Money. Money. Grief hadn't stopped their slaphappy singing, had it?

'We've received considerable legacies, Edna, Alec and I.'

Money. Swag masquerading as inheritance? At once Ember offered the Misks a balanced, beautifully shaped response: 'Always I'm confused in such cases about whether to offer congratulations or commiserations, since a legacy clearly implies, as you say, a death, perhaps of a greatly loved one.' He gave this fine, sympathetic gloom, but not too much, in case the legacies mattered a sight more to them than the loved one, who might have been hardly loved at all, just loaded, full of years and double incontinent. That is, of course, of fucking course, supposing there had ever *been* a loved one to confer the supposed legacies, and not simply a lumpy lump-sum dollop to Articulate—and therefore to the Misk women—from the emptied Holborn bank. Very constructively, however, Ralph went on: 'I reconcile such opposites by thinking that the departed, though much missed, would wish his/her bequests to affect positively the future lives of those so favoured. This would be his/her motive, surely, in selecting them as beneficiaries.'

'Due sadness and regret, but yet, as you say, a positive aspect also, Ralph,' Mrs Misk said.

And Ralph sussed it was this positive aspect that put the clang and assurance into her voice, almost like religious conviction: boodle zealotry. 'Certainly,' he said. The ICDS

252

product, as he heard it, varied from £21 million to £12 million. Even the larger amount did fall a whack short of Belfast, but both these lesser figures were clearly satisfactory millions, all the same, and so were the eight possibles between—that is, 13, 14, 15, 16, 17, 18, 19 and 20. Articulate collected a sweet slice? Ralph and most other people familiar with Misk would have considered this sortie beyond his class, dogsbody role or not. Several accounts said he'd been an outside man, sentrying in case of police; others that he ran the phone link at one of the hostage homes.

Anyway, tales putting him on the operation persisted, and lately, Ralph had noticed a new jauntiness in Articulate. That's how Ralph would describe it, 'jauntiness'. In his view, jauntiness in an established Monty member such as Alec often meant a portion of recently obtained safe loot, 'safe' signifying two factors: (a) it had been lifted from someone's *safe*, for example a Holborn, London, bank's, and (b) the notes were old and, therefore, reasonably *safe* to spend, though unostentatiously.

Usually, Ralph saw in Misk the standard, niggly, comical, defeated self-obsession of a small-time crook who pathetically believed that next week he'd be big-time, and who'd pathetically believed it for an age, these next weeks having long ago slipped into the doomed, exceptionally small-time past. His present Monty profile would rate him like that.

Wrong? Out of date? Alec's nickname came the satirical way some blubber lump weighing 300 pounds might be called 'Slim'. More than any other quality, Articulate lacked articulateness, so, joke of jokes, label him with it. People had mocked his taste for sullen silence. And, until now, in Ember's opinion, Misk was the feeble sort who put up with mockery, possibly even expected it, not someone formidable and esteemed enough to get asked on to an enterprise like the ICDS, all expenses paid, retrospectively. Things changed? Things changed.

'I remarked to Edna and Alec, "We'll have to—*absolutely* have to—have to talk to Ralph Ember about this,"' Mrs Misk said.

And now, of course, of fucking course, he knew Iles had heard the truth somehow. Often he heard the truth somehow, of course, of fucking course. Just the same, Ember had refused to accept this slice of Iles-type truth until the boom and lunacy of Mrs Misk's '*absolutely* have to—have to talk to Ralph Ember about this.' Naturally, there'd been a moment when he'd wondered if the motive for her eagerness to get him close was merely, rampantly, sexual. These old birds had their needs and hots and some could still get antiquatedly aroused by his jaw scar and general charm. But, no. They aimed higher than his trousers. This was about the Misk gains laughably fictionalized as three bumper legacies: the Misk gains and the Monty.

'Our bequeathed monies we wish to be used . . . well, that word again, Ralph . . . positively,' Mrs Misk said. 'We would like to enhance.'

'If I may say, this is what I would expect of your family,' he answered. 'Positivism.' Keep it unspecific, vague. But he realized now that using capital in something like the Monty redevelopment might look highly wise to them. It would be discreet, confidential. They mustn't flaunt the wealth. Crucially, the funds should not be spent in a style that drew attention or people would start asking how Articulate and his family grew so rich so fast. Such people might be police people, such as Iles or Harpur. Hazardous. Or they might be villain people who'd decide that if Articulate had a lot they'd get some of it, at least some of it. Hazardous. But money committed to the Monty would probably not come to the notice of outsiders.

'We do not want these gains frittered,' Mrs Misk said.

'I'm always gratified to hear of the responsible use of money,' he said.

'Or to put it briefly, Ralph, we want to share in—to aid—to share in and aid some scheme we can admire and feel spiritually enlarged by,' Edna said. Fervour ruched *her* voice, too.

'In which respect?' Ralph replied. A waiter brought more brandy glasses and Ember poured for the four of them.

255

'Such a worthwhile project,' Mrs Misk said.

'That's what we seek, you see, Ralph—something worthwhile, something we can tangibly improve.'

'It's not easy,' Edna said.

'Yes, to be a part of it,' Mrs Misk said. 'Of your vision.'

'Of *my* vision? In which respect?' Ralph replied. Oh, God, he knew which respect, and Iles knew which respect: they wanted to use their dirty boodle to buy into the new Monty. They actually thought he'd let them invest in the club, take an ownership share of the Monty—the transformed Monty, as it soon would be.

She said: 'We know you have wonderful ambitions for this place, Ralph—makeover ambitions. Well, *everyone* knows it.'

'These inspire us,' Rose Misk said. 'We wish to be involved.'

'Yes,' Articulate said. He had always seemed a bit passive as well as tongue-tied. His mother, and especially great aunt Edna, handled family policy. Mrs Rose Misk would be over sixty and Edna well over seventy. Their combined life experience left Articulate doing catch-up. Even now, although Articulate somehow gave off the impression of a new confidence and bounce, he did not speak very much. The women dominated, maybe domineered. Edna almost always wore flashy red or green leather—trousers and tasselled

256

jacket—including to major, formal Monty events such as the après funeral. Today, red.

'Our admiration for your plan is why, as Rose remarked, we wish to be part of it, Ralph,' Edna said.

Ralph saw now why he'd sensed a religious flavour in what Mrs Misk had said: resurrection of the Monty *was* a religious project, but for Ralph, and only for Ralph. Of course, of fucking course, this approach squared with that sod, Iles's analysis: they'd make the offer when Ember's morale seemed low following the death of Brown. They considered he'd be especially vulnerable, malleable. Yes, these things interlocked. Or the Misk women *thought* they did. A slight case of error. Ralph and the Monty would survive the wipe-out of Joachim Brown.

'The funds—the legacies, that is—could be *so* vital, *so* supportive here,' Rose Misk said.

'Definitely,' Articulate replied. It sounded forced from him, though.

'Your plan, your brilliant scheme, will cost you considerably, Ralph,' Edna said. 'Now I know you're not by any means poor, and I hope you won't regard this as presumptuous, but we could help bankroll the transformation—would be proud to help bankroll the transformation.'

'Exactly what I meant by not frittering,' Rose said. 'An estimable and, in our view—Edna's, Alec's and mine—a magnificently promising commitment.'

'Definitely,' Articulate replied.

Edna said: 'Without, I hope, being cruel or snobbish, Ralph, we look at the club as it is now—the type of member, the need for a freakishly decorated bulletproof slab up there to guard you, that frightful, yet necessary, quelling incident just now with Unhinged—we look at all this and cannot believe the Monty today—a virtual hotbed of criminality—we can't believe it satisfies someone of your taste and refinement. We join in the singing, yes, because we . . . because we're here . . . in the Monty as it is now . . . and we don't want to seem aloof . . . but . . .'

'No, no, not a shield,' Ember said, with what he regarded as a fair show of rollicking amusement. 'It's a board to maximize ventilation by helping control air currents. But please don't ask me how!'

'All right, all right, we can understand why you don't want the Monty considered a pot-shot range,' Rose said. 'You know the value of reputation and seek to guard the club's as much as you can. It's inspiring to watch, and yet also sad.'

'Some consider your hope of creating a new Monty a delusion,' Edna said.

'Bravely you persist, though,' Rose said.

'We feel you've earned our help,' Edna said.

'Which we readily give,' Rose said.

'Right,' Articulate said.

'We're talking of an infusion to the Monty development funds of at least hundreds of thousands, Ralph,' Edna said. 'As starters.'

'That's it,' Articulate replied. New self-belief still brightened his features, but a kind of misery and opposition clothed these words.

'Your first move has to be expulsion of nearly all the present Monty membership, hasn't it, Ralph?' Edna said. 'You won't draw the type of people you want while the Monty still looks like Low Life Inc. Which decent London club would have Unhinged on its books? Initially, you'll have to take some mighty losses—ending of membership fees and, obviously, a collapse of bar takings. This could be where our funds become useful—perhaps crucial—crucial and creative, a necessary bridge.'

Because her survey of the problems was spot on, Ralph loathed Edna, nearly to a point where he might have followed Unhinged and reached out to throttle the cow. To him there seemed something foully tactless and sadistic about describing his cull plans with such disgusting, far-sighted accuracy. It was exactly the kind of unforgivably truthful approach to sensitive things that ensured Edna in her damn gaudy gear would be an early victim of the coming Monty clear-out, plus Articulate and his mother. They were up there, high on the expulsion list, almost with Unhinged, as a matter of fact, and Dean Knighton.

Did Edna, this pushy, leathery and leather-garbed old doll, imagine she and the other two were 'the type of member' he wanted? And did she imagine there were people around the Athenaeum like her, suppose the Athenaeum let women into membership at all? Did she think the Misks could not just buy assured places in the new Monty with their bank haul, but perhaps take a share of the proprietorship and the profits through the size of their investment? She had her scheming old eye on the club deeds. Ralph regarded that as farcical and arrogant. It massively riled him. The money they wanted to use in the new Monty would be flagrantly, brazenly criminal. This struck Ralph as a central snag: not just criminal cash—which Ralph knew he could hardly object to—but *flagrantly*, *brazenly* criminal. Ralph would never claim total purity for the Monty's finances, either in its present or the projected, changed club. The Misk money reeked, though. There'd been so much amazed talk about Articulate's coming of age at the Holborn bank. Obviously, nobody would believe the legacy tale.

And, on top of the grubby nature of the funds, came an additional smelly fact: these were Misk funds. Even if he swallowed the inheritance talk, it would be a *Misk* inheritance, and the Misks could have no entry to the new Monty, not even basic membership, let alone favoured investor status. Ralph recognized that these moral arguments might look sham to some, but they bound him. He said with a happy lilt: 'Many people come to me with ideas of development of the club, and I'm heartily grateful to them. And I'm heartily grateful to you now, Edna, Rose, Alec. These approaches—so positive and well-meant—show how fondly some members regard the Monty.'

'The Monty's underachieving on its possibilities, Ralph,' Rose Misk said. 'Yes, it's just a hotbed of criminality.'

And did they imagine he hadn't realized this? Did they think they could advise him about his own cherished club, cherished even in its present radiantly vulgar, recidivist state? The singing and comb accompaniment resumed with some slow slop: 'I Dreamt that I Dwelt in Marble Halls'. 'To each of these proposals I listen with full interest and, as I say, gratitude,' he replied. 'It is encouraging to know there's a groundswell of workable ideas among the Monty's faithful. I ponder all these ideas, let me assure you, and at some stage ahead I might act on one of them, or perhaps a mixture of several. But at present those ideas have to remain as such—ideas only.' He gave a small, regretful, but determined smile. Would they want to change the Monty's name to 'Misk's'?

'This is the moment for it, Ralph,' Edna said. 'We all think so. There has been a tripartite meeting.'

'Yes, we all think so,' Rose said.

'Definitely,' Articulate said after a while.

'These things can't be rushed,' Ember said.

'But accelerated,' Rose said.

Ember stood. 'I have to get to my chores now,' he said. 'I'll leave the bottle. There's still enough for toppers in it. You chat on, by all means. It's been bracing.'

'We haven't really got anywhere,' Rose said.

'I certainly would not say that,' Ralph said. 'I've filed away in my head the very promising suggestions you've given me tonight. In due course, or even sooner, I will bring the file out and consider it properly in context.'

'What does that mean?' Edna said.

'What?'

'"In context",' Edna said.

'Yes, true, Edna. This has to be the way of it—in context,' Ember replied. 'Competing proposals to be weighed against one another. In a way, I'm fortunate to have such choice. It's a responsibility, though.'

'Well, part of the fucking context now, Ralph, is that we have the funds entirely available and entirely ready,' Edna said.

'You're well placed, indeed,' Ralph said.

'Cash, as it happens,' Edna said.

'Oh, really?' Ember said.

'What does *that* mean?' Mrs Misk said.

'Such a large amount,' Ralph said.

'We like currency,' Mrs Misk said.

262

'There's much in its favour,' Ralph replied.

'But this availability might not be so *"in due course"*,' Edna said. Mockery there, the old schemer. 'We wish to apply these legacies as an immediate priority, not "in due course",' she went on. 'Lumps of cash about like this—unwise. There are other openings for investment. We chose to put you and the Monty first on our schedule, sort of favoured client—potential client. I hope you agree this is a natural preference: we've known you and the Monty a long time. However, if our offer does not attract an instant response, we might feel it right to turn elsewhere.'

'That choice would certainly be yours,' Ember said.

'So?' Edna said.

'I've come to learn that in this kind of business a review of all options is vital.' Ralph gave that finality. He left their table. He felt proud of how he'd managed the meeting with those three. At no point did he allow his rage at their gross cheek and clumsiness to show itself. Snarls had ganged up inside him ready for use, but these he suppressed. None of the trio, nor anyone watching and listening, could have guessed he meant to ban the Misks eternally from the new Monty. Diplomacy Ralph regarded as one of his chief strengths.

He went to the bar and gave orders that, as soon as the choir paused, musak should be switched on to deter any more singing. Then he did an inspection of the snooker and pool tables to see there were no rips after so many people pressed around, perhaps putting pint mugs on the baize. He ran a hand carefully over the green playing surfaces to assure himself they were all right. This movement struck him as a picture in miniature of the whole Monty situation. He wanted perfection, smoothness, elegant suavity at the club, and yet these qualities were constantly and gravely menaced by the club's murky membership. Rose and Edna had this correct, no question, the cruel derelicts. But why couldn't they see that they, personally, plus Articulate, were a hopelessly ridiculous and unacceptable part of that murky membership?

C.P. Brown came and stood near him. He waited politely while Ember finished his inspection. 'I'd greatly value a one-to-one talk for a moment, Ralph,' he said.

Ember smiled to show he might approve. He had expected an approach by Brown. For one thing, Ralph thought there must be a kind of actorly link, because of his blatant, embarrassing resemblance to the young Charlton Heston. Ralph believed also that Brown would feel an obvious, natural comradeship with another 'clubman', Brown representing the Garrick, Ralph the Monty. But it would be the Monty as not simply the present Monty: no, the Monty with a clear capacity to become, in time, at least the equal of the Garrick or the Athenaeum. Brown would definitely appreciate this, even if someone like that provincial slob, Harpur, couldn't see these grand prospects for the Monty, and resorted to cheap, destructive sarcasm. Ralph prized the word 'clubman'. To him it spoke of fine, civilized, convivial, reliable, unflamboyant, British qualities, not entirely based on class, but implying a certain status and affluence.

However, Ralph did realize he must be careful talking to Brown. It would be foolish to get over-relaxed merely on account of those undeniable links—Chuck Heston and the clubs. Brown was almost certain to have been to 15A Singer Road to deal with Joachim's possessions. Those 15B neighbours might still be very alert and would hear him there, perhaps even see him arrive if they continued watching the road for strangers interested in 15A. They'd come nosying downstairs again. By then, of course, they'd have known of Joachim's death, through the press or broadcast news, and would be even more tense than when Ember called. They'd be reassured when they found that Brown was Joachim's brother and would probably give him a history of callers at the flat, and mention the apparent surveillance carried out by the man in the car using a mobile phone. Ralph must decide how much he should show he knew, or half knew. Life was so often like this, wasn't it?

Just the same, Ralph thought that a private conversation with Brown would have a good foundation to it, so different from the ludicrous exchange with the Misks—ludicrous mostly on their part, of course, but tainting him because they actually considered he would accept their crude, idiotic offer. Although he knew he would never agree to such a proposal, their assumption that he would, and at an eager gallop, was an unpardonable insult. Because the family had produced a successful fucking bank robber, they calculated this entitled them to talk to him, Ralph W. Ember, as a possible business partner. Some sodding logic! And the kind of job Articulate was trusted with in the bank robbery would most likely have been minor, piffling, marginal—though well paid, to keep him quiet. Ralph found it pathetic and infuriating that they could imagine this gave them parity with him, and especially infuriating because they raised the matter direct, unabashed, in his own club. The Misk lot lacked all notion of protocol and status. Understandable. They'd never been required to use protocol until now. And they entirely lacked status, except possibly sudden money status. Money status did not impress Ralph or any other true clubman, particularly not sudden money. You could win ten million on the Lottery and still fail to get elected to the Garrick.

They were absurdly jumped up. Ralph had

detested the way Mrs Misk sounded off with that word 'enhance'. She obviously loved it— as if they had some high-minded mission to bring improvement, like school inspectors or landscape gardeners. God, the cheek! And the principal—the only—the principal object for their *enhancing* programme was the Monty. The condescension nauseated. These were people who big-mouth chanted 'Mares Eat Oats and Does Eat Oats and Little Lambs Eat Ivy' in a public arena and did not mind being seen at it. True, Edna said they only sang so as not to seem 'aloof'. Oh, so sensitive, so damn democratic! If they had to make an effort so as not to seem 'aloof', it must be because they considered they *were*, and should be, 'aloof'. But when Ralph booted them out of the new Monty it would not be on account of their 'aloofness'—disguised or plain—but because they had fuck all to be aloof *about* other than, maybe, a nice, lumpy bit of recent pilferage, thanks to Articulate.

Ralph found a table for him and Brown on the opposite side of the room from the Misks, and near the framed, enlarged, black and white photograph of old sailing and steam vessels moored in the docks. Ralph liked to remind Monty members that they lived in what had once been a great seaport, and that the names of areas like Valencia Esplanade commemorated the busy trading then with Spain and other foreign cities. These days, much of the local drugs dealing took place at 'The Valencia', as the district was often known now. Ralph's people worked there, of course. But this did not mean the district's good— even great—past should be forgotten, in Ember's opinion. The Monty probably hadn't existed so far back, but, if it had, the membership would almost certainly have been chandlers, well-to-do general merchants, master mariners between voyages, coal factors. Estimable, solid people. Ember felt envious. 'So much I don't understand, Ralph. Gossip, rumour, hints, that's all I have,' Brown said. 'I seem to meet continual shut-off points.'

'Gossip, rumour, hints are all anyone has, I think. Such information—if one can even call it that—is always unsatisfactory.' Ralph thought Brown might at least have said something decent and appreciative about the club as a conversational start, instead of just plunging into his own damn problems. But Ralph acknowledged that the problems were great, from Brown's point of view. Did he want to play private investigator here—another of his roles? Ember had time to study this theatrical 'star's' face close-up now they talked. A disappointment. Ralph saw no true distinction there. It seemed an ordinary, two-a-penny sort of face, especially taking into account the rather dated spectacles.

'I don't feel as if I'm discovering anything about Joachim's life, nor about his death,'

Brown said.

'His death *is* a mystery,' Ralph said. Nobody was ever going to tell Brown he looked like the young Charlton Heston, nor like any other Hollywood leading man. In Ralph's opinion, Brown had a face entirely unsuitable for a star—theatre or cinema—but which might look all right bchind a grille selling tickets for a theatre or cinema. Although Brown's face was not exactly unpleasant, it lacked zing and authority. Maybe they gave him parts that actually needed a very ordinary face. Ralph wished he knew something about that character, Bosola, Iles had mentioned.

'I went to Joachim's flat to sort out his things,' Brown said.

'Singer Road.'

'You've been there?'

'I felt I should. I called onc night when he'd been out of touch for a while.'

' "Out of touch"? Were you, then, in touch with him individually through work? Did he have some special project for you?'

'When he'd been missing for a while,' Ember replied. 'Many noticed it.'

'But you took the trouble to call at his flat personally.'

'He was a valuable member of the company.'

'The people in 15B heard me and came down.'

'Yes, I met them, too.'

269

'They seemed nervous—said there'd been callers just before Joachim's body was reported found. "On edge", they described themselves as. They wondered if I knew what kind of work Joachim did. They seemed to think that might be relevant. I had to say no. Well, it's true: I don't really *know*, do I? It was as if they feared being dragged into an area of life they knew nothing about and felt scared by. They'd chosen a flat in respectable suburbia and then these links with an entirely different kind of milieu began to show themselves.'

'I would have been one of those callers,' Ember replied. He wanted Brown to see him not just as owner of a potentially brilliant club and chief of a fine business, but a leader who felt solid responsibility to each of his workforce, no matter how insignificant. Ralph would certainly not like to be thought of merely as a distinguished figurehead famed for his unforgettable features. Incidentally, he had seen that the woman from 15B was slightly mesmerized by his looks, despite the shadowiness around the door of 15A. Ralph had grown used to such reactions from women, of course. Occasionally, he might respond, but Sally from 15B hadn't excited him, though not at all untidy.

'And a young girl also called,' Brown said.

'Yes, they mentioned that to me.' Ralph decided to admit this, so he could show doubt

270

about its importance. He had to keep Venetia out of an increasingly grim mess. She was a girl he'd paid big euros to nuns in Poitiers and Bordeaux for, hoping they'd implant restraint and refinement. Besides, Ralph saw a danger that, if Venetia were identified as the visitor who shouted through the letter box at 15A and left a note, the suspicion might grow that he, Ralph, had done Turret Brown. People knew how much he fretted about Venetia and her strong, dodgy, romantic urges. By 'people' Ember meant Harpur and Iles. They, in their intrusive, disrespectful way, would understand why her father had sent Venetia off to France. And they would understand in their intrusive, disrespectful way—or *think* they understood— how Ralph might decide to deal with one of his crook underlings, twice her age or thereabouts, if it looked as though he meant to move in on Venetia, and vice versa. Very much vice versa: he could visualize his child yelling her plaintive calls into an unresponsive hallway of an empty flat through an indifferent letter box. Poor, avid Venetia. He longed for her happiness. How Ralph wished she could be content with Low Pastures and her ponies and the paddocks and gymkhana wins, and her good school. Of course he would occasionally talk over these anxieties about her with Margaret, his wife. Responsibility for keeping the child safe must be entirely his, though. He could not dodge that, would not try to dodge that. Ralph believed in fatherhood.

Perhaps, in fact, he would really have considered doing something serious about Turret if he'd lived, and if Venetia continued to stalk him. But he hadn't lived. Ralph thought he'd spotted Venetia with her bike in the funeral crowd having an immense, soul-sick, mouth-gape, oh-gone-from-me-love-of-my-life weep. He'd felt irritated by this stupid, toothy display, but her performance could lead to no catastrophes. She'd recover, as she always recovered, and Ralph would be on guard for the next one.

But, at the moment, he had to deal with C.P. Brown. 'I don't know much about Joachim's private life,' Ember said.

'A young girl—thirteen or fourteen.'

'Yes.'

'The 15B couple said they'd noticed her before in Singer Road, apparently watching the flat.'

'Yes,' Ember said.

'And did they tell you she seemed a quaint, grown-up sort of kid—spoke of having been sent by "an associate" with a message that "brooked no delay". They remembered the strangely weighty words.'

'Not always easy to get the age of some girls right. Fashions. She might have been several years older.'

'They've told the police about her.'

This Ember knew. 'They'd have to,' he said.

Of course, as Turret's employer, he'd been interviewed by detectives about his death. They wanted information on his life apart from the firm. Ember replied he knew nothing about Joachim's life apart from the firm. More or less true. Did Turret like young girls, for instance, they asked. So, yes, they'd heard about the unidentified child caller. Or Ember *assumed* unidentified. Perhaps they knew more than they showed—a customary cop trick. Ralph had to play ignorance and hope it worked. He gave them an absolute blank and turned snooty: would he, for God's sake, go poking into an employee's sex life? he said. The main interviewing officer was Chief Inspector Francis Garland, who, apparently, had charge of the inquiry: another one, besides Harpur, reported to have been close, and very close, to Iles's wife, though perhaps not quite simultaneously with Harpur. No wonder many of Garland's questions focused on sex—his special study. 'Ralph, neighbours gave us a description of someone who could be you—in fact, could *only* be you—calling at 15A,' he'd said.

'Certainly I went there. A colleague missing. I felt concerned. A visit to his home seemed the least I could do. There'd been no phone response.'

'It struck us as unusual for the head of a firm to take that kind of trouble over someone minor,' Garland had said.

273

'On the contrary, *any* head of a firm meriting such a title would surely feel anxiety about a disappeared member of staff.'

'Did he have any special duties for you—special duties that made for an exceptionally powerful bond?'

'He was a colleague.'

'The woman from 15B said the male caller had a remarkable resemblance to the young Charlton Heston. *Ben Hur* vintage. She was impressed. We guessed it must be you, Ralph.'

'Me, like Charlton Heston? Never heard that before,' Ember had answered.

'No? The woman's husband/partner seemed a bit put out by her swoon at your looks, Ralph. But you're probably used to that kind of thing.' Yes, Ralph had noticed this. And, yes, he *was* used to that kind of jealousy in women's husbands/partners. It could be a bore.

Now, in the club, Brown went on: 'And the 15B people told me the girl claimed to have seen a man watching 15A from a car and speaking into a mobile phone. Did you hear that?'

'They did mention it.' Ralph hoped this might take some of the interest away from the mysterious girl who had to stay mysterious.

'Who are these people, Ralph? How are they connected to Joachim?'

'No information so far.'

'The 15B couple said the girl wrote a note

to Joachim. They actually provided the paper and saw her post it. Yet when they looked later through the glass front door it couldn't be seen.'

'I was there when they tried to spot it. But a piece of paper, not in an envelope—it could drift, couldn't it?'

'I imagine the police have this now. The neighbours said detectives and uniformed officers came round to 15A in numbers once Joachim's body was found.'

'They'd need to search for anything in the flat that might explain his death.'

'Someone in a car watching and talking into a mobile—it could actually *be* the police, couldn't it?'

'It could be anybody, anything, suppose the girl had it right in the first place.'

Brown hesitated, sipped some armagnac. Then he said: 'Look, Ralph, one story I hear is of a full-out rivalry between you and Shale. That's why I spoke of a war. Is my brother's death part of this? Forgive me for the frankness, but I must ask. You'll understand, I'm sure.' Suddenly, he had become intense, confidential, demanding. Perhaps the Bosola character was like that.

'As you say, rumour, gossip, hints. These are poor indicators.'

'I know, I know. And I see you and him apparently so friendly here tonight and dealing jointly with that lout in the morning suit.'

'We've known each other a long time, Manse and I. I'm to be his best man.'

'Just the same—*is* there a sort of movement towards war? Joachim the first casualty?'

'They say the first casualty of war is truth,' Ember replied.

'Have you thought you might be at risk yourself, Ralph?'

'Life is risk.' Ember felt proud of this answer. It could have come from a play—terse, correct, thrumming. But he sensed reproach in what Brown had said. Wasn't he virtually asking whether his brother—one of Ember's staff—had been killed by Mansel Shale, or on Shale's orders, yet Ralph did nothing: continued the friendship with Shale and, in fact, extended it to bestmandom? Was he calling Ralph a poltroon, someone capable of felling a nut case in a bar with a bottle, but not much beyond that? 'Yes, life is risk,' Ember repeated. He wanted to sound like someone who knew danger, and knew it well, but would never retreat from it, cringe to it. Had this sod, Brown, heard among the rumours, gossip and hints, that some enemies referred to Ember as Panicking Ralph, or even Panicking Ralphy?

He left Brown then and did a short tour of the premises. He believed the party could run itself safely now. Some people had left and the club no longer looked overcrowded. Ralph thought Unhinged would not cause any further upheavals. He went home to Low Pastures, for

276

a meal, a talk about the day with his wife, Margaret, then a nap, and, as was routine, returned to the club at just after midnight— not via Singer Road this time—to supervise close-down for the night at two o'clock. Almost everyone had gone. A couple of men played pool, and Ralph would wait for them to finish the game before locking up. He sat at his shelf-desk behind the bar with another glass of Kressmann's from a fresh bottle, admiring the mystical William Blake pictures on the metal screen sheltering him. Ralph thought Blake must have been a fascinating thinker. How the hell could that bitch, Edna, refer to the drawings as 'freakish'?

Articulate Alec, alone now, entered the club and took a high stool opposite him on the other side of the bar. He still wore the fine, made-to-measure pinstripe suit and wide silver and yellow tie he'd had on for the funeral and drink-up. Ralph poured him another armagnac. 'They won't abandon the idea, Ralph.'

'Who?'

'Great aunt Edna and my mother. I suppose you're counting on that. You'll play reluctant, negative, so, when you finally relent, you can ask more, and tie them to tougher terms. All that stuff about not rushing and having competing proposals to consider is to get the pair bidding. They're bidding against no bugger, of course, but they can't be sure of that. I don't blame you for the tactics, Ralph. It's how business works.'

'They're real Monty fans, I'll say that for them,' Ember replied with a fine warm chuckle.

'Such out-and-out bollocks,' Articulate replied.

'What?'

'That notion—to put good money into the club.'

'"Good" in what sense—because it came from a legacy left by somebody good who had built up the wealth in a good, lawful way?'

'Good because it can be used to make our lives better.'

'Oh, so it's not the money that's good, but what might be done with it?'

'Yes, what's done with it. My mother and great aunt Edna—they're confused.'

'I appreciated their affection for the Monty,' Ember said. 'Constructive. You're lucky to have such family.'

'Idiotic.'

'Oh?'

'Like throwing money down an old coal pit.'

'Oh?'

'Everyone else with a bit of brain—except you and my mother and Edna—everyone knows the Monty is never going to change, Ralph. Perhaps even you know it, but have to hope—this crazy ambition, like somewhere over the rainbow in the ancient song. That might be what keeps you going. When I say it'll never change, I mean not change as they and you would like, anyway. Your idiotic dream. I suppose the police might shut it down one day because of your drugs game etcetera. But you'll stick to your hopes, and you'll come round in your own time and grab the boodle from them, for the sake of this loony plan— maybe grab more boodle than they intended offering now. You'd feel stupid if you didn't work the price up.'

Ember thought about hitting the brassy prat. Ralph could have stood, leant forward quickly and reached him across the bar. Although Ralph had never heard Articulate put so many words together before, when he did grow verbal now, it was to insult Ralph and the Monty. Ember could have failures of courage and decisiveness sometimes, at dangerous moments during business operations outside, but not in the Monty, and certainly not when some jumped-up jerk questioned the club's sanctity. Should he physically squash this sod? Sometimes one *had* to get rough, as with Unhinged. 'I wouldn't say your great aunt Edna or your mother lacked brain, Articulate,' he replied. 'The opposite.'

'The money has shoved them off balance.'

'The legacies?'

'That's it, the legacies. Yes, the legacies,' Articulate said. 'As if they feel they have to compensate for something.'

'Compensate for what—for receiving a legacy?'

'That's it, Ralph. For receiving a legacy.'

'A sort of guilt—even though the money, or what you—you, personally—what you personally want to do with it is good?'

'Yes, like guilt.'

'Guilt because they and you have profited from a death? This does happen to legatees sometimes, I know—to the sensitive ones, and I'm sure that would include your mother and Edna, not to mention yourself, Alec. They suffer guilt over where the money comes from.'

'Yes, right, *so* right—over where it comes from, Ralphy.'

'"Ralph", not "Ralphy".' Cunt. 'Or "Ember", Alec.'

'Why it's in cash, of course.'

'I don't follow,' Ralph said, face deadpan.

'So, to rid themselves of this shame, they want to find some noble project where they can put the lucre—and get a return. They're compensating. It's a genuine, worthwhile wish. But what they pick—sorry to say this, Ralph— what they pick is a noble, dud, *mad* project.'

'I don't see it like that,' Ember replied.

'No, I shouldn't think you do. Why I had to come back tonight for a chinwag, on our own. I thought you'd be here. Your routine. The captain's last to leave the ship.'

The pool players finished, settled up the

280

bets and said goodnight to Ember.

'Look, one thing my mother and Edna had right is the gutter rating of the Monty membership on the whole,' Alec said. 'Again, apologies for the harshness, Ralph, but that's how it is. Gutter and troublesome. Maybe *continuing* troublesome. Take the ding-dong with Unhinged tonight. He's not going to forget it, hammered in public like that, despite a hyphenated name. Anyone togged up in such a suit has pride. He could bring you more unpleasantness in the club. And he thinks he was grassed from the Monty, doesn't he?'

'It's bollocks.'

'His perception, though. So, multi-motived retaliation. It's just what you don't want, isn't it? I don't mean you don't want it because it's going to become a grand new place like Edna and my mother were talking about, dreaming about, in their daft fashion. But you don't want that sort of unclassy carry-on in the Monty as it is now because . . . you're not dim, Ralph, and you know that really the Monty is the dregs and when things happen like that with Unhinged, the more dreggy and eternally hopeless the club looks. Unhinged could be long-term pestilential.'

Ralph said: 'Very kind of you to look in, Alec, but I don't really think someone like Unhinged could—'

'He'll come back when he's got one of his moods going and start more p.m. gaudy behaviour.'

'I think it can be handled.'

'Another whack with a brandy bottle? Iles and Harpur have seen that once. Think: if the Monty gets a reputation for such crudity you might have big bother renewing the licence. You're a drugs wholesaler, Ralph, a shady middleman, and into God or the devil knows what other dicey activities. Iles lets all that go unnoticed up till now, for his own reasons. But changes in the air? Suddenly, he might want to knock you. He's good at that. And he's got a new Chief, who possibly starts hounding him— ordering him to behave like an Assistant Chief, not like Iles. As it were, your use of a Kressmann bottle could be used against you. You've got to act, Ralph, or the Monty will have sunk so far it's past recovery. But, yes, saving it needs money. Plenty of. Not Misk money, though. *Not Misk money*. It will never come your way. Instead, what you must go for, Ralph, is monopoly in the drugs game, isn't it? This sharing with Manse—no good. It's *been* good, but not any longer. They say he knows it. And they say you might know it, too. That's why you put Turret in as a spy, and that's why Turret's dead. You're making things too complicated, Ralph. Move direct. This is what I've learned lately. No fiddling about. Go straight at the target. I hear you and Shale take more than half a million each out of the businesses every year. Well, think—he might

282

be removed. Twice more than half a million is more than a million. With that sort of pay jump you'd be able to start on your fantasy future for the Monty—exclude people like Unhinged, once you're rich enough to do without their membership fees. I call it a fantasy future because—because, like I said, I don't see it ever happening. But you could have a go. *Would* have a go. I know it. I'm as sure of that as I'm sure none of my fucking fortune's going into it.'

'I have to lock up,' Ember said.

'Here's the bargain, then, Ralph,' Articulate replied in a ringing, generous voice. 'It's simple.'

'Bargain?'

'Bargain. I'll get rid of Mansel Shale if you promise you won't ever pick up on that offer from my mother and great aunt Edna.'

'Get rid?'

Articulate became intense. 'Listen, Ralph, I don't want my money flung away like that by two old dames gone ga-ga. You said you'd file their notion for another consideration sometime. That's a bargaining ploy, and very clever, yes. What I'd expect from Ralph Ember. But I want you to keep it really filed away, or, even better, ditch it, forget it.'

'*Your* money? It wouldn't all be yours, would it? I thought there were *three* legacies.'

'Yes, well let's not play about any longer, all right? *My* money. *My* earned money. Cash,

cash, cash and more cash. Mine but . . . Ralph, I've always let my mother and great aunt Edna organize the big things in my life, you know.'

'That so?'

'Look at me, Ralph.'

'Yes?'

'I'll tell you what you see, shall I?'

'What I see is—'

'You see a bloke of thirty-two in a suit that cost over two grand, physically sound, and suddenly very successful.'

'Successful. You mean getting the legacy?'

'Right, getting the legacy.'

The description Articulate gave of himself was not bad, although it didn't deal with the wide shoulders on a thin body and his longish, deadpan face, as if purposefully manufactured to thwart interrogation. He had a large but unmirthful mouth, skimpy fair eyebrows and bleak blue eyes, maybe a lookout's eyes.

'I respect mum and great aunt Edna, naturally,' Articulate said. 'That will never alter. There's so much I owe them. Not these acquired fucking funds, though. I can't be run by those dear ladies any more. I'm me, Ralph. Me. I've learned getting big money is a chancy game, so, once you've got it, don't play about with it. Sorry, Ralph, but I consider any investment by us in this place as a total no-no, because it might be an absolute waste. Perhaps I'm wrong, and you can really bring it off. Not with our cash, though. *Not with our cash. My* cash.'

Ember saw the bank raid had transfigured Articulate. This was not just what Ralph thought of at first as 'jauntiness'. That could come and go. But Alec had climbed a little late into maturity and would stay there. He could string words—'perception', 'compensating'. He could do fruity phrases and alliteration—'multi-motived retaliation', 'fantasy future'. Some of this was disgustingly offensive, but no question he could dish it out. He knew oratory—repetition and stresses. He fancied himself as a proven warrior now—a warrior who could still show token deference to his mother and great auntie Edna, but who also knew that a true warrior's main and perhaps only real role must be to scrap, starting, as a matter of fact, with a crafty, secretive fight against his mother and great aunt about his own money, sort of. He'd grown up—had drawn selfhood from the Holborn bank.

Ember said: 'There's a term for this kind of character development—"rites of passage".'

'Fine! I could get fond of terms like that.' Articulate put an arm across the bar, skirting the Kressmann bottle. This seemed more than just a physical movement. It reeked of overtones, symbolism. 'A handshake will do for us, I think, Ralph,' he said. It was clipped, matey, seasoned, foursquare, seasoned man to seasoned man. 'You keep turning down my mother's and great aunt Edna's crazy scheme for my funds, and I see to Shale for you.'

'See to?'

'See to,' Misk said.

Ralph took his hand with wholehearted firmness. Naturally. This agreement, whether it worked or not, could be only a bonus. As to alliteration, he would never have given, never *would* give, great aunt Edna, Mrs Misk and Articulate the faintest fucking financial foothold in the Monty, anyway, and, yes, a trade monopoly might help Ralph do all the things he wanted for the club. In any case, as Articulate said, Manse might have monopoly thoughts himself. If Turret had survived he could have told Ralph of Manse's intentions and plans. But Manse most likely wanted those intentions and plans kept confidential, the sickeningly calculating sod, and so he'd silenced Turret.

Now, Ember yearned to be resolute, or, at least, to let someone else be resolute on his behalf. That hint of condemnation from Turret's brother upset Ralph, made him feel flimsy and uncertain, not worthy of the new Monty image. Ralph had indomitable faith in this image, and in the club's potential to become brilliant, enduring, exclusive: clearly much too exclusive for Edna, Rose and Alec. Articulate didn't believe in that potential. Irrelevant: he could still have a try at 'seeing to' Mansel Shale and so possibly contribute despite himself to Ember's grand, inspired quest.

'This conversation hasn't taken place, Ralph.'

Oh, Lord, he'd picked up tough-guy, under-your-hat lingo, as well as basic spiel flair. 'Nobody would believe you could be so articulate, Articulate, anyway,' Ember said.

CHAPTER NINE

Harpur had watched Articulate go alone into the Monty at about 1.30 a.m. and then reappear half an hour later and drive off. The club car park was better lit than the Agincourt's, and Harpur thought Articulate looked happy and resolute when he left, even triumphal. That could be a perilous combination in someone as inept as Articulate: perilous above all for himself. He might try something dangerously beyond his range. But maybe this estimate of Articulate's range no longer fitted. Possibly he wasn't inept any longer, if he'd really been picked for the Holborn bank coup: people risking their liberty and life for a stack of gold wanted very ept colleagues, even in the smaller jobs—and, perhaps, especially in, say, a lookout job. Whatever job he'd had, it apparently worked, and he'd probably collected a nice fee—part gratitude, part to cement his silence. How long had they all been misjudging Articulate?

Harpur didn't follow him, but went back to Arthur Street. 'Surveillance,' he said, as he joined Denise in bed again.

This time she woke up, or wasn't asleep, and put her arms around him, held him to her with some power, even desperation. She played lacrosse for the university and did a lot of training. He valued being gripped like this. It made him feel he really mattered to her. There were times when he could hardly believe that, and not only times when he looked in the mirror. 'You smell of mud,' she said. 'Like someone from the trenches.'

'How often have you been in bed with someone from the trenches?'

'I worry about you, Col.'

'I'm old enough to be out in the dark late. But not as old as mud in the trenches.'

'I never think of you as old.' She had a little sob then, because, obviously, she did sometimes think of him as old, and would have been stupid not to. It might become a factor one day.

'I didn't say "old". I said old *enough.*'

At once she brightened. 'Yes, "old" is a comparative term.'

'A what?'

'Comparative.'

'Compared with what? "Young"?'

'Is it dangerous, the surveillance? Why mud?'

288

'I'm grateful that you worry about me,' Harpur replied. 'But, no, not dangerous at all.'

'What's the use of it?'

'I don't know yet—if anything.'

She loosened her arms around Harpur, pushed him over on to his back and straddled him. 'Well, I think you deserve to take it fairly easy after all that,' she said.

'How will *you* take it?'

'This way. As starters.'

'This way seems a good way. As starters.'

'No ecstatic yelling, regardless of the ecstasy,' she said. 'The girls have been on edge a bit. They wonder about all this surveillance. You know what they're like.'

'What are they like?'

'Fretful.'

'Yes, it was surveillance,' Harpur said.

'Anyway, the girls might not be sleeping well. They'd be puzzled if they came in and smelled mud.'

Of course, he could have explained the mud, but he didn't want to make things sound chancy, even dangerous, and, in any case, he'd rather not waste his breath and concentration on words now. He and Iles had stayed at the Monty funeral shindig until just before midnight. Then Harpur drove Iles home to Idylls, his house in Rougement Place. 'What would you say was the most interesting feature of this evening, Col?' Iles had asked.

'This would depend on viewpoint, sir.'

289

'Of course it would depend on fucking viewpoint. That's what I'm asking for—your viewpoint.'

'You'll have your own viewpoint, I expect, sir.'

'Yes, I have my own viewpoint and I'd like to know whether *my* viewpoint is the same as *your* viewpoint, which, if so, would suggest these viewpoints are probably the right viewpoints in that they confirm each other. We'll, as it were, pool our viewpoints. Would that upset you, having your viewpoint commingling with mine?'

'Ah,' Harpur said, 'I—'

'Exactly,' Iles said. 'The meeting between Ralph, Articulate and the two women.'

'I saw the meeting between Ralph, Articulate and the two women as a very interesting feature. That is, from my viewpoint.'

'In which respect interesting?' Iles said.

'I certainly noticed them in conversation.'

'Yes, well, as Naomi said, if people are in a club together some conversation is to be expected.'

'She'll be a real asset to Manse, pointing out the obviousnesses.'

'I thought the women with Articulate Max looked full of big-time purpose,' Iles said.

'He's always been dominated by them.'

'But it's Articulate who has the money now, yes?'

'If rumours about the bank raid are right.'

'Articulate might have the money but Rose Misk and great aunt Edna would want to say how it's spent, because Articulate is—because Articulate is the way he is, a nonentity, entirely unused to boodle on a possibly, probably, considerable scale.'

'Or was.'

'Shrewd, Harpur.'

'If he helped lift the International Corporate Diverse Securities treasure it might have done something for his personality.'

'What might be called "a rite of passage". That's why I say the conversation with Ralph is the crux of the evening.'

'In which respect, sir?'

'Some deal with Ralph proposed by the women?'

'Ah, yes. They need his help? We think Ember does some laundering of ill-gottens. It's subtly handled. So far the actual evidence is thin.'

'In my position, I have to see beyond the blatant, the trite, Col.'

'You're famed for that, sir. People say to me, "That Mr Iles, he would never be satisfied with the blatant and/or trite."'

'To me, those women looked set on something considerable, something magnificent, something, perhaps, grandiose.'

'Property? Ralph probably has estate agent contacts who don't quibble about accepting dubious cash, for a special commission—and I mean fat cash in cash form.'

'Always you reach for the banal, Harpur.'

'I'm famed for it, sir. When I introduce myself, people say, "Harpur? Harpur? You must be the one who always reaches for the banal." It's a real ice-breaker.'

'By "full of big-time purpose", I meant elevated purpose. Ralph Ember may be part of that elevated purpose.'

'Ralph has some good sides to him.'

'Perhaps these two women want to help him emerge,' Iles said.

'From where to where, sir?'

'From the Monty to the new, dignified, reputable, exclusive, magnificent Monty.'

'Back his sad, mad plans for the club?' Harpur asked.

'Back his sad, mad plans for the club. What was it Oscar Wilde said, Col?'

'This will be another of those books you had your head stuck in as a child.'

'"We are all in the gutter, but some of us are looking at the stars." That's Ralphy. The women think they can help him get out of the gutter by freshening up the Monty project with their funds.'

'*Their* funds? Is Articulate going to agree to that?' Harpur said. 'He's earned that loot. Not a pushover. I know he is, or was, dim and a doormat but—'

'Articulate looked as if he loathed the

idea—if that *was* the idea on the table. I'm guessing, Harpur. I'm not infallible.'

'I've heard people say your guessing is not infallible but wondrous nonetheless. This was one of the phrases that has remained in my mind, "wondrous nonetheless".'

'Which people? Did they all say "wondrous nonetheless"? It would sound like a put-up job if so.'

'You think great aunt Edna and Rose will browbeat Articulate?'

'They might try. That's supposing Ralph would touch their money. Articulate and the women are the kind of members he wants to kick out as a condition of turning the club into the new, dignified, reputable, exclusive, magnificent Monty. He's not going to welcome them as partners.'

'Ralph *can* bc fussy.'

They drew up at Iles's house. 'What we have to think, Col, is that Articulate himself may have *emerged*, as you hinted. I certainly don't dismiss *all* your attcmpts to analyse a situation.'

'Thank you, sir.'

'Anyone could see—and I include you in this, Col—anyone could see that if it's true Articulate helped at ICDS he's lived through big hazard, even possibly shown big skills. He's had a victory. Yes, perhaps he feels he's somebody at last. He'll want to keep on being somebody. He'll know he won't do that by throwing his cash at Ralph and the Monty pipedream. He might try something else, though.'

'What kind of thing, sir?'

'We ought to keep an eye on Articulate, Col.'

'In which respect, sir?'

'Oh, yes. Possible crucial developments there, Col.' Iles climbed out of the car, waved, disappeared into Idylls. If Iles forecast crucial developments, there would most probably bc . . . crucial developments. Harpur had sat for a while outside the house thinking. Then he drove back to the Monty. It was just before 1.30 a.m. The club would still be open. He wanted to see if discussions between Ralph, Articulate and the women had resumed. Perhaps he—Harpur—could come up with supposed insights the way Iles had, or even do some eavesdropping: that would be more in his workaday line.

But as he approached the Monty he saw an old Mercedes enter the car park, and Articulate get out and hurry into the club. He and the women must have left earlier. Now, it looked as if Articulate was returning alone. This seemed to endorse Iles's non-infallible guesswork, though Harpur couldn't have said exactly how. He kept going and parked out of sight around the corner from Shield Terrace, then returned on foot. Articulate had found wisdom and not ostentatiously blown some of the bank money on a new car, supposing he really had a slice of the bank money. Or the two women had *imposed* wisdom.

Harpur realized he must switch tactics. It would be too obviously a spy ploy if he actually went into the club now and found Ember and Misk in one-to-one conversation. Road works were under way opposite the car park. A reasonably deep hole had been left overnight, surrounded by red and white warning barriers. Harpur climbed in. The mud felt moist, but not impossible. His feet rested on a hefty piece of piping. Water? Drainage? Gas? Telephone lines? He crouched. Dugouts must have been something like this in the First World War. What was that saying his father had told him the troops used then? 'If you know a better 'ole you go to it.' Harpur didn't know of a better 'ole, for now. From his chosen spot he could see the Monty door into the car park and observe all movement. There wasn't any, until, just before 2 a.m., Articulate came out and went to his vehicle. Harpur crouched lower and tried to merge with the mud when Articulate's headlights made an arc as he drove away. Yes, like being under star shells on the Western Front in 1916.

Harpur had climbed out of his cover then, gone home, and, instead, climbed into bed. 'Surveillance.'

CHAPTER TEN

When Manse's fiancée, Naomi, turned up on her own next afternoon at the club looking for Ralph he felt damn surprised at first. Although women at Monty functions would often seriously embarrass Ember by coming on at him in what he considered foolishly intense, hungry style, he couldn't recall any of that from her yesterday, just lively, plain chat, plus persistent, sometimes tactless questions.

'Naomi!' he said. 'Alone?'

'Is that all right?'

'All right?'

'I'm not a Monty member, am I? Yesterday, I was a member's guest and therefore *persona grata.*'

'We'll stretch a point.'

Oh, yes, Ralph did suffer terribly from eager women. The club might not yet be entirely as he wished, but its ambience obviously tickled the mainspring of certain female guests and members, particularly at major festivities such as to honour territory grabs, or mark burials or cremations, or celebrate court victories. Special functions seemed to stir hormones. In addition came what Ember regarded as the bizarre fascination with his jaw scar, plus that idiotic, tedious business of the undeniable resemblance to Charlton Heston as Chuck used to be, and possibly an improvement on him: Ralph thought the boniness of Heston's face might be slightly too much, and his own face, fortunately, did not suffer from this. But, of course, Ralph *did* deny knowledge of any resemblance if it was mentioned to him, or he might have seemed grossly, coxcombly vain, a quality he considered quite against his nature.

These factors combined apparently gave him a special sexual attractiveness, which, added to what could be called 'the Monty effect', seemed to rally some women's blood and lavishly boost appetite.

'I think you'll come to see why I couldn't bring Mansel,' Naomi said.

To Ralph, this seemed a pretty fast approach, even viewed alongside some of the fast approaches he'd grown used to. Naomi obviously had dash. On the whole, Ralph approved of dash in women, as long as it was backed up by appearance, of course. 'The Monty effect', as he termed it, came from the fact that he ran and owned the club and therefore had a position of masterfulness and eminence. Women always went for that sort of thing. Although their enthusiasm could be a drag for Ralph, he tried to put up with it, even when they were old and/or ugly and/or unspruce. As Monty proprietor, regardless of its present state, he felt he had an absolute duty of respect and politeness to all members however crummy and/or monstrous. He thought of it as like *noblesse oblige.*

This was why he had joined the Misks when Rose called him over so blatantly. In Ralph's experience women these days *could* become blatant. Also, he'd wanted the talk with Alec, and couldn't seriously think that someone of Rose's age would still be touting for it in a public place, although the elderly, desperate ones could sometimes be the worst. His reasoning had turned out OK, even if the proposal she and Edna did put was just as unacceptable to Ralph in its own comical, big-headed way.

He spotted no signalling from Naomi yesterday, though, and Ralph considered himself extremely sensitive to women's cries from the heart and so on, even when discreetly concealed. But, then again, he'd naturally looked for nothing like that from Naomi. Good God, how could he possibly have expected such an approach? This woman was to marry Mansel in a full church ceremony very soon. Her focus would be exclusively and wholeheartedly on him, wouldn't it, for heaven's sake? Many might find this incomprehensible, even sickly, but it must be the case, mustn't it? The fact that Manse lacked altogether an intriguing jaw scar, and also lacked any resemblance to the young Heston, or to the young, glamorous anyone else, need not affect her commitment to him, surely. Luckily for Manse, beauty of face and physique was not the only desirable quality.

Of course, Ralph had been the first to offer Naomi gallantry by disposing of Unhinged when he made his lunge for her neck. Manse's response came only later. Almost *too* late and, in any case, redundant. Also, rather crude: knuckledusters suggested thuggery, whereas the Kressmann armagnac bottle had class and possibly wit. Ralph could imagine Unhinged might experience a kind of pride at being felled by the Kressmann. Probably Naomi felt a special thankfulness to Ralph. He understood thankfulness and would accept it, though in an offhand, say-no-more-please fashion. He hated to have too much fuss made of his accomplishments. Ralph did not mind tall, thinnish, frank, argumentative women too much as long as they had looks, decently curvaceous arses to counter the thinness, and some idea of fashion. But there'd clearly be health concerns after Manse.

'A drink?' he said.

'I get scared, Ralph.'

He thought she sounded puzzled rather than afraid. 'Unhinged—that's to say, Humphrey—*can* become a little ungovernable,' he said. 'His mind—his so-called mind—goes its own way. But you dealt with that unpleasantness well. You certainly didn't *look* scared. Capable, in fact—flung into an unpredictable, seesawing situation, yet markedly unfazed. I'd imagine Mansel was proud of you.'

'Oh, yes . . . Mansel . . . well . . .' She made her face expressionless. Not everybody could do that when talking about Shale. Ralph waited for her to finish, but she didn't. He tried to guess at the rest of it. *Oh, yes . . . Mansel . . . well, he doesn't throw praise around. Oh, yes . . . Mansel . . . well, he was so concerned about the foxes and stoats nuzzling Turret he didn't know much else until almost too late. Oh, yes . . . Mansel . . . well, Mansel is Mansel and who knows what he's thinking?* Ember could have agreed with that. Who *did* know Manse's thoughts, besides himself? And when, sometimes, he tried to describe them he came over unintelligible. Ralph doubted whether Manse genuinely worried all that much about the foxes and stoats nosing into Turret. After all, Manse had probably dropped Turret there dead, or had him dropped there dead, careless of whether he got nuzzled.

'Actually, I didn't mean scared of Unhinged Humphrey,' she explained. 'But, obviously, I'm in your debt for the vintage armagnac thumps on him.'

'Routine.'

'Really?'

'Oh, yes.'

'So swift. *So* decisive.'

'Necessarily.'

'Manse told me some call you "Panicking Ralph" or "Panicking Ralphy" because they felt let down by you in crisis circumstances. But this must, absolutely *must,* be a slander. I saw nothing like that—nothing panicky—the opposite, indeed—and Unhinged with his fingers on my neck could be called a crisis circumstance, I believe.'

Oh, thanks, Mansel, you big-mouthed Pre-Raphaelite-loving, grammar-mincing fucker. All right, Ember would acknowledge that now and then he did suffer those more or less disabling, pathological panic symptoms—loss of limb power, sweats, the fear that his mesmeric jaw scar had opened up and begun to weep something lurid and unspeakable. There'd been a few bad episodes long ago during tense team jobs on security vans and so on, yes, and word travelled: that malicious nickname went around, he knew, though nobody but this blunt bird and Turret would use it to his face, even to deny *absolutely* its rightness, as she did. And why had Manse told her? The act of a mate? *Was* that sodding schemer a mate now, though?

'People who fear one do try to diminish one by grotesquely false accusations,' Ralph remarked in a quiet, relaxed, almost casual style. 'The Goebbels big lie technique. In its perverted way, a compliment. They seek to make one sound weak because they are so aware one is anything but. Contemptible and, in the long run, self-defeating. One is what one is, and nothing can damage this central integrity.'

They sat at a table in the centre of the club with coffees. Ralph's wife, Margaret, had said she might call in on her way to shopping later, so he wanted nothing that looked hole-in-the-corner. This was a friend-to-friend conversation, friend-to-new-friend, friend-to-engaged-new friend. If she had a damn pash for him he didn't want it causing awkwardness today in the club. It might be possible to work out something else for later.

There were a few members at other tables nearby. Ember liked the way Naomi pulled her lips back over her teeth when she spoke fruity phrases such as 'vintage armagnac thumps' and the repeated 'crisis circumstances'. Teeth as teeth in a beautiful girl didn't do all that much for Ralph, but the efficient unveiling of them, then reveiling, only for them to be unveiled again during chat, did buck him up, could have a kind of hypnotic effect on him.

Ralph wondered why someone like this should go for Manse Shale. But, then, Ralph often wondered how lovely women with fine bodies—though a little skinny, in this case—yes, he wondered how such women could get interested in the kind of men they did seem to get interested in, even though he might have made it as obvious as he could that he, personally, would definitely not turn them away short-term. Of course, one reason that sod, Manse, had told her about the obnoxious nickname could be his fear Naomi might get a yen for Ralph: most probably a tactic to diminish him in her sight. Ralph knew well that men, frightened of his definite, very proven, allure, would try all kinds of sly, hurtful tricks to put their women off him. But any female who had seen Charlton Heston as El Cid on the movie channel would regard those tricks as what they were—filthy backbiting.

'But no, it isn't, wasn't, Unhinged Humphrey that scared me,' she said. 'Some of the conversation, though—so dark and impenetrable.'

'Which conversation?'

'Yesterday. Near the bar.'

'Whose?'

'Almost everyone's.'

'Mine, for instance?'

'Some of yours, yes,' she said.

'Well, I'm sorry. We must clear that up.'

'People talking to conceal, not disclose. A sort of semaphore, but by someone behind a wall.'

This woman possessed cleverness as well as all the rest of it. So how could she think of marrying Manse? Of course, Manse did have the money and the art and the big ex-rectory. These might count, but he didn't think Naomi would be captured by all that. Somehow, Manse had always been able to do a bit of pulling, though. Ralph wondered about

303

women sometimes, or more frequently.

'So many topics came up—I mean, serious, often terrible, topics—and they'd be on show for a moment but then seemed just to disappear,' she said. 'Seemed *made* to disappear.'

'Oh, I didn't notice that.'

She laughed. 'Look, it's happening again now, isn't it?' She tried to make her voice gruff and male. ' "Oh, I didn't notice that." '

'I don't follow,' Ember replied, following.

'You say you didn't notice some comments just sort of . . . sort of got buried. And is this now, today, another blackout?'

'I think I *would* have noticed something like that.'

'Well, for instance, Unhinged thought it weird, and more than weird, that you and Manse should be talking chummily about the death of Turret. I asked why, but no answer. Not just no answer—I sensed a feeling around that I shouldn't even have asked why. Way off limits. Suddenly, all the discussion was about Unhinged and whether he'd been grassed.'

'People tend not to spend much time on ideas coming from Unhinged,' Ralph said. 'Ideas are not his long suit.' He smiled. 'His morning suit is his long suit. Sorry! But subjects raised by Unhinged will not occupy people for more than a moment or two.'

'But what did he mean? He found it unbelievable that you and Manse should be friendly and peaceful with each other "after what happened to Turret". Words like that—they stick. We know what happened to Turret, but why should this affect your relationship with Manse and vice versa?'

'About almost any matter Unhinged always has some jumbled theory—if one can call it as much.'

'Well, I don't know. Patches of lucidity, I thought.'

'Few.'

'Then, that man, Brown, speaking about the death of his brother—a terrible, vicious death—and you—you, Ralph—you ignore it and ask about his club and the Monty,' she said.

'No, I wouldn't say ignored. The talk just flowed that way.'

'You directed it that way.'

'Not at all, Naomi. I—'

'It's important. Why I'm here today.'

'Because we spoke briefly about the Garrick and the Monty?'

Her tone became super-methodical, super-rational, as if she were expounding a lesson, laying out a theorem to someone backward. 'I'm supposed to be marrying Manse,' she said 'Have you got hold of this idea? Not just shagging him, as Unhinged so sweetly and decorously put it. *Marrying* him. A church job. A life job.'

'Yes, of course. Supposed? I don't

understand. I thought it a fact. What's going on?'

'It is a fact, was a fact.'

'Which?'

'I'm not sure. Let me tell you what I got from that conversation yesterday—from what was said, and what wasn't. All right?'

Ember didn't much like this. She had a brain, but no notion of custom and practice here. And if she did come to understand the scene, she probably wouldn't think much of it, or comply with it. 'From what *wasn't* said?' he muttered. 'But wow! That puts us on to infinity, doesn't it?'

'Silences. Evasions. They could be felt. They could be measured. They dominated.'

'I really can't say I—'

'Mansel killed Joachim Brown, or had him killed.'

'What? My God, what?' Ralph detested blaring declarations of the totally obvious, and not just from women. She despised tact. That might be fine and healthy in some settings. This was not one of them.

'That's the message I got,' she stated.

'From the semaphore flags behind a wall?' Ralph replied. He had quite a belief in wit, though he tried never to do bad injury with this, except to Iles, and certainly never to injure a presentable woman.

She said: 'It's what Unhinged seemed to be hinting at. It's what the cop, Iles, meant, wasn't it, when he said Manse looked "profoundly stricken" about the death. This was a sort of joke—his sort. You could have filled a truck with the sarcasm. That one knows things.'

'Which?'

'Iles. What did he mean by saying Brown was an "intelligencer"?'

'The ACC acts all-seeing and all-powerful. Part of his job. Most of it is show and bluff. Standard cop tactics. Keep the populace down. That's us, Naomi.'

'But "intelligencer"?'

'Some word to baffle people, impress people. He reads a lot and goes to the theatre. That might seem strange for a major police officer, but he *is* strange. Probably he saw that word in some ancient volume or heard it in an old play. He'd stick it in his ready-to-use bag. It would be like him to try to sound clever with it in front of you for his own reasons. He'd want to get superior to Manse in your eyes. Manse is never going to use a word like "intelligencer".'

Always Ralph tried to be gentle and understanding with people from outside trying to make sense of the way things ran in this domain, and especially gentle and understanding to women: all women—not just the younger, attractive ones, though this sympathetic approach did sometimes provide a way into the attractive, younger ones. Of course, the terrible trouble was that the unattractive older ones also responded, and often responded more strongly, shamelessly. Ralph found it to some extent painful having to repel them. Overall, he naturally realized that folk new to the area must find some features of life here baffling, and he would try to treat them all with patience, lookers or not.

'And the other cop—Harpur. He says less, but probably is at least a step ahead of Iles all the time.'

'Ungifted. He lives in a very ordinary street.'

'There seemed a sort of conspiracy to make sure everything stayed close. I can't see why, I admit. But is there a bizarre, disgusting solidarity between you and Manse, even though he might have done you and yours harm? You'll settle it between yourselves somehow—and nobody should ask what the somehow might be? An old business tradition, I suppose—that is, in the kind of business you and he do.'

'You're reading a lot into—'

She leaned forward to get nearer to Ralph. For a couple of seconds he misinterpreted this and thought she'd decided to make her inevitable play for him. He could admit to a quiver of excitement. It would have been an insult to her not to feel that. She spoke more quietly: 'Of course, I twigged a while ago that Manse's firm had murky aspects. A lot of murky aspects. I'm a grown-up woman. I'm not totally naive. I knew I shouldn't ask too much, and I didn't. All right, this was weak and self-deceiving and shifty. But I wanted him. Oh, he's got some oddnesses, but who hasn't? At core he's all right. At core he's great. And he's needy—his wife gone, kids growing up. That's vital with me. I like answering needs, if I can.'

She paused, shrugged, as though suddenly conscious that Ralph might have other views of her motives. 'His money and the art and the property? I'd say they helped persuade me, a bit. Only a bit. I think I'm being honest about that. So, yes, I wanted him, and on a settled basis. I knew he'd had women living in at the old rectory for spells, but only for spells. I'm in search of permanence. And I had the idea he wanted permanence, too. There was the proviso we've mentioned, and I accepted it—not to pry unduly. It looked as though it might work. It *was* working. Yes, it was working until . . . until I heard Turret and his end talked about and *un*talked about yesterday. All right, I never knew Turret Brown and can't pretend to any great grief. That isn't what I'm saying. I found I couldn't blind-eye what might have happened to him, and Mansel's possible involvement. Things became suddenly very precise, very exact, very awful, although people tried to get them—keep them—covered up.'

'You've allowed imagination to take over, Naomi, I'm afraid,' Ralph declared.

'And, I have to wonder now whether I want to—whether, in fact, I *could*—marry someone who kills and disfigures, or had killed and disfigured, an associate of one of his alleged main chums, and might have that main chum himself lined up for slaughter soon,' she replied. 'Which woman wouldn't wonder? This is not just standard business viciousness. This is major butchery.'

'But . . . but . . . and but again—it's all absurd, Naomi, I assure you. You're building a—'

'Iles and Brown talk about a war. Ask "Between whom?" and there's a flurrying gallop away into some other subject, harmless subject. I'm not to know. I'm due to marry one of the main men in any "war" but I must be told nothing.'

'People exaggerate,' Ember replied.

Margaret came into the club and joined them. Ralph had told her about Mansel's fiancée but they'd never met. Ember introduced the two women. 'Naomi dropped in to check a few things for the big day with Mr Best Man,' Ralph said.

'We're all so excited over the wedding,' Margaret replied.

'And me, too, of course,' Naomi said.

After all, Ralph thought, she must have learned something about the evasions she'd described. 'It will soon be upon us,' he said very heartily.

CHAPTER ELEVEN

Iles called a small meeting in his suite to hear how things were going in the Joachim Brown investigation and discuss points arising. Harpur attended, with Francis Garland, the Chief Inspector handling the case day-to-day. 'This is nice, isn't it?' Iles said, looking around the room and putting up something like a smile but not very.

'What, sir?' Harpur said.

'Cosy,' Iles said. 'Us. The Three-team.'

'Well, yes,' Harpur said. 'Although the topic might not be cosy—someone's death.'

'Oh, don't go worthy on me, Col, for fuck's sake,' Iles said.

'We think a professional operation,' Garland said.

' "Professional". That means someone shot him and he's dead, does it?' Iles asked. 'Three bullets in the head even from a total amateur would do him, you know, Francis.'

'We find no weapon,' Garland said.

'Of course you find no weapon,' Iles said. 'This is Manse, or someone employed or hired by Manse, disposing of a spy. Unlikely to leave a gun around. Shale's Cambridge Ph.D. is in how to mess up any detection attempts to fit him to a crime.'

'That's what I meant by professional, sir,'

311

Garland said.

This type of ACC's conference could be difficult. Personal aspects might intrude. And often larger considerations arose than the mere problem of deciding—trying to decide— who might be guilty of what. Iles, and Iles's mind, had not been made for the nitty-gritty. Or rather they could do nitty-gritty, but were not confined by it. They also looked at a wide scene. However, others might not be aware of what the scene actually consisted of. 'Others' could mean people like Harpur and Garland, although Harpur and Garland tried to fathom him, especially Harpur off and on.

The ACC required that the nitty-gritty should be made to fit into a large, fairly fixed, Ilesean overview. This had become even more true since the new Chief Constable took command of the force. Sir Matthew had not yet been fully broken in to Iles's way of looking at things. Iles believed that an Assistant Chief, such as himself, could only assist properly if the Chief Constable he was supposed to assist accepted the style of assistance the Assistant Chief felt right to offer. Iles needed to put in more work yet at shaping and generally improving Sir Matthew, teaching him the value and wholesomeness of street peace, through unspoken treaties with drugs overlords. And Iles seemed to think the Turret business might provide key chances.

'When I described this meeting as cosy I

had in mind that we three are quite interestingly, perhaps uniquely linked,' Iles replied. 'I expect you both see how.'

'There's a common interest in the murder of Brown, yes, sir,' Harpur said hopefully, hopelessly. 'We could be regarded as an investigative triumvirate, Francis actually running the inquiry, you and myself, sir, in support.'

'My wife,' Iles replied.

'As you know, sir, we've unearthed several strange factors to do with 15A Singer Road, Brown's latest domicile,' Garland said. 'The neighbours upstairs have made some quite useful—'

'Perhaps I've put this to you before, Harpur, Garland,' Iles said, 'but do you think there's another police force in the country or the world, for that matter, where three officers of notable rank, one of *considerable* rank, sit or pace in a pleasant, prestige room, with innocuous watercolours on the walls . . . yes, sit or pace here chatting amiably, although the two of only notable rank have sexually pillaged the wife of the one of considerable rank, who is au fucking fait with this? Might it be regarded as unusual, even in, say, France or Peru?'

'Ember called at 15A, of course, one night,' Garland said. 'This is established.'

Iles's voice took on the high, chant-like fervour that would sometimes come when he

313

referred to his wife, Sarah. 'But, obviously, I mustn't grow obsessive about her and you two in the past,' he said. 'That would become self-destructive. I would never allow memories of that degenerate era to impose upon my present thinking. I have to be alert, unimpaired for my current duties, under a Chief Constable who may or may not get somewhere near competence in due course or later. He will prove himself one way or the other, I'm convinced. He has that look. But meanwhile I have to accept the extra burden of making up for him. I cannot—absolutely cannot and must not—let unpleasantnesses from some way back affect my mentality. In fact, I will tabulate for you what I'm absolutely determined to avoid, because it would be pervy, prurient, brain-corroding, Othello-like. Thus:

'One, I never try to visualize the kind of flea-pit rooms, or municipal park flower beds, or police vehicles, or back lanes, or beaches, or train lavatories which you and she would utilize.

'Two, similarly, I never speculate mentally about whether she was running both of you simultaneously or one succeeded the other, and, if the second of these, in what order? It is, of course, incomprehensible to me why she should want either of you—and incomprehensible to *her* now—many's the puzzled yet unrestrained laugh we have

314

together some evenings over the ludicrousness, as she and I see it in retrospect—the ludicrousness of what went on in those flea-pit rooms, municipal park flower beds, police vehicles, back lanes, beaches, train lavatories which I never try to visualize . . . Indeed, it's so incomprehensible to me that I can't possibly guess at the priority she might have given one of you or the other. Can anybody put in order of merit different kinds of dross? Would it be what is called in politics, I believe, "Buggins' turn"?'

'Of course, Ralph has an entirely reasonable explanation for calling at 15A,' Garland replied. 'He is the benevolent Mr Mighty, concerned for the welfare of his understrappers. If someone is missing, he might legitimately try to find out why.'

'Three,' Iles said, 'because I have absolutely no wish to visualize those encounters in flea-pit rooms, or municipal park flower beds, or police vehicles, or back lanes, or beaches, or train lavatories, I, similarly, do not seek to imagine the sounds raised—the gasps, shrieks and exclamations. For me to imagine compulsively these unkempt outbursts would be another sign of a sick mind. Madness lies that way, even for someone of such robustly stable faculties as mine. And what if householders working in their garden at twilight heard such evil hullabaloo over the wall from the back lane—is that really a civilized manner to treat others' quiet enjoyment of their property?'

Iles shook his head with massive sadness, obviously not thinking of Sarah in flea-pit rooms, or municipal park flower beds, or police vehicles, or back lanes, or beaches, or train lavatories, but thinking how painful it would be if he *did* cave in and think of such episodes. Only small amounts of froth came to the ACC's lips, and his voice remained clangy but mild. Had he been on a Staff officers' course in unmadness? He could be remarkably conscientious. Iles walked about the suite as he spoke, but not in a loony, jerky, frenetic style. There was a gorgeous athleticism to it. Might he have in mind that sinuous caged panther? He wore full dress uniform today for some function later. Harpur and Garland had easy chairs.

Garland said: 'And then a series of enigmas around 15A. Perhaps I should list these:

'One, an unidentified girl of possibly fourteen years of age with a bicycle calls at 15A, presumably rings the bell, then, when this is unsuccessful, shouts through the letter box, obviously hoping Brown is inside and will hear her. This would suggest she knew him.

'Two, the girl is still unsuccessful and posts a note for Brown. She claims to be delivering an important message that will "brook no delay" from "an associate".

'Three, did someone enter the flat secretly
316

and remove this note and other mail? Nothing was in the hallway when we arrived after his body had been found. This could not have been Brown himself because the pathologist puts the date of his death much earlier than when the girl called. We found no sign of break-in, so whoever entered appears to have been skilled at that kind of operation. Plastic on the front door lock?'

'Did you get in there, Harpur?' Iles said. 'So, where's the damn note? With all the stuff you took from the body, is it?'

'And then: Four,' Garland said. 'This unidentified man in an unidentified car—according to the girl, that is. Or, rather, according to the neighbours' report of their conversation with the girl.

'Five, the car's gone by the time she tells the neighbours, and they don't get a proper description of him or the vehicle.'

'Four,' Iles replied, 'also, I can say—happily say—that I'm not one to harbour resentments about matters now unquestionably at an end. This was what I mean, you see, about the laughter over these recollections that Sarah and I happily share now. I can look at you two and see perfectly acceptable, indeed, admirable colleagues—colleagues who, it's true, were disgustingly and deceitfully—'

'Six,' Garland said, 'this man in the car was, according to the 15B version of what the girl told them, speaking into a mobile telephone, while intently watching 15A—perhaps briefing someone about the scene in Singer Road and 15A.'

'Perhaps briefing someone *inside* 15A, Dumbo,' Iles said. 'You had a watchman, did you, Col?'

Harpur never wondered how Iles had made it to Assistant Chief despite his frequent lapses into radiant mania, sometimes loud. He could show this fabulous intuition. Perhaps that was the other side of radiant mania. And his intuition and other gifts had taken Iles a long way, but not quite to the summit. Something else seemed necessary to lift him from Assistant Chief to Chief. He appeared to be stuck with his intuition, his other gifts and his radiant mania at where he was. What extra quality did the selection boards for Chief want? Consistency? Gravitas? Likeability? Moderation? Unobsessiveness? Radiant non-mania? Most of these he would find obnoxious and/or trite. Was he a career Assistant?

And did he, perhaps, know himself to be a career Assistant? Possibly, he never even applied for Chief Constable posts. He would not tell Harpur if he did. And Harpur had not heard anything from the rumour machine. Maybe Iles needed, and knew he needed, one of those *contexts* he'd spoken of: that is, people below him, but also someone immediately above. He'd mentioned unofficially usurping the Chiefdom while Sir Matthew was made manageable. But, at least, Sir Matthew would be there, nominally supreme, and in charge of Iles. Likewise, his predecessor, Mark Lane, had apparently been Iles's boss, though Iles generally ignored him, and had helped drive him into breakdown and then the Inspectorate of Constabulary. Yes, Lane was feeble but Lane was *present*, until his collapse. Iles accepted a place in Lane's regime, and, using his splendid talents, set about trying to fuck it up, but not wipe it out. He could not do without subordination.

Now, as to those splendid talents, Harpur wondered whether Iles also intuited that the young girl who called at 15A and shouted through the letter box might be Ralph's daughter, Venetia. If he did, he wasn't saying. Harpur could certainly make this guess at her identity. The note he'd picked up in the 15A hallway referred to a Welsh cob. Ralph's place had horses and Harpur knew Ember's daughters rode. Hadn't Ralph boasted to Harpur about the paddocks and grounds at Low Pastures, so suitable for what Ember called Venetia's 'equestrian side', and so different from Harpur's home in Arthur Street? Harpur knew, too—so did many—that Venetia tended to fall hard for older men. According to Lamb, Turret had been up to Low Pastures at least once. Was that enough to captivate Venetia and send her desperately calling when he didn't reappear? She'd discovered his address somehow? Harpur had heard those piping, passionate tones through the 15A letter box before she posted her note, a young girl, lorn, baffled and hurt. Nothing else that Harpur found in the hallway or in Turret's pockets added up to much. He had £3K in his current account and subscribed to the *National Geographic Magazine.*

'Ralph and Manse,' Iles said. He spoke the names with big warmth. 'Manse and Ralph.'

'They're certainly involved somehow in the Joachim death, sir, but I can't see exactly how or why, yet,' Garland said.

'I've had new thoughts about them,' Iles said.

'Ah,' Harpur remarked.

'Yes,' Iles said.

'New in what sense, sir?' Harpur said.

'Yes, new,' Iles said.

'This is interesting, sir,' Harpur said.

'The theory, of course, is that they are lining up to fight each other for ultimate supremacy in the trade, and that Ralph sent Joachim in to report on Shale's plans,' Garland said. 'Joachim was rumbled and slaughtered. To date, though, it's hard to get evidence to back this theory.'

'New in the sense that these most recent thoughts rather contradict what I've said previously,' Iles said. He grinned as he confessed to this. This grin was different from the smile he had used when referring to the cosiness of the meeting, and came close to making him seem almost genial and unharmful, even benign. The uniform followed the lines of his body splendidly, and you could believe that, although the grin made him seem almost genial and unharmful, even benign, he would, at the same time, be always ready to do his formidable best for whatever he might believe in. Harpur considered that what Iles believed in would most probably be OK, give or take a few enormous details.

'Contradict former ideas?' Harpur said. 'Oh, you were never one to be shackled by a mind-set, sir.'

'I see Ralph and Manse as human beings,' Iles replied. He spoke quietly, like someone awed by a sudden revelation, possibly of a spiritual nature, but, in any case, life-changing.

'Human beings? That's a point, yes, sir,' Harpur said.

'Do you recall a time in the club when Ralph claimed Monty special occasions showed the humanity of his clientele? This seemed rather fruity then. Yet, perhaps humanity *is* important. I don't know whether you've ever thought at all about humanity, Harpur. It might not be within your range, but those two—Ralph and Manse—are not mere elements to be pushed about by a political theory. I'm afraid this goes back on what I described to you, Col, only a little while ago. My view then you see, Col, Francis . . . my view then placed Ralph and Manse as fated, doomed, by the pressures of market demands to seek monopoly. And therefore each must try to dispose of the other, despite their long affiliation and possible friendship. This theory seemed feasible, coherent. It appeared academically convincing. However . . .' He paused lengthily. Harpur and Garland waited, silent. Iles said: 'However , I wholly reject this notion now. It might be academically convincing but does it square with Life?' He spoke with the capital letter. 'There are more things in heaven and earth than are dreamt of in your philosophy, K. Marx.'

'That's almost poetic, sir. It's a treat the way these thoughts just seem to come to you.'

Iles stopped strolling and held up two hands, as if in surrender. 'No, no, don't say anything out of your habitual good nature to excuse my volte-face, Col. I am routinely grateful for that kindness, even from someone who casually yet repeatedly debauched my wife in flea-pit rooms, or municipal park flower beds, or police vehicles, or back lanes, or beaches, or train lavatories, but I must not accept such kindness now. Would you say it was casually yet repeatedly, Harpur? I'm not certain what answer I want to that. Which do you think would be preferable to me, Col—the casual or not casual debauching of my wife? "Casual" would suggest no serious attempt to take her from me. Non-casual might mean

322

intent.'

'Has anything specific brought about this change of mind on monopoly, sir?' Harpur replied.

'Yes, something specific,' Iles said.

'This is fascinating,' Harpur said.

'Naturally, I'm speaking of Unhinged Humphrey.'

'Ah,' Harpur said.

'Clearly, this is what lay behind my reference to Ralph and Manse as human beings,' Iles said.

'Right, sir,' Garland said.

'Obviously,' Harpur said.

'Unhinged, as we saw, insulted and assaulted Mansel's fine and, for all I know, at this stage, clean and reputable, fiancée in the Monty.'

'Unhinged can be like that,' Harpur said.

'This is someone very precious to Manse,' Iles said. 'He is ready to take her on full-time, despite the experience he had with that earlier, wandering piece, Sybil, the mother of his children, though that didn't seem to bother her much when she hopped it.'

'Manse and Naomi met through art,' Harpur said. 'It's rather inspiring. I hear there's a lot of picking up done in galleries. People loiter and make themselves receptive to the stuff on the walls. In that state, conversations can occur with other loiterers. Some women get turned on by almost anything in a suitable frame.'

'Now, who was it who first took action against Unhinged during that disgraceful attack in the Monty?' Iles said.

'I heard Ember hit him with a Kressmann armagnac bottle,' Garland said.

'I find that so meaningful,' Iles said.

'Ralph usually has a bottle of Kressmann's near,' Harpur said. 'When there's plenty in it this can give a very effective smack.'

'I see an unshiverable bond between Ralph and Manse,' Iles said. 'If something of Mansel's is threatened—for instance, his fiancée—Ralph regards it as an inescapable duty to protect her, a duty more compelling than even that capitalistic duty to compete. He acted regardless of the fact that, as far as I've discovered, Ralph isn't doing anything with her himself at this stage. Knightliness—we witnessed a kind of knightliness. We saw unbreakable comradeship. They stand by each other and, I now think, on this evidence and my accumulated knowledge of them, always will. They are part of the fabric, a lasting, proven part. Further—oh, yes, magnificently further: further, there comes the notable way Manse expertly backed up with his knuckleduster Ralph's use of the bottle as bludgeon. This is two men beautifully in concert, two men viscerally connected, Col, Francis, in that case via a woman, but also generally, profoundly. On the face of it these

324

may seem small, accidental incidents. In a way, yes. But they are also indicators. They tell us of larger issues—or, at least, they tell *me*, who is, possibly, exceptionally attuned to such hints owing to my reservoir of empathy.'

'You don't any longer think they'll try to wipe out each other in the predestined fight for capitalistic dominance, as proposed by Marx?' Harpur said.

'My point now is, they are bigger than any mere woolly claptrap about the inevitable need for commercial monopoly.' The ACC tightened his jaw to demonstrate certainty. 'Bigger in which respect, you may ask.'

'Bigger in which respect, sir?' Harpur said.

'Oh, don't you see it—don't you *sense* it, Col, Francis? Bigger because they are human, human, human, gloriously, unimpeachably human.' Iles almost sang, almost chortled. He beamed. This hugely surpassed a smile or grin. It tried to warm the room. Yes, it was as if the ACC had seen a vision, a happy one, unique to him. 'They will act according to human impulses, not formulae,' he said. 'They will, in fact, deliberately, unenslavedly, resist those formulae.'

'But we still have Turret dead, sir,' Garland said.

Iles frowned. Here was that sodding nitty-gritty, to foul up those splendid abstractions. 'Yes, Turret dead. I think they both now suffer major regrets over Turret—Ralph for placing him secretly, treacherously, in Manse's outfit, Manse for killing him, or having him killed. Both acts violate perfect blood-brotherliness.'

'But how can you know they repent like that, sir,' Harpur said, 'if I may ask this, too?'

'Yes, Col, ask, ask away! How? I'll tell you: I feel it.' Iles struck the uniform at stomach level with the palm of his right hand. Harpur thought it must be to show how visceral this, also, was. 'Perhaps we shouldn't push too hard at the Turret inquiry, Francis,' Iles said. 'After all, what *was* Turret? Offal. We have a balance to keep. That balance will see Ralph and Manse maintain their long, fruitful tolerance of each other in the trade. We then enjoy continuance of assured peace on the streets. This is precious. To make too much of the Turret death will endanger such peace, cause finger-pointing. Let's avoid that.'

'His brother is still around, sir, pressing for a rigorous inquiry, as you might expect from a brother,' Garland said. 'He has some clout—a famous actor. Press friends, possibly. I wouldn't want him or them to regard us as slack.'

'Famous, certainly—and deservedly. My wife and I will definitely try to get up to London to see him in *No Man's Land*,' Iles replied. 'That's the kind of joyful, open, stimulating trip she and I often take together these days—a bit damn different from your activity in—to list at random—flea-pit rooms,

326

or municipal park flower beds, or police vehicles, or back lanes, or beaches, or train lavatories, wouldn't you agree? Theatre—such a wonderful link between us!'

Garland said: 'On the whole I accept the word of the neighbours at 15B, but that word doesn't take us very far.'

'Neighbourhood fucking Watch,' Iles replied. 'I should think the young girl with the bike was Ralph's daughter, Venetia. Did you recognize the hopeful, sad, teenage, loving, letter-box voice, Col? Have you ever met her? I hear Turret went to Low Pastures for a discussion, perhaps discussions, with Ralphy. If this girl saw him there she'd probably take a fancy. Wispy beard? Moustache? She's rather that way, isn't she? Even in the condition we found him, Col, one could see he might have had some third-rate, short-term, underclass attractiveness. But I'd say, keep her right out of things, please, Francis. I don't know how it could affect Ralph if we start harassing his daughter. True, Ember wouldn't have liked Venetia making a play for Turret, but possibly he'd feel angry with Mansel for bringing her distress. I'd rather he was not angry with Manse. Things between them seem good now, but might also be delicate for a while. We seek peace, don't we, Col, Francis? It is our duty to preserve the Queen's Peace, God bless her. We are, as Colin said, her triumvirate, her happy, united triumvirate. This doesn't mean I forget you helped your respective selves to my wife, but we are professionals and can be happy and united in that boundaried, workaday fashion.'

CHAPTER TWELVE

Ember and Shale had one of their routine, private business pow-wows in Manse's house, the former St James's rectory. Shale wanted to finalize some accounts before his wedding and honeymoon. Suppose he got through the ceremony alive, Manse and Naomi would leave immediately afterwards for Stockholm. Shale had told Ralph he didn't want any of those 'touristy', 'obvious' spots, such as Venice or Las Vegas. 'Them northern countries, such as Sweden, Norway, Finland—there's a sort of *cleanness* to them, Ralph. As you know, I'm always seeking that—cleanness. Such as fjords for Norway—that clear blue water and snowy cliffs—and islands all around Stockholm, more beautiful water, some sea, some fresh. I hear they got what's called an "ice bar" in Stockholm, which is a bar in an hotel where everything is ice. The bar itself—what they serves the drinks off of—is a big lump of ice and you can see right through it because ice is so pure. Great! There's a lad over there, Upsalla way, running a really sweet H and coke operation, and it will be nice to call in on him and check any new angles we could learn from, Ralph.'

Ember and Shale talked now, as they often did, in what Manse termed 'the den-room'. Ralph reckoned Manse didn't care for the word den on its own, because it would make him sound like an animal, and not an attractive or odour-free animal. Ember thought Manse's eyes looked ferrety, so you could understand his worry about the word 'den'. This was not a cruelly personal view of Manse's eyes: several people had mentioned the blatant ferretiness of them to Ember. He found ferretiness difficult to define exactly, but the eyes radiated something stony, clever and unmerciful.

Shale had told him once that he liked to work in here doing the accounts and so on because he felt it put him in touch with vicars and rectors who might have used this room to draft sermons, and write testimonials. Manse loved that sort of connection with the upright, even holy, past. Maybe it chimed with what he described as the desire for cleanness via Scandinavia. His den-room had a large mahogany table-desk and a suite of furniture in red leather. Original paintings hung on the walls, one of a plumpish woman who looked as though she would be Dutch. On their way through the house, Ralph had seen other paintings in the hall and, through an open door, in a larger room off it, some more daubs, probably from that Pre-Raphaelite movement Manse adored. They drank coffee. It was early evening.

Ember would never allow these meetings to take place at Low Pastures or even in the Monty. Not at all fucking on. Ralph felt committed to keeping his home and the club clear of any contact with a trade he knew to be generally viewed as crooked. Naturally, he recognized that Low Pastures could not be wholly clear of his trade because trade money helped buy it. But he'd prevent any further link between the property and the business. Making sure the Monty stayed separate from the trade was less easy. After all, the club had its tainted, villainous, aspects, regardless of any connection with Ralph's other career: why Ralph wanted to transform it. Just the same, Ralph greatly disliked the thought of making the Monty a site for regular strategy meetings about the drugs game.

Inevitably, he realized that Manse might ask why, then, *his* place, with its evident religious history, should be considered suitable for their meetings. Ralph didn't have much of an answer, but often he'd bring a bottle of Kressmann's around to solace him. He could tell that Shale, in his fucking small-minded, niggly way, was not totally convinced by this. Ralph certainly regarded Manse's attitude as regrettable, and, ultimately, Manse could go stuff himself.

330

Immediately the two lots of figures had been agreed—one set for Manse and Ralph, the other for the general, companies' dinner at the Agincourt—Shale said: 'What I appreciated above all, Ralph, was the way you looked after Naomi in the club the other night when Unhinged turned rancid, like he so often does.' He sounded genuinely warm and matey, though his eyes couldn't match this.

'Oh, an automatic response, Manse—nothing extraordinary.'

'An automatic response for *you*, yes, Ralph. But for many another it would not of been that. This was something deep and personal in you—in you, Ralph Ember. And I felt proud to join you in this flattening of Unhinged. Such cooperation, Ralph. Such very special, brilliant comradeship.'

'True.'

'It thrilled Naomi,' Shale said.

'She's a fine girl.'

'Now and then she gets her doubts about me, Ralph.'

'Doubts? About *you*?' Only someone mad *wouldn't* have doubts about Shale.

'I can tell. These doubts might be natural.'

'You're very forgiving, Manse.'

'It wouldn't be right to blame her too much, seeing the sort of life she've come from.'

'Which?'

'She got to adjust. All right, every couple got to do that. But for her it's a really big item.

Not so easy, maybe. This is a woman with her own mind. In a way, I admire her for that. It can be a fucking plague.'

'What *kind* of doubts, Manse?' as if Ralph didn't know.

'She don't like some of the . . . well, she thinks there might be untoward things she haven't been told about, like not quite as things seem, and this worries her. Women goes in for all sorts of worries, as you know.'

'Untoward?'

'Like this Turret Brown.'

'In what sense, Manse?'

'She wonders who killed him. They can be like that, women. Somebody gets killed and cut about, so they'll start with questions. They see that as natural. It's their way. Silence? They never fucking heard of it. They haven't got a lot to do, and so they're always on the lookout for topics.'

'Whom does she think killed him?' Obviously, Ralph knew the answer to that one, but it would be best for *Manse* to tell *him*, not for *him* to tell *Manse*. He said 'whom' because it was correct and he did not want to patronize Manse by going down to his fucking grammatical level.

'This nosiness can make things dodgy, Ralph.'

'Everyone wonders who killed Brown, including the police.'

'Yes, we all do, I know. It's an absolute

332

mystery.'

'Does she want to name someone?'

'She thinks she picks up pointers—such as from Unhinged. Very sickening hints.'

'What sort of hints?'

'It can make things tense, Ralph.'

'You tell her what Unhinged is like, don't you?'

'That his mouth takes over? Yes. It takes over until something else takes over, such as the throttling.'

'Pointers from Unhinged mean nothing. Well, she ought to be able to *see* what he's like. Half crazy. Naomi's an intelligent woman.'

'Yes, I think she does see it. And because of what you done on Unhinged and the way we acted so harmonious together, flattening him—I think that affected her in a truly helpful style. I don't say she's forgot the doubts—not totally, that will take time—but I believe it's going to be all right—the wedding and so on. I got to say moments used to come when I couldn't be sure. This is a major church all lined up and willing to do it, and I still worried she'd back out because this Brown gets hisself killed in very worrying conditions—I mean, it was more than worrying for him hisself, clearly, but worrying for others, as a result. A poor situation, Ralph.'

'Hard on you.'

'Yes.' Shale did some mourning. Then he bucked up suddenly. 'But what I wanted to explain, Ralph, is how I—I mean I myself, in person—how I learned so much from that little carry-on with Unhinged. You might not know it, Ralph, but there are some who say businessmen like us are bound to fight each other, because we all want to be top dog with no other dogs around at all. It's what known as a theory. You heard of "dog eat dog"? It's like that. Of importance. Some thinker come up with it as an idea, I heard. They can be like that, thinkers—famed for theories. They'll look at certain conditions and they'll decide, Ah, these need a theory. You and me, Ralph, when we think of something it's just ordinary thinking. But when one of these real thinkers thinks most likely they'll come up with a theory. Famed for it.'

'They're always at something.'

'Anyway, I don't believe it. Never did, and less now. What I'd say, especially after that Unhinged trouble, is we're friends, you and me, Ralph, and *eternal* friends. No theory from no thinker can upset that. Them thinkers can go fuck theirselves. If they think thinking's so grand, why don't they think about something useful, not just theories? We'll act like we always did, two firms, but two firms who give each other total respect and understanding.'

'Right, Manse,' Ember said.

'We don't usually talk about such matters, I know. We don't *need* to talk about such matters because they are there, like natural.

But now and then it's good to talk about such matters. They deserve it, because very few others got anything like it, or none at all.'

'True.'

'This is not one of them theories, this is just how it is, and OK to discuss.'

'Highlights things.'

'Spot on.' Shale stood suddenly. 'Look, Naomi is here, with the children. I'd like to call them all in so they can see us together, companions for ever, in total trade harmony. This they should witness, and share the joy.'

'Right, Manse,' Ember said.

Shale went and opened the den-room door. He called out to Naomi and the children, in an excited, fulfilled voice. After a moment, the three appeared and sat down on the leather chairs and settee, Naomi, Laurent and Matilda. The boy and girl were still in their private school uniform, blue, trimmed with black. They looked refined, despite Mansel. 'Here's Ralph,' Shale said, with terrific affection. 'He didn't want to go until he saw you all. It's the way he is. Of course, he'll see you again at the wedding, but that's still days away.'

'We're all looking forward to it, I'm sure,' Ralph said.

'So much,' Naomi said.

And Ralph thought she might mean it now, although she seemed to have learned fast how to use conversation to hide things as well as say them. Perhaps that very personal interview with him at the club helped her. He guessed she had not told Manse about the visit. Their meeting, plus the Unhinged incident, could have worked on her, together convinced Naomi that Shale might just about justify the risk, marriage being such a risk, anyway. Many women would gamble. Also, she knew art, and had decided that at least some of Manse's stuff was genuine and valuable. Plus, there had been so much talk about this wedding that she probably thought she couldn't get out of it now—big church, very helpful clergyman, lots of invitations sent. Ralph believed he might be able to give her some consolation later on in the marriage. She'd probably expect this from him. But not immediately. He would regard that as gross, and probably she would, too.

'Naomi's not our mother, of course,' Matilda said, 'in the biological meaning, but she's going to be our new mother, anyway.'

'Yes,' Laurent said. 'Our real mother's quite good at it when she wants to be, but she's not here lately.'

'No,' Naomi said.

'Isn't it great?' Shale said. 'How things sort theirselves out.'

'Great,' Naomi said.

Ember left soon after this. He'd certainly thought about getting Manse on his own to let Shale know that Articulate meant to kill him as part of a deal with Ralph, but then decided

Manse could probably protect himself. Perhaps, in any case, the sod deserved whatever came. After all, he'd done, or he'd *had* done, Joachim Brown, someone very carefully selected and approved of by Ralph, and by his daughter. It was difficult to forgive that, despite all the endless brotherly windbagging and buddy-mush just now.

Yet, Ember didn't want to be entirely negative and harsh. Maturity, in his opinion, brought an ability to compromise, and he thought of one way he could respond to Mansel's thoroughly inspired show. Ralph decided he'd tell a couple of his people to watch out for Sybil on the wedding day, assuming Manse lived that long, and, if she looked likely to turn rough and loud, cart her off somewhere secure and soundproof until the ceremony ended, though with no more than necessary violence, and definitely nothing sexual. Ralph knew he, personally, would hate a disturbance in this top quality church as much as Manse.

*   *   *

Ember was at the Monty late again a day or two later and did a routine tour of the club yard to satisfy himself no mysterious packages had been left against outer doors. He must not get unvigilant. It could be a mistake to think any attack from Shale would be against him,

Ralph, physically. Instead, the tactics might be shaped to reduce him, break him, gradually. So, for instance, knock off Turret, a valued, favoured, honoured, member of Ralph's firm. And then? Do the Monty, and with it, many of Ralph's golden hopes. Destruction of the Monty could mean destruction of Ember's mind and selfhood and will to fight.

An unmarked Volvo drove into the yard and parked. Iles and Colin Harpur left the car and walked towards him, Iles looking what Ember thought of as deeply unwinsome. These two would sometimes arrive at the Monty after midnight, on the face of it to see all licensing conditions were observed, but actually, in Ralph's view, to terrorize the clientele and enjoy a few free drinks. 'Hunting firebombs, Ralph, dear?' Iles said. 'Isn't it a gross world, though?'

Ember took them to the bar and set the pair up with their usuals, then poured himself a Kressmann's. Twenty or so members remained in the club, mostly at the bar or playing snooker and pool. Iles did his usual arrogant glare about, as if he couldn't believe how some of these people were out of clink, or any of them. Ralph felt this sort of attitude would be utterly improper once the Monty had been relaunched. Perhaps it should be regarded as improper *now*, though Ralph would admit that some members who got Iles's disbelieving stare tonight might have been locked up except for very talented QCs and/or the overcrowded jails.

They sat at a corner table. Harpur said: 'I gather Articulate was here alone recently for quite a dialogue. Had he suddenly turned *really* articulate? He'd emerged somehow?'

'I see such one-to-one conversations with long-time members as a very worthwhile and, indeed, pleasurable experience,' Ralph replied, 'and an essential factor in one's job as host.'

'How true,' Iles replied.

'One to one?' Harpur said.

'Articulate's a valued "Montyist", as I term our regulars,' Ember replied. Had this sod, Harpur, seen Articulate turn up alone, on a return visit the other night? But how could that have happened? Articulate arrived very late. Had Harpur been watching the Monty? Why? Or had someone in the club at the time given Harpur or Iles a whisper? It always badly hurt Ralph to think the Monty housed members who watched things here and straight off reported to the police, for some contemptible fee. He might be able to trace the guilty voice this time, if that was how Harpur knew. There'd been very few other people in the club. Ralph believed he could remember who.

'And then Articulate and his mother and great aunt Edna in earlier that evening,' Harpur said. 'We saw them, of course. A previous conference.' It wasn't a question, but he gazed at Ralph, as if expecting an answer. Harpur always looked slabby, harsh, aggressive—yes, some said, like Marciano, though fair-haired. Alongside him, Iles appeared dainty, but to Ralph's knowledge, lacked all daintiness. 'This sounds like real activity,' Harpur said.

'What does?' Ember said.

'These visits,' Harpur said.

'This is a club. It has a social aim. People drop in,' Ember replied. 'You drop in yourselves, don't you, Mr Harpur?'

'We wondered, Mr Iles and I, whether you could recall the gist of your talk with Articulate, or even with Articulate and his mother and great aunt Edna.'

'As a matter of fact, I didn't know of the later tête-à-tête with Articulate,' Iles said, 'but Harpur mentioned it to me. He'd found out about that in some way. We won't inquire how, Ralph, shall we? We'd get no fucking answer. Occasionally, Harpur does mention things to me, if it suits him, but edited.'

'I talk to many members over any twenty-four hours, you know,' Ralph said. 'I see it as my function—a necessary and pleasurable one.'

'They're lucky to have you,' Iles said. 'Everyone realizes that. But, look, don't piss Col and me about, Ralph, there's a chum. Just give us what Articulate said, what you said, what the women said, would you? Something agreed at the first meeting and then Articulate comes in late to confirm? Or cancel? OK?'

'Casual conviviality, that's all. You make it all sound very purposeful and businesslike, Mr Iles,' Ralph said, 'whereas—'

'Yes, purposeful and businesslike,' Iles said. 'That's our reading of things.'

'It could be wrong—with respect,' Ralph said.

'It's the later conversation—just you and him—that really interests us,' Harpur said.

'Generalities, I should think,' Ember said. Ralph produced a frown to show he meant to try seriously to help them and recollect. 'Weather. Holidays. Cricket. The usual small talk. We try to avoid politics—too controversial. Most of them support David Cameron and the new Conservatives, of course, because of Eton and Oxford. I don't mean any of them actually *went* to either place, but they'd like to be noticed backing classiness. They think it will persuade me to accept their membership when the Monty changes. I bump into so many people here and have a few unimportant yet, I trust, comradely words. These little exchanges seem to merge into one pleasant and not very significant encounter. I don't know whether Alec would recall things better than I. It might be in your interests to talk to him, if you feel something significant might have come up.' Obviously, Articulate would tell them nothing. He wasn't going to chirrup: *Oh, yes, Mr Iles, Mr Harpur, I went into the Monty to arrange a bit of reciprocity—I'd do Manse for him if he'd promise not to let my mother and great aunt put any of my money from the Holborn bank expedition into the Monty black hole.* 'I'd not object to your asking him. Why would I? Nothing controversial or private. You can tell him, if you wish, that it's OK with me for him to go over what was said.'

'The thing about Articulate is he's dead,' Iles replied.

'My God,' Ralph said. The shock was real.

'Which is why what he talked about with you might be to the point,' Harpur said.

'Is this certain—confirmed?' Ralph said.

'*I* confirm it,' Iles said. 'You can't get anyone deader than that.'

'Generalities,' Ralph said. 'We talked generalities.'

'Done by multiple shots,' Harpur replied.

'Oh,' Ralph said.

'It looks as though he meant to bop Mansel Shale, but got bopped himself,' Harpur said.

'As most of us would have forecast,' Iles said. 'Alec as executioner? I mean, sure to cock it up.' He sniffed boisterously for a while and did an imitation weep for Articulate. 'These things tend to sort themselves out nicely, don't they, with next to no interference from us? A bit of neat domestic tidying. Brown, dead, Articulate dead—both wholly inpenetrable cases, I'm afraid.'

'The whisper's around, isn't it, that he was in on the ICDS robbery with some sort of stooge function,' Harpur said, 'but nicely paid to keep his gob shut? Did that make him feel suddenly big and mature and competent—and free up his voicebox, at least for chats with you?'

'Poor deluded prat,' Iles said. 'He gave himself a kill mission on your behalf? Has Mansel seemed a threat lately, Ralph? That's how we read the scene. I expect you know the theorics about monopoly, the commercial imperative, that eternal, grisly capitalistic struggle for dominance.'

'Interlocking factors,' Harpur said. 'You'll remember that Mr Iles is quite a dazzler at charting these. So: Joachim Brown, Karl Marx, Naomi, monopoly, Unhinged, Manse Shale, Articulate, the lady Misks—Rose and Edna.'

'And, of course, yourself, Ralph,' Iles said.

Yourself. Ember wondered, did these two want to nick him as accessory? Were they saying he commissioned Articulate to remove Mansel Shale? Perhaps in a way he had. Articulate and he shook hands on the plan. Articulate had offered, Ralph accepted, though regarding it as fantasy. That might be criminal. Must be. Luckily, however, it was deeply, blessedly unprovable. Possibly, Harpur saw Articulate come late to the Monty, but he couldn't have heard the conversation, and no stooly club member had been near enough to eavesdrop. Harpur and Iles pressed him to tell them what was said, but must realize they'd get only horse shit. They hadn't put him under caution. Iles considered this and the Brown case 'impenetrable'. They'd never charge anyone with either. So, how could Ember be an accessory? Accessories had to have somebody to be an accessory with.

'Mansel, a threat?' Ember replied. 'In which way?'

'Thrilled by his new gangster gloss, did Alec offer to knock Shale over for you?' Iles said. 'Suddenly the retard thinks he's one of Nature's hit men? Were you and he talking some kind of deal? You'll see why we're concerned about his appearances here, Ralph, especially the second one, without his minders, the crones. He needed confidentiality? I wonder if he wanted to say something to you they shouldn't hear?'

'Deal?' Ember said.

'Quid pro quoism of some sort,' the ACC said.

Ember saw Iles needed to show he had guessed the arrangement between Articulate and Ralph. As ever, this fucking know-all craved credit for being a know-all. That was probably enough for him. There could be no arrests. 'Yes, generalities,' Ralph replied. 'We spoke generalities.' He replenished their drinks and took more armagnac himself. 'I

344

think about his mother and great aunt Edna,'
he said.

'Those two are provided for, we believe,'
Iles said.

'I mean their grief,' Ralph said. He gave it
solemnity, though clipped, not unctuous.

'Did they want to buy into the club with
Alec's loot?' Iles replied. 'They longed to be
part of the new, redeemed Monty, right? A
grand, sparkling wish. But Alec objected, did
he? Perhaps he didn't consider it a sane way to
use his distinguished earnings. Not everyone
has your special, visionary flair, Ralph. Some
cannot believe the Monty will ever change itself
into something different. Did Articulate think
like that? People used to find him a bit slow
and stupid. But had he altered somehow—felt
entitled to his own views now? Instead of the
women's funding plan, he offers to take out
Manse. You could then boost your trade
takings and use the increase for recreating
the Monty—without touching Articulate's
gorgeous funds? Was that the situation?'

'The club's in for another after-funeral do,
Ralph,' Harpur said. 'The Monty's a real social
fulcrum, even *un*transformed. Maybe *because*
untransformed.'

'Your fine ambition will linger, though,
Ralph. Possibly now Articulate's a goner the
two ladies will try offloading their loot in your
direction again,' Iles said. 'The Heston pull
pulls.'

CHAPTER THIRTEEN

At home in Arthur Street, Hazel said: 'We were thinking of going to have a gaze at the Manse Shale wedding, dad. St James's. Is that all right? It's a crook wedding. You didn't much like it when we went to the Turret Brown funeral. I thought we'd better clear it with you in this instance.'

'The bride's not a crook,' Jill said.

'There'll be the same lot as guests,' Hazel said.

'Weddings are all right,' Harpur said. Hadn't Iles decided Ralph and Manse were brilliantly, humanly, *unenslavedy* free from the dictates of economic theory and wouldn't be trying to kill each other, for the present?

Jill said: 'How about you, dad?'

'No, I don't think I'll come,' he said.

'I meant, do you ever think about getting remarried—like Mansel Shale,' Jill said. 'We wouldn't mind if you married Denise.'

'I do think about it,' Harpur said.

'Does *she*?' Hazel said.

'Probably not,' Harpur said.

'I don't think you're *terribly* old,' Jill said.

'Would her parents kick up a fuss?' Hazel said.

'Why should they?' Jill said. 'Dad's got good sides as well as the . . . Shall we talk to Denise

346

about it for you one day, soon?'

'No, I wouldn't want that,' Harpur said.

'Why?' Jill said.

'She might feel pressured,' Harpur said.

'Maybe she should,' Jill said.

'Not a good way to start,' Harpur said.

'You haven't got time to waste,' Jill replied.

'I thought you said I wasn't old,' Harpur said.

'Not *terribly* old,' Jill said. 'Think of Mandela.'

The girls were away for a few hours and then came back, full of delight and excitement. 'Lovely, dad,' Jill said.

'Another horse-drawn vehicle. But this one an open carriage for the bride and groom to go off to the reception,' Hazel said.

'And then, just after they'd left, some crazy woman comes running down the road screaming she'd been kidnapped, and wanting to get into the church,' Jill said. 'Too late, though.'

Chivers Large Print Direct

If you have enjoyed this Large Print book and would like to build up your own collection of Large Print books and have them delivered direct to your door, please contact **Chivers Large Print Direct**.

Chivers Large Print Direct offers you a full service:

✧ **Created to support your local library**

✧ **Delivery direct to your door**

✧ **Easy-to-read type and attractively bound**

✧ **The very best authors**

✧ **Special low prices**

For further details either call Customer Services on 01225 443400 or write to us at

Chivers Large Print Direct
FREEPOST (BA 1686/1)
Bath
BA1 3QZ